"I run a shelter fo__ __ not a dating service for their fathers."

"My father dates all the time. I'm talking about someone who'll marry him. It shouldn't be hard to find somebody. He's good-looking and rich. Don't you know some nice women who would like him well enough to go out with him?" Cynthia asked.

Kathryn didn't want to tell Cynthia how easy it would be for a woman to like her father very much. Neither did Cynthia need to know Kathryn found her father so attractive she temporarily forgot that though they seemed to have a lot in common, they disagreed on most fundamental matters.

"Your father will remarry when he's ready."

"He needs somebody who'll take care of him, somebody who's not interested in his becoming the most famous businessman in the world. He needs someone like *you*."

Pocket Next Page

Dear Reader,

Love is in the air, but the days will certainly be sweeter if you snuggle up with this month's Special Edition offerings—and a box of decadent chocolates. First up, award-winning author and this year's President of Romance Writers of America®, Shirley Hailstock is a fresh new voice for Special Edition, but fans already know what a gifted storyteller she is. With numerous novels and novellas under her belt, Shirley debuts in Special Edition with *A Father's Fortune*, which tells the story of a day-care-center owner and her foster child who teach a grumpy carpenter how to face his past and open his heart to love.

Lindsay McKenna packs a punch in *Her Healing Touch,* a fast-paced read from beginning to end. The next in her widely acclaimed MORGAN'S MERCENARIES: DESTINY'S WOMEN series, this romance details the trials of a beautiful paramedic who teaches a handsome Special Forces officer the ways of her legendary healing. *USA TODAY* bestselling author Susan Mallery *completely* wins us over in *Completely Smitten*, next up in her beloved series HOMETOWN HEARTBREAKERS. Here, an adventurous preacher's daughter seeks out a new life, but never expects to find a new *love* with a sexy U.S. marshal.

The fourth installment in Crystal Green's KANE'S CROSSING miniseries, *There Goes the Bride* oozes excitement when a runaway bride is spirited out of town by a reclusive pilot she once loved in high school. Patricia McLinn delights her readers with *Wedding of the Century*. Here, a heroine returns to her hometown seven years after running out of her wedding. When she faces her jilted groom, she realizes their feelings are stronger than ever! Finally, in Leigh Greenwood's *Family Merger*, sparks fly when a workaholic businessman meets a good-hearted social worker, who teaches him the meaning of love.

Don't miss this array of novels that deliver an emotional charge and satisfying finish you're sure to savor, no matter what the season!

Happy Valentine's Day!

Karen Taylor Richman
Senior Editor

Please address questions and book requests to:
Silhouette Reader Service
U.S.: 3010 Walden Ave., P.O. Box 1325, Buffalo, NY 14269
Canadian: P.O. Box 609, Fort Erie, Ont. L2A 5X3

Books by Leigh Greenwood

Silhouette Special Edition

Just What the Doctor Ordered #1223
Married by High Noon #1295
Undercover Honeymoon #1452
Family Merger #1524

LEIGH GREENWOOD

has authored twenty historical romances and debuted in Silhouette Special Edition with *Just What the Doctor Ordered*. The proud parent of three grown children, Leigh lives in Charlotte, North Carolina. You can write to Leigh Greenwood at P.O. Box 470761, Charlotte, NC 28226. An SASE would be appreciated.

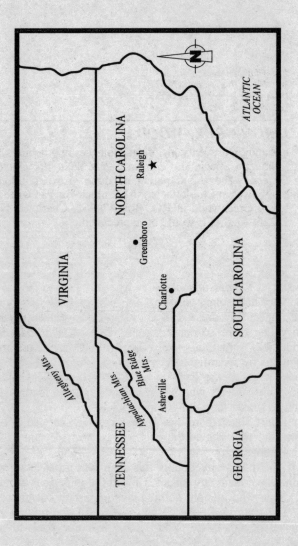

Chapter One

Kathryn Roper suddenly found herself face-to-face with one very handsome, very angry man. Tall, neatly groomed and impeccably dressed in a custom-made suit, he looked too young to be so conservatively dressed. The gray pinstripe was something her father would wear. This man ought to be wearing a cream-colored Polo shirt and tan slacks. He had the body of an athlete, though she didn't know any athletes who had such good taste in clothes and such bad taste in visiting hours.

"Don't stand there staring at me," he snapped. "I've flown halfway around the world to get here. I want to see Miss Roper."

If she'd had any doubts this man was Ron Egan, she didn't have them any longer. He had the imperious attitude of a man who thought nothing was important but himself.

"I'm Kathryn Roper," she said, "and I don't allow visitors after nine-thirty. You'll have to come back tomorrow."

His angry gaze narrowed its focus, bore into her like a laser. "You're too young and pretty to have turned into a battle-ax."

Kathryn couldn't stop a spurt of laughter. "Who says a battle-ax has to be old and ugly?"

He appeared to be weighing her up, calculating his approach. He was just like many upper echelon types she'd run across, ready to shout at people they thought unimportant but immediately taking a different tack when they encountered someone they considered on their level.

Yet she was having a very different reaction to him than what would have been usual for her—one of a purely physical nature, one that caught her off guard. She felt attracted to this man. She had never denied the possibility of instant chemistry between two people, but this was the first time it had happened to her.

What a tragedy his outside should be so beautiful when his inside was rotten. But that's the way it seemed to go with her and men.

In a way, she was just as impressionable as the girls who came to her for help. All too often they had been seduced by a man's appearance. Only she was older, more experienced and had her physical desires firmly under control. She might have a gut-clenching reaction to Ron Egan, but he'd never know it.

"I want to see my daughter. Where is she?"

"She's in bed, as are all the girls in this house. You can see her in the morning."

"I've come all the way from Geneva. I got on the next flight out after your phone call and spent the last eight hours on a plane. I'm six time zones away from where I started, and I'm tired. It won't hurt her to miss thirty minutes of sleep."

"It's not the sleep I'm concerned about so much as that your visit will upset her. It's extremely important that she remain calm. She's going through a stressful experience."

They still stood there in the entrance hall, facing each

other like gladiators, each trying to decide how to manipulate this conversation to their own advantage. At least that's how Ron read it.

"She's a minor," Ron said. "I can force you to give her up."

"It's not a matter of my giving her up. She came here of her own free will. She wants to stay. If you care for her, you'll let her stay."

Ron didn't know quite how to respond. From the moment he'd received a call from a stranger telling him his daughter was pregnant and had run away from home, he hadn't known what to think. He hadn't expected to find his daughter housed in an elegant old mansion in the heart of the oldest and most fashionable neighborhood in Charlotte. Kathryn Roper wasn't at all what he'd expected, either.

His first impulse was to shout at this woman for having the effrontery to imply he didn't care for his daughter. Who was she to make such a judgment? She didn't know anything about him. Cynthia had every right to be upset, but he was sure if he could talk to her, they could straighten things out.

Still, there was something about this woman that caused him to look at her again, to reevaluate. He was used to women being visibly affected by his appearance. She didn't show any reaction whatsoever. She didn't appear the least bit intimidated by him, by his size, his reputation or his gender. She looked quite young and slender, even fragile, but she acted as if she thought she was as tough as any man.

"I can have you arrested for kidnapping."

"But you won't."

"Why? It's not because I'm too honorable."

"I imagine you know enough dirty tricks to fill a book, but you wouldn't want any of this splashed over the front page of *The Charlotte Observer*."

"I don't give a damn about that paper."

"I don't believe you."

"What you believe isn't important. Since it's my daughter we're talking about, it's what *I* believe that's important. And if you don't know that, I'll get a judge to explain it to you."

"Who are you planning to ask—Frank Emery? He's my godfather. Emily Anders is a friend of my mother. I think my brothers have worked with every other judge in Charlotte."

"Are you telling me the judges can be bought?"

Much to his surprise, she flushed. "No, and it was quite wrong of me to imply they could be. Come into the living room. We'd better sit down."

"I don't want to talk, and I don't want to sit down."

"If you hope to convince me you flew halfway around the world because you care what happens to your daughter, you'll sit down."

"Why should I care what you think?"

"Because Cynthia does."

He didn't want to believe her, but there was no other reason he could think of for Cynthia's presence in this house. He still had every intention of taking her home, but maybe it would be better to hear what this woman had to say. After his wife died, he'd had an increasingly difficult time communicating with his daughter. He didn't understand how the lovable, biddable little girl who used to climb onto his lap to read had turned into the silent, sulking, angry teenager who sometimes refused to eat breakfast with him and often made excuses to miss dinner as well. Maybe he should have taken some time off before now, but he had to have this one last deal to put his company into a position where its success didn't depend solely on him.

He intended to hire the best therapists he could find, but if Kathryn could help, he'd be foolish not to listen to her. Cynthia had chosen to come here, and she always had a reason for anything she did.

"I'd like something to drink," he said.

"I don't serve liquor to guests."

"I don't drink liquor. Ice water would be fine."

"I'll be right back."

Ron watched her leave, the sight of her backside causing a surprising reaction in his groin. He hadn't felt like that in years, certainly not with a woman who seemed ready to oppose him in every way she could. Yet Kathryn wasn't like any of the women who faced him across a board table or the functionaries who kept his various offices running smoothly.

He had worked with single-minded determination from the time he was ten to get where he was today. He'd sacrificed leisure, friends, nearly everything most men would consider the rewards of success so Cynthia would have all the advantages.

It was clear Kathryn Roper looked down on him. That was all the more reason to be angry he was attracted to her. Hell, it was nearly impossible to be angry with a woman when you found yourself wondering what it would be like to get closer to her. How was he supposed to concentrate on her shortcomings when her body distracted him?

Just then Kathryn returned with a glass of ice water. Her front looked just as good as the back. It was a good thing she couldn't read his thoughts. She'd probably throw the water in his face.

"Now let's talk about your daughter," she said after she'd handed him the water and allowed him time to take a few sips.

"Tell me what you do," Ron said. "I still can't figure out why Cynthia would come to you."

She looked as if she took that as a personal insult, but surely she had to know a father couldn't just take for granted she was qualified to be responsible for his daughter.

"I maintain this house as a shelter for unwed young girls who become pregnant."

"How much money do you owe on it?"

"My aunt left it to me."

"I don't imagine your neighbors are thrilled with what

you're doing." People don't pay upwards to a million dollars for a big house to find themselves next door to a halfway house for pregnant teens.

"Not everybody likes what I'm doing, but I'm a good neighbor. The girls are quiet and well behaved. I don't allow visits from boys unless I'm present and then only brothers or the fathers of their babies."

"How many girls do you have here?"

"I have room for ten, but I only have four now."

"Who looks after them when you go to work?"

"This is my work."

"You mean you have a trust fund that allows you to do nothing."

"I have an income that allows me to provide a service to the community."

Just what he thought. A rich woman with nothing to do, who excused her meddling by thinking she was providing a social service these girls couldn't find elsewhere.

"How do they know about you? Do you advertise?"

He'd angered her. She sat with her clenched hands in her lap, her back ramrod straight, her knees together.

"They learn of me through their friends or from girls who have been here. When they come to me, I urge them to go to their parents immediately. I tell them all the reasons that would be preferable to staying here. I'm proud to say most of them do go home. Two have come back afterward, but most found their parents were more supportive than they expected. Mostly the girls fear their parents will hate them for what they've done."

"Don't think you're going to convince me Cynthia thinks I'll hate her. We don't always agree, but she—"

"Cynthia believes your work comes before her."

"It keeps me away from home a lot, but nothing is more important to me than Cynthia. Why do you think I hired so many people to take care of her?"

"I imagine what she wanted and needed was you, your

time and attention, your assurance that *she* was more important than your work.''

"She knows that."

"She told me she came here because she doesn't want her having a baby to get in your way."

That was such a ridiculous statement he could hardly believe his daughter made it. He wasn't even sure what it meant. "Cynthia couldn't possibly get in my way. I've hired four people to take care of her. If she wants anything, she only has to ask for it."

"She still doesn't believe she's as important to you as your next merger."

"Of course she is. If she wants, she can go to Switzerland with me as soon as school is out." He realized with a terrible sense of guilt he hadn't even considered that until the words came out of his mouth. If she had wanted to go vacationing with one of her friends, he'd have been happy to let her.

"She wants to stay here. She doesn't want to hurt you or the baby's father."

"That's something else I want to know. Where can I find the boy who did this?"

"I have several rules. One is I never ask the name of the father. Another is even if I know it, I never reveal it."

"You're a regular paragon of virtue, aren't you?"

She must have a difficult time with her shelter. He didn't imagine many fathers would have been as calm as he had been so far, but he couldn't work up the will to rant and rave at Kathryn. He intended to take Cynthia home, but he didn't think Kathryn was an evil person. She was just a well-meaning busybody who couldn't keep her nose out of other people's business.

"My only purpose is to help these girls. I want to give them a safe place to stay where they can continue their education, have their babies, then decide what to do with the rest of their lives. I don't provide a permanent solution, just a temporary refuge from all the pressure."

"All that sounds fine and noble, but what are you getting out of this?"

"I beg your pardon!"

"People don't do things like this without a reason. You're rich. I imagine your friends are building careers, going to parties and having children. There's got to be some reason you'd give all that up to baby-sit pregnant teenagers. And there's no point glaring at me. I don't intimidate."

"Neither do I."

"Good, then answer my question. Why are you doing this?"

"Because something like this happened to my sister," she said after a pause. "I saw the damage it could do when it was handled badly."

She meant it happened to her, he thought. People always put traumatic events off on a relative, a friend, even a neighbor. They only reacted like Kathryn Roper when it really happened to them. She didn't seem like the kind of woman to let her emotions get the better of her. But then who better to learn to control her emotions than someone who had failed to do so and paid the price?

He looked at her, sitting so stiffly in the chair opposite him and felt some of his aggravation melt away. It couldn't be easy. She must relive what happened to her every time a girl came to her for help. Most people would want to put it behind them, to forget, pretend it never happened, but she'd had the courage to turn her personal tragedy into a benefit to the community. He had to admire her for that. And it was a real community service.

He wondered what had happened to her baby.

What did Cynthia mean to do with her baby? For the first time it hit him that he was about to become a grandfather. He had just turned forty.

"I want to see Cynthia."

"As I told you before, she's in bed."

"I heard you the first time, but you can't really think I'll just get up and walk out that door."

"It would be better if you waited until the morning."

"It would be better if this had never happened, but it has and I'll deal with it. Now I want to see my daughter."

Kathryn didn't move.

"You can get her for me, or I'll get her myself. It's your choice, but I'm going to see her."

"I won't let you yell at her, and I won't let you force her to leave."

"I hope I won't yell at her. I imagine she's extremely upset already, but I can't make any promises. How would you feel about leaving your only child in the hands of a stranger?"

"I wouldn't do it, but you've been doing that all her life."

This female didn't fight fair. "My work makes it impossible for me to be at home all the time. My staff has been with Cynthia for more than ten years."

Kathryn got to her feet. "I'll ask Cynthia if she wants to come down."

She left the room before he could make it plain that in this instance, at least, the decision wasn't up to Cynthia.

He was extremely tired, but he was too full of nervous energy to sit still. He got up and walked about the room. It was impossible not to notice that even though the furniture looked extremely comfortable and well used—the window treatments subtle, the carpets not new—everything had the look of being quite expensive. It was the kind of furniture that said *I'm so expensive and well made I don't have to look expensive.* Ron had studied such things. The trappings of success he made sure he acquired. He hadn't had anything when he was a kid. He was determined everybody would know that wasn't the case any longer. He finished his water and set the glass in what looked like a candy dish.

He wondered how things had gone with the meeting in Geneva. He was sure his colleagues Ted and Ben would do an excellent job of explaining why the two companies would do better under new management. It was just that he'd never before left the start of negotiations to anyone else. It was essential to know people's starting positions, prejudices and all, if he was going to bring them together in the end. Part of his reputation had been built on personal attention to every detail. If Ron Egan came after your company, you knew you were going to be meeting with Ron Egan *all the time*. He wondered what his absence now would do to his reputation.

Oh well, he'd be back in Geneva tomorrow. Or the next day. He could sleep on the plane if worrying about Cynthia didn't keep him awake again. This was one merger that wouldn't be easy. It wasn't merely a matter of money or paperwork. It was people and politics. You had to find a way to bring both together, and nobody could do that better than Ron Egan. It was how he'd raised himself from a kid whose parents didn't have enough money to buy him decent shoes or a winter coat to a man whose income had reached nine figures this last year.

He turned abruptly away from a mirror that showed him a much too realistic view of himself. He had the look of a successful man—the clothes, the carriage, the confidence—but right now that left a bad taste in his mouth. His daughter had become pregnant. Worse, she had turned to a perfect stranger for support rather than to him. It didn't take a rocket scientist to know something was wrong there. He was an expert when it came to analyzing people, figuring out what made them tick, knowing what to do to make them come down on his side.

How had he managed to fail so badly with his own daughter?

Why was she afraid of him? What would he have done if she had come to him?

The door opened, and Kathryn reentered the room. Cynthia followed. Ron felt almost as though he was looking at a stranger.

She had put on jeans and a T-shirt, allowed her dark-blond hair to fall over her shoulders. She displayed none of the sullen anger he'd seen the last time he was home. She faced him with a new calmness. Only her twitching toes—she was barefooted—betrayed any uneasiness.

Ron hadn't realized how much her facial features had grown to resemble her mother's. It was almost like seeing Erin the way she looked the first day they met. Cynthia was tall with slim bones, though right now she carried some extra weight. He remembered how much being overweight had affected his life. It had to be worse for a girl. They were under so much more pressure to be slim.

Like Kathryn.

He cursed silently and brought his mind back to his daughter.

In his mind she'd remained his little girl. He'd been too busy to realize she'd gone ahead and grown up on her own. And now she was in trouble, and he had to figure out some way to help her.

"Why did you come?" Cynthia asked. "I don't want you here."

"I'm your father."

"I'm sixteen."

Was there a single teenager in America who *didn't* think turning sixteen made him or her an adult? "I'm still your father. If you hadn't come home soon, Margaret would have called the police. I would have had the SBI and the FBI combing the state looking for you. You should have told me you were in trouble."

"You can't do anything about it."

"I could have tried to help."

"I don't need your help. I can do this on my own."

Despite the twitching toes, she didn't appear frightened or overly angry. It was almost as though he were a momentary obstacle she had to deal with before she could move on.

"When were you going to tell me about the baby?"

She didn't answer.

"How were you going to keep it a secret?"

"I'll stay here until after it's born. I don't have to go to school when I really start showing. Miss Roper has people come teach us. I can get my GED."

He spent ten thousand dollars a year to send her to the best private school in Charlotte, and she was talking about a GED! Didn't she have any idea how important it was to graduate from the right school? No matter what he had to do, he was determined Cynthia would do that.

"We'll worry about that later. Are you okay? You look pale."

"It's because I'm pregnant." Cynthia stumbled over the word that described her condition. "Mrs. Collias fixes meals especially for pregnant girls. She says she can make sure I have enough for the baby without getting fat."

Ron had almost forgotten Kathryn was still in the room. She had taken a seat near the door and was leafing through a magazine. She didn't trust him alone with his daughter, but at least she had the decency to pretend she wasn't listening to everything they said. He wondered if she was this protective of her other girls.

"All expectant mothers are supposed to gain weight."

His wife had gained forty pounds then lost it within a few months.

"If I get fat, I'll never get it off."

Ron didn't know how the conversation had drifted onto something as trivial as weight.

"What about the boy?" Ron asked. "The baby's father."

"He doesn't know."

"You have to tell him."

"No, I don't. It's my baby. Besides, I don't want to ruin his life, too."

"This is not going to ruin your life. I won't let it."

"I'm a pregnant, unwed teenager," Cynthia said, anger now rising to the surface. "There's nothing your money can do to change that."

He felt as if he were being punished for working so she would never have to endure privation. "You still have to tell the father. It's his baby as much as yours. He has a right to know."

"No, he doesn't."

For the first time since seeing her, he sensed fear. "I'm sure he'll guess when you don't return to school."

"I told everybody we were moving to Connecticut."

Ron knew it would be impossible to keep her baby a secret even if they did move to Connecticut, but he would deal with that later. Right now he needed to get Cynthia home and settled into her own room. And he needed to get out of Kathryn Roper's house.

"Get your things," Ron said. "I'm taking you home."

Cynthia pulled back from him. Something about her expression changed, something subtle that made her look less like a child and more like a woman.

"I'm not going home. I'm staying here."

Ron knew his relationship with his daughter wasn't the best in the world, but she'd never refused point-blank to do anything reasonable. "Why not?"

"I just told you," Cynthia said, sounding impatient. "I don't want anybody to know."

"They'll know soon enough."

"Not if I stay here and you go back to Switzerland. They'll believe we moved to Connecticut, just like I said. I told them we were keeping the house with Margaret and everybody else in case we didn't like it. I told them I didn't want to go but some of your Yale buddies had talked you into it because it would put you closer to New York, that it would be good for your business."

Ron didn't bother pointing out that such a story was so full of holes it probably wouldn't last a day. The school would call if she missed more than one day without an excuse. Her friends would call. Neighbors would ask questions. There was no way she could keep her disappearance a secret.

"Why don't you let me take you home?" Ron asked. "We can both get a good night's sleep and try to come up with a plan in the morning."

"A plan for what?"

For the rest of your life Ron thought, exasperated. She didn't appear to realize nothing would ever be the same after this. She would be a mother. That was a barrier that would separate her from her friends almost as effectively as moving to Connecticut.

"Everything is going to be different after this," Ron said.

"I know that," Cynthia said. "I'm not stupid."

"I never said you were, but even intelligent people can have trouble thinking through unfamiliar situations. There are so many things you can't know at your age—"

"If you tell me even once I don't understand because I'm too young, I'll walk out of this room."

"You don't understand," Ron said, "not only because you're too young but because this is beyond your experience. Hell, your mother and I didn't understand, and we'd been planning for you for three years."

"Age and experience have nothing to do with it," Cynthia said as she got to her feet. "You've been a father for sixteen years, and you still don't understand a thing about children."

"I don't understand why you're more upset about your friends knowing you're pregnant than you are about having a baby. I half expected you'd be nearly hysterical begging me to help you get an abortion."

"I'd never do that! I want this baby. I *need* this baby."

"Cynthia, you've just turned sixteen. You're in the tenth grade. How can you need a baby?"

Tears sprang to her eyes. He reached out to her, but she backed away.

"You never let me have a cat. I begged you over and over again, but you wouldn't let me."

"I'm allergic to cats. You know that."

She started toward the door. "I would have kept it in my room. You never go there. I would have taken care of it myself."

She ran out leaving Ron wondering what had just happened. He turned to Kathryn who'd remained silent during the whole conversation, quietly turning pages in her magazine. Now she was looking at him with an expression of pity mingled with something that seemed to say *You poor, dumb clod. You don't have a clue, do you?*

"What? You're looking at me like I've dribbled ketchup down my shirt."

"You don't understand her, do you?"

"Are you saying you do?"

"Of course."

That irritated him. "There's no *of course* about it. Has she told you something I don't know?"

"Not in so many words."

Erin used to say that. She said men weren't supposed to understand women. "How about putting it into words a poor, dumb male can understand."

She stood and came toward him. She really was a lovely woman with a beautiful body. It was hard to concentrate on his daughter when he was having such a visceral reaction to this woman. Why wasn't she married? What was wrong with the single men in Charlotte that she was left alone to oversee other men's daughters?

"Cynthia wanted something to love," Kathryn said, "something of her own that would love her back."

"I offered to buy her a puppy, but she said she didn't want a dog."

"Did you get her one anyway?"

"No."

Kathryn sighed, and he felt even more out of it. "Now what?" he asked, becoming extremely frustrated.

"She would have taken the puppy."

"She said she didn't want it. She said she wouldn't even give it a name."

"She would have taken it and been happy. Didn't any one of those women you employ tell you that?"

"I was in Chicago. My secretary talked to Margaret."

"Did it ever occur to you that since you've hired a staff to take care of your daughter, it might be a good idea to ask their opinion, maybe even let them handle the situation?"

"Margaret has authority to buy anything Cynthia needs."

"Cynthia's wanting a cat was a cry for help. She wanted more attention than she was getting."

"It was a cat, for God's sake, not a security blanket."

"It might as well have been."

"Boys ask for dogs all the time. They'd never compare it to having a baby," he insisted.

"You don't understand women."

"I know that."

"And you don't understand your daughter."

They were standing there, facing each other like two antagonists squaring off over some kind of prize.

"I know that, too."

"I expect you tried," Kathryn said.

"You're too generous."

"You were probably too involved in your work to take the time to learn to really listen."

"I listen to her all the time."

"Maybe, but you're not *hearing* her. You're insensitive to women's issues. You need to spend more time—"

"I don't have more time," Ron broke in. "Do you have any idea how tough it is in the international market? Half the men out there would cut my throat if they could gain anything by it. And if I survive them, there's a new, young wizard popping out of the woodwork every day brimming over with ideas of how to do what I do cheaper and faster."

"I'm familiar with the business world. My father has spent his whole life in it, and he's just like you."

"So you're telling me it's hopeless?"

"Not if you really want to try. If you don't—"

"Would I come halfway around the world if I didn't?"

She seemed to accept that. She turned away and walked toward a bookcase built into the wall. "I can recommend several excellent books."

"I don't have time to read one book, not to mention several."

She turned back to face him, her expression impatient. "Then how do you expect to learn to be sensitive to your daughter's feelings? You need training."

"Then you train me."

"I doubt I'd be able to do that."

"How hard could it be? I'm bright, I'm willing and I'm ready to start now."

Chapter Two

"Are you sure everything went okay?"

Ron had called Ted the minute he got back to the house. It was 7:21 a.m. in Geneva. Time to be preparing for the second day's meeting. He was the one who was up past his bedtime. More than six hours past.

"Lord Hradschin is in favor of the merger," Ted said. "There's nothing that old pirate likes as much as money."

There really wasn't much that was difficult that had to be done during the first few days. It was mostly laying out the plans for the merger, explaining how they meant to restructure the company, answering questions, giving the costs and income projections. Ted was good at making difficult things sound simple and Ben could make you feel good about a root canal, but could they read the people, know who was going to be trouble, figure out the arguments necessary to bring them around, figure out how the politics played into the decision? That had always been his job.

"Don't move to a second point until you're certain

everyone understands the first one," Ron said. "It'll only get worse as you go along if they don't."

He'd already rejected the idea of flying back to Geneva in the morning. Something had happened to him when Cynthia suddenly broke into tears and ran from the room. This wasn't the same as having a tantrum, sulking or being obstinate. She was deeply hurt, and he had no idea how to fix it.

Kathryn said she could teach him to understand his daughter if he really wanted to. He couldn't imagine why she would have any doubt. He had left his meeting just as it was getting started. What more proof could she want?

"Call me if you hit a snag. I'll have my cell phone with me... No, I don't know when I'll be back. In the next couple of days, but I can't say exactly when."

He was certain Kathryn would say he'd need more than one session, but he didn't have time for more. If she was as good as she thought, she could teach him everything he had to know in a couple of hours. After that it shouldn't take him more than a day to sort things out with Cynthia and get her back home.

"I've got to go. If I don't get some sleep, I'll be a zombie. You've been wanting a chance to do this on your own, so make the most of it."

He hung up the phone and fell back on the bed without bothering to take off his clothes. He would undress in a minute, just as soon as the muscles at the back of his neck and shoulders unknotted enough for him to move his arms. Then it struck him, the million-dollar question.

Had he screwed up so badly with Cynthia she wouldn't give him another chance?

He hoped not. Their relationship wasn't perfect, but they'd been going along with only an occasional bump until this pregnancy thing happened. He couldn't wait to get his hands on the boy who'd done this to his little girl. It was always the boy who was so anxious to have sex he didn't stop to think of the consequences.

* * *

"Is Daddy really going to let you try to teach him to understand women?" Cynthia asked Kathryn over a bowl of oatmeal sprinkled with brown sugar and pecans.

"That's what he says," Kathryn replied. "But he may be too angry at me to listen to anything I say."

They were sitting in the breakfast alcove in Kathryn's bright, cheerful kitchen. Sunlight streamed in through the windows despite the canopy of oaks that shaded the backyard.

"How can any man be angry at you?" Lisette asked. "You're beautiful." She had requested French toast, which she had promptly drowned in a sea of maple syrup. She had yet to swallow the vitamin and calcium pills that Mrs. Collias had placed by her plate.

"My dad never notices women, even when they're as beautiful as Miss Roper," Cynthia said. "I used to think it was because he could never love another woman after my mother died."

Kathryn couldn't imagine a man as handsome, energetic and vital as Ron Egan ignoring women. She was certain women didn't ignore him. She hadn't been able to.

"That's so romantic," Lisette cooed.

"Now I think it's because he'll never like any woman as much as he likes his work."

"But he's rich," Lisette reminded her. "All rich men like beautiful women, and he isn't even ancient with a potbelly and bald head. Please tell me he's not fifty."

Kathryn couldn't help laughing. "Fifty is not ancient, Lisette. You wait until you get there."

"I never want to be fifty," the young girl said. "I want to die while I'm still young and beautiful, just like Princess Diana."

"Well, speaking as one who has passed her thirtieth birthday, I can tell you I plan to live well past fifty. And I don't intend to become an old hag in the process."

"Of course not," Lisette said, smiling as she popped a

vitamin in her mouth and followed it with half a glass of orange juice. "You can have all the plastic surgery you want."

"Will you do that?" Julia, the third of four girls at the table, asked.

"I hope to age gracefully."

"Why would you do that when you could still look young and beautiful?" Lisette asked.

"Because I want my husband to think of me as a wife and companion, not as someone who's concerned with nothing but her looks. I want to enjoy every phase of my life, to live each age honestly whatever its challenges."

"Kerry doesn't want me to look old," Lisette declared. "He wants me to be as beautiful as possible. I want to go to parties, wear beautiful clothes and have men follow me with their eyes when I walk past."

Kathryn decided somebody needed to explain to Mother Nature that some girls, regardless of their age, were just too young to have babies. Lisette should have been at the top of that list. This wasn't about rich husbands or beautiful clothes. She was about to become a mother. It was about learning to act with the maturity and responsibility necessary to make her a good mother.

"I want lots of children," Cynthia said. "I want a thousand pictures of when they learn to walk, start school, go on their first dates, of their proms and their graduations. I want books of pictures of their weddings, even more of their children. I want movies, too. After Mama got sick, she used to watch movies of me when I was a baby. She said I was her touchstone. She said as long as she had me she never felt lonely."

"Kerry will never leave my bedside when I get sick," Lisette said. "He'll be holding my hand when I die."

"Has your father dated?" Julia asked Cynthia.

"No."

"He must have loved your mother very much," Kathryn said.

"Both of them were only children whose parents died early," Cynthia said. "I think they were friends more than lovers."

"Would that bother you?" Kathryn asked.

"It would bother me," Lisette said. "If Kerry doesn't love me to distraction, I'll divorce him."

"Mama said she was happy because she had me to love," Cynthia answered. "Maybe a woman doesn't need more than that. What do you think?"

Kathryn realized what she thought was uncomfortably close to Lisette's feelings. Her own mother had been content to spend most of her married life waiting for her husband to return from business trips. When the split came between her sister and their father, her mother had backed their father's position without hesitation. Away at college at the time, Kathryn had been too furious to give any thought to her mother's position, but now she wondered. Could a woman be happily married to a man who was away from home more often than not?

"I can't speak for anyone but myself," Kathryn said, "but—"

The sound of the doorbell caused her to break off. Lisette bounded up from her chair. "It's Kerry. He can't stand to be separated from me."

"He must stay in the living room," Kathryn called after her. "I'll be in as soon as I fix my coffee."

"Do you think their parents will let them get married?" Julia asked as the door banged shut behind Lisette. "They're nuts about each other."

"It will depend on what Kerry's father says when he gets home."

"Where is he?"

"On a business trip. No one seems to know when he'll get back."

"My dad was on a business trip, too, but he came home right away."

Kathryn didn't know quite how to interpret Cynthia's

expression. It seemed to be some combination of pride and anger. Kathryn concluded that Cynthia loved her father deeply but just didn't happen to like him very much right then.

Lisette came back into the kitchen looking dejected. "It's Cynthia's father. He said he's come for his sensitivity lessons." She made a face. "Nothing personal, Cynthia, but that man's not normal. It's Saturday morning, and he's in a suit and tie."

Kathryn felt something in the region of her stomach flutter uncomfortably. "I didn't expect him so early," she said, getting up to put her coffee cup on the sideboard. "I'm not even sure I thought he'd come."

"If my father says he'll do something, he does it," Cynthia said, as though that was not a trait she admired.

"Does he do everything in a suit and tie?" Julia asked.

"I've never seen him wear anything else outside the house," Cynthia said.

Kathryn was about to say it was an attitude that was as outmoded as the twentieth century, but she was flattered Ron Egan had taken such care with his appearance. He could have come dressed in jeans and a T-shirt. That was *not* a wise thought. Just imagining Ron Egan in jeans and a T-shirt caused her belly to tighten.

"What'll I do when Kerry comes?" Lisette asked.

"You can use the TV room as long as Mrs. Collias is in sight," Kathryn said.

"She hates me," Lisette wailed. "She never lets me—"

"Do anything foolish," Kathryn finished for her. "That's why I hired her."

"I can watch her," Cynthia offered.

"Your father might want to see you. Now I've got to go. Make sure you both finish your breakfast. Good nutrition is extremely important now."

Ron turned from the window when Kathryn entered the room. It was 7:58 a.m. on a Saturday morning, and he looked like he'd just stepped out of *Gentleman's Quarterly*. Foolish, though, to be feeling like a young girl meeting a date.

"You're earlier than I expected," Kathryn said.

"I want to get this over so I can get back to Geneva," Ron said, coming toward her. "I left my assistants to handle some very difficult negotiations."

The thaw that had begun in her feelings toward him stopped. She didn't know why he'd bothered to come home. He could have saved himself a lot of trouble by shouting at her over the phone.

"I'm sure there are lots of people in Geneva far more qualified than I to help you with sensitivity training," she said. "If you'll tell me where you're staying, I'll see if I can line up someone. I don't know about Saturday flights from Charlotte to Geneva, but I'm sure Atlanta or New York—"

Ron looked at her like she had lost her mind. "Who said anything about my flying back today?"

Kathryn took a moment to gather her thoughts. "I interpreted your remarks to mean you planned to return almost immediately."

"Well you interpreted them wrong." He seated himself on a sofa. "Come on, let's get this over with. I want to talk to Cynthia, and I want to be sensitive enough to understand how the hell she could get herself in such a fix."

Kathryn broke out laughing. She didn't know why. There was nothing funny about the situation, but she couldn't stop.

"What are you laughing about?" Ron demanded.

"I don't have a magic potion I can pour over you like Achilles's mother."

"She didn't have a potion," Ron said. "She held him by his heel and dipped him in the River Styx."

Kathryn was impressed despite herself. "Sorry. I'll try to avoid sloppy classical allusions."

"I like mythology," Ron said.

She wouldn't have expected that of him, but maybe he associated himself with the godlike humans of antiquity. He'd certainly accomplished enough to give him an exaggerated opinion of himself.

"I'm more attracted to early nineteenth century English literature," she said.

"The romantic period."

"Yes, I suppose you could call it that, though the term usually refers to poetry."

"What else would you call the Brontës?" He seemed to realize he was off topic and give himself a mental shake. "But I didn't come here to discuss mythology or literature."

"You came here to learn how to become sensitive in one easy lesson."

"I don't expect it to be easy."

"Good. You can begin by not glaring at me. You have to be receptive to the feelings of others, able to interpret the slightest hint of what they may be feeling inside. As long as you're angry at me, you're too busy projecting feelings to be able to receive any."

"I'm not angry at you."

"Look at your facial expression," she said pointing to a mirror mounted in an ornate gold frame on the wall.

He was so slow to rise she thought he wasn't going to move. But once he stood, he moved quickly.

"What's wrong with my expression?" he asked.

"You look like you're about to chew somebody out."

"That's how I always look."

"Then it's a good place to start. Smile."

It was more of a grimace.

"Like you meant it. Imagine—"

"I don't need any help knowing what to imagine."

His smile was brilliant, warm, sexy. A mistake. It transformed him into a person she found even more attractive. "Okay, we know you can smile," she said, turning away from the mirror. "Now let's see how you sit."

He sat on the edge of his chair, leaning forward from the waist as if he were ready to pounce at any moment.

"Relax. You look like you're ready to attack the first person who disagrees with you, or so eager to speak you won't be willing to listen."

"I have to convince people they're making the best decision they can when they accept my offer."

"And if they don't?"

"I keep after them."

"Why?"

"I can't stand it when people make stupid decisions."

"You can't be judgmental," Kathryn said. "There's no right or wrong with people's feelings. All feelings are okay."

"That's ridiculous."

"What would you say if I told you your feelings for Cynthia and her situation were all wrong?"

"I'd say you were nuts."

"As long as you feel like that, you'll never be able to understand her or make her care how you feel."

"But you don't want me to tell her what I feel."

"She already knows."

"Then what's this sensitivity mumbo jumbo all about?"

"She needs to feel you're not angry at her, that you're not condemning her. Most important of all, she needs to feel you still love her."

"Of course I love her. But I'm not going to tell her I'm glad she's pregnant at sixteen, or that I'm looking forward to meeting the horny kid who's responsible for this."

Kathryn supposed she couldn't blame him for being upset. "Mr. Egan, you can't say anything like that to Cynthia."

"Why not?"

"Because it will prove to her you don't understand her feelings."

"I don't."

"Then it's up to you to change enough so you can."

He sat there a moment, apparently thinking of one response after another and rejecting them all.

"And how do you propose I do that?" he asked finally.

"You can begin by asking Cynthia how she feels about what's happening, about the kind of future she wants for her and her baby. You don't have to agree with what she says, but you have to make her feel you're not condemning her in any way. And when you do make a decision, she has got to feel you're putting her wishes ahead of your own."

"She's sixteen. She doesn't know what's best for her."

"Then you have to be so sensitive to her thoughts, you can guide them without her knowing you're doing it."

"I can't do that."

"Isn't that what you do in your business, convince people your way is the right way?"

"I don't waste time letting them think they're right in the first place. I knock the props out from under them within ten minutes. I destroy their security so completely they can't help but look for another way out."

"Maybe you should have talked to your wife more."

"Erin never asked me to stay home from a meeting or to leave the office early. My success was as important to her as it is to me."

Kathryn couldn't understand any woman feeling that way. "I don't think it's important to Cynthia."

"Then what is?"

"You are."

"She goes to the best school, we live in a new house in the best part of town and she has four people who are paid to see she has everything she needs. What else can I do for her?"

"You can stay home more. You can make her feel she's more important than your work."

Ron reacted as though she'd slapped him. "My work has never been as important as Cynthia!"

"Then why were you in Switzerland?"

"Because it's my job."

"Are you sure it's not about making more money, about control rather than making a company more efficient?"

His lips had thinned to an angry line. "What do you know about business?"

"Not as much as you do, but my father is a businessman and he's never home. Not one of his four children believes we or our mother are as important as his work."

He looked at her for a long moment. "Okay. Since you feel what I'm doing isn't working, what do you propose I do?"

"You could begin by taking a leave of absence from your job. You've got enough money to retire right now."

"And sit around all day understanding my daughter and some boy I have yet to meet?"

"That's a good place to start. Cynthia obviously isn't as materialistic as you. You need to try to see the world from her viewpoint."

"Did you ever ask your father why he worked so hard?"

"Yes."

"What did he say?"

"For his self-respect."

"Did you understand that?"

"Not really."

Ron suddenly seemed charged with energy. "Tell your housekeeper we'll be gone for a few hours."

"I can't leave."

"You're teaching me to be sensitive. Remember? Well, you can't do that if you don't understand *my* feelings, and you never will unless I show you a few things you know nothing about."

"Where are we going?"

"Somewhere I'm sure you've never been before."

Chapter Three

Kathryn had ridden in several Bentleys before but never in one she was certain cost more than three hundred thousand dollars. She was just as certain the car had never been down these particular roads. Neither had she.

"Where are we going?" she asked.

"Where I grew up," Ron said.

They had left Charlotte and were somewhere in what she presumed was the far reaches of southern Mecklenberg County. It was an area where small farms were either still in production or had been allowed to grow into young forests. Some areas next to Lake Wylie had been developed into upscale resorts. Ron pulled off the road into the parking lot of a local fish camp, turned away from the restaurant, and drove into a strip of woods. When they emerged on the other side, she saw the trailer park.

Ron pulled the Bentley to a stop near a small trailer. The grass around it had been cut recently, but the steps had collapsed and the trailer had rusted badly. "That's where I grew up."

"Does anyone live here?"

"No. I still own it."

"Why?"

"So I never forget where I came from."

Kathryn looked at laundry hanging on lines, children playing in the spring sun wearing nothing but dirty underpants, two women looking tired and worn down, and a hound dog lazing in the sun. Kathryn felt as if she were gazing at the set for a black-and-white movie set in the fifties.

"I lived here until I was fourteen," Ron said. "I was ten years old before I knew enough to hate it."

"What happened?"

"We had court-ordered busing for desegregation. I got sent to a wealthy white neighborhood where I saw kids I thought existed only on TV. I came home and told my parents, but they didn't care that I didn't have a winter coat or shoes without holes in them as long as they had enough booze. The rich kids had so much stuff they didn't bother keeping track of it. I got a coat from the lost and found. I even found a pair of shoes my size."

He sounded as though he were talking about somebody else, but Kathryn knew he would never have held on to the rusting trailer if he didn't still feel the hurt.

"When I heard one of the boys say Charlotte Country Day School was giving scholarships to smart kids, I made up my mind to get one. My parents didn't want me mixing with the rich kids. They thought it would turn me into a snob. I didn't know what was at that school, but I knew it was something I wanted."

"I gather you got that scholarship," Kathryn said.

He nodded. "But I didn't get what I wanted. I was overweight, wore glasses, was smarter than anybody else in my class, and I was a trailer park kid. I had nothing to do but study hard so I could win a college scholarship."

"To Yale."

"And Harvard for my MBA."

"Your parents must have been very proud of you."

"My parents were supposed to come to my high school graduation. I was valedictorian. I wanted them to see what I'd accomplished. I wanted them to be proud of me."

Ron's voice had taken on a different tone, one she could only describe as trying to keep some fierce emotion in check.

"A friend talked them into going drinking instead. They were killed when he lost control of his car trying to outrun the police."

"I'm sorry." She couldn't think of anything else to say.

"Don't be. I don't think they cared much."

"Is that why you care so much?"

He turned to face her. "You can't understand where I'm coming from because you've never been there. You can't understand what drives me because you've always had everything—looks, money, acceptance."

"Try me."

Ron retrieved an envelope from the glove compartment. He opened it and pulled out a picture. "That's me at sixteen, fat, glasses and all." He pulled out a second picture. She was stunned to see it was of her debutante ball.

"Where did you get that picture?"

"Newspaper archives go back years." He pulled out another picture. "This is what I looked like at eighteen when I worked at Taco Bell." And another picture. "This is you." The picture had been taken just before a group of students from her boarding school went to France on an exchange program.

"I won't apologize for having advantages others don't."

"I'm not asking you to. I'm just saying you don't know what it's like to be poor, to not have proper food, warm clothes, toys at Christmas. Even worse, what it's like being ignored, realizing nobody knows you exist, wouldn't care if you didn't. That *really* gets to you. You've been accepted your whole life just because of who you are. I've had to earn recognition, sometimes force people to give it to me. Well, nobody is going to ignore Cynthia. I'll see to that.''

She was beginning to understand. It really wasn't about the money. ''But Cynthia does feel ignored…by you.''

''I've done everything I could for her.''

''You've paid someone else to do it. She'd rather it had been you.''

After an uncomfortable silence, she picked up the second picture. ''You don't look like that now. What happened?''

He grinned, and something inside her went all open and tender. She wished he wouldn't do that. She didn't like the effect on her.

''I had a late growth spurt, lost my baby fat, took up intramural sports and got contacts.''

''No hormones or steroids?''

''Just decent food and exercise.''

She smiled. ''And shoes without holes.''

He smiled back. ''And not from the lost and found.''

''Was it hard being a scholarship student?'' She didn't know why she asked that question. All the schools she'd attended had scholarship students. She knew they usually felt left out and unwanted.

''I hated it. I felt I ought to at least be given a chance to prove I could fit in. The other scholarship kids didn't seem to care, but it ate away at me all the time. From that first day in the fourth grade, I swore one day I'd be so successful nobody could ignore me.''

He'd certainly done that. He'd made the cover of several business magazines during the past year. *The Charlotte Observer* had run a feature article on him. ''I won't pretend to understand,'' Kathryn said, looking at the rusted hulk of the trailer, ''but everybody knows who you are now.''

''But they don't *accept* me. I went to their schools and played touch football with them. I have the money, but I don't have the pedigree. I don't have the family history.''

Kathryn remembered how her friends made comments

about people with less money, looks and sophistication. There had always been an unspoken barrier that separated them, that constantly reminded them they weren't good enough. She'd never really stopped to think how that must have made them feel. Rather than discriminate against them, she should have admired them for having the courage to tackle and overcome obstacles she didn't have to face.

"Not all our families have a history I'd want."

"It doesn't have to be good. It just has to be well-known. Well, Cynthia's going to have a history, even if it's short."

"Maybe she doesn't want the same things you want."

"Maybe not, but she doesn't want to be a nobody."

She felt sorry for him. His parents had died without giving him the love and acceptance he needed. His wife had died before he was much more than another Harvard MBA struggling to make a place for himself in the business world. Cynthia was too young to appreciate her father's accomplishments. He had turned to the public to give him the feeling of acceptance and approval he couldn't get anywhere else.

Her life hadn't been perfect, but at least she had a family that loved her. Still, as much as she sympathized with Ron, she couldn't lose sight of the fact her first concern was Cynthia. Ron was tough. He'd proved he could take care of himself. Cynthia had proved she couldn't.

"Let's go," Ron said. "We're conspicuous."

Like a three-hundred-thousand-dollar car in a squalid trailer park wouldn't be! He pulled to a stop at a boardwalk behind the fish camp that overlooked the lake. They got out. The breeze coming off the lake was refreshingly cool. It smelled of crisp water and honeysuckle.

"I used to watch the boats," Ron said. "I'd try to imagine what it would be like to roar across the lake in one of those big boats without caring that my wake might capsize some little boat."

"I always hated people who did that. Did you ever buy a boat?"

"Lake Norman is the place to be now. It wasn't the same."

Her father had bought a house at Lake Norman. He said Lake Wylie was for the middle class. "Did you do the other things you dreamed you'd do when you were finally successful?"

"I bought a house in the best neighborhood and sent my daughter to the best school in town. She has the best of everything."

"What if she considers you the best of everything?"

"Cynthia knows I have to work, or we won't have the money for all those things."

"Maybe she doesn't want them."

"She would if she didn't have them."

"Maybe not so much."

"Look, I can't go to a company and say I'll only do seventy-six thousand dollars worth of work because I need only seventy-six thousand dollars this year. They'd think I was a fool and hire someone else. I have to charge top dollar, or they won't think I'm good enough to hire."

"Even if it's a million dollars?"

"You're talking companies worth thirty, fifty, a hundred *billion* dollars. A million is pocket change to them. More than the cost, what's important is the quality of the service, the expert personal attention to every detail. I have an office of fifteen full-time staff. That can double or triple depending on the job. Then there are bonuses and percentages. I have to get paid well. A lot of people depend on me."

"That doesn't change the fact that nothing can replace you in your daughter's life."

"Who do you think I'm doing all this for?"

He wasn't getting the point. "Maybe you've reached the point where your success has isolated you from Cynthia."

"I know it's kept us apart more than I want, but I have to go where the work takes me."

Now he was making excuses for doing what he wanted to do. She wouldn't let him get away with that. "Every decision is yours to make one way or the other. Everything is a choice. Some of the choices you've made have hurt Cynthia.''

''I can't help that.''

''Of course you can. It doesn't matter that some decisions don't work out the way you wanted or planned, they're still your decisions and you're still responsible for the results, for seeing that something is going wrong and doing something about it.''

She wondered what was going on in his mind as he stared out over the lake. Was he remembering his parents and his childhood here, his progression from school to school, or was he thinking of his wife and daughter? She wondered if his career left him time to think of anything else.

She wondered why he hadn't remarried.

He was relatively young—the *Observer* article said he was forty—handsome and rich, characteristics that would make him the target of beautiful women the world over. Add to that intelligence, a vibrant personality, excellent taste in clothes and cars, and you had a catch of the first order. She was certain he wasn't immune to women. She'd seen the way he looked at her.

Yet for some reason, she didn't think he'd spent the last ten years traipsing through available bedrooms on both sides of the Atlantic. She had no knowledge of his personal life, but the articles she read failed to mention a constant companion. Even business articles these days rarely overlooked such interesting facts.

''Erin encouraged me to put my career first,'' he said without turning away from the lake. ''She didn't want a family to hold me back. She said she would take care of things I forgot or was too busy to do. She wanted me to be successful.''

Kathryn remembered reading that Erin Egan had died of ovarian cancer.

''After she died I worked even harder. I felt guilty because I hadn't achieved the success she desperately wanted for Cynthia, for all the other children we planned to have. She said we had to sacrifice in the beginning to get where we wanted to be in the end.''

Kathryn wondered if he was still so much in love with his wife he was still living his life for her.

He turned his gaze from the lake to her. ''I'm not going to pretend I did everything for Erin, but we were like partners, each willing to do our part.''

''Do you miss her?''

''Yes.''

His smile seemed bleak, in contrast to the glorious spring day filled with sunshine.

''We were friends bound together by a mutual goal. I think that brought us closer than passion could. When she died, I was left to carry on alone. I realize now I should have known I had to reassess, but I thought Cynthia was too young to need me. I planned to work hard then so I could take some time off when she grew up. I guess I got too busy to realize the situation had changed.''

''She always needed you,'' Kathryn said. ''She just couldn't tell you how much.''

''What can a grown man do with a little girl?''

''Love her.''

''I did love her.''

''I'm sure you did, but in a child's eyes, love means being there, holding her hand, playing with her, telling her stories and kissing her good-night. Your physical presence counts far more than what you say.''

He turned back to the water. ''So you're saying I'm a failure as a father.''

Was she? She certainly considered her own father a failure, but she hesitated to make the same decision about Ron. If he hadn't loved his daughter, he wouldn't have left his meeting in Geneva. She didn't know much about big business, but she did know people at his level weren't expected to let anything interfere with their work. There was always somebody willing to make whatever sacrifice was necessary to reach the top. She wondered what his coming home would cost him.

"No. I'm just saying you haven't understood what your daughter needed from you."

"Do you?"

"In general. My own father has a career that keeps him away from home most of the time, but everybody's different. Cynthia may not need what I needed."

"What did you need?"

She hadn't expected the spotlight to be turned on her. "What I needed isn't important. It's what Cynthia needs."

"You've just said we're not communicating well. If I can understand what you needed, maybe I'll have a better chance of understanding Cynthia."

She wondered if he looked at his clients the way he was looking at her. He was so earnest, so *sincere,* she found it nearly impossible to resist him. "Mr. Egan, I make it a point to keep my relationship with the families of the girls impersonal."

"You have to try to understand the parents, or you can't help restore a relationship that's broken down."

"I don't attempt to restore relationships. I leave that to the girls."

"How can you possibly say you're doing your best for these girls when you leave out the most important part of all, helping them restore a family relationship that has broken down so badly they've turned to you for help?"

"My purpose is to provide a place for them to stay, a way to continue their education, a way to have their baby safely. I've taken classes in psychology and counseling, but I don't consider myself a professional psychologist or counselor."

"Then you're not qualified for your job."

She pushed back the anger. She had attacked him, and he was attacking back. It wasn't much fun, but she guessed she could understand it. "I don't think you understand my role here. I'm the administrator. I hire qualified people to do the teaching, counseling, career planning, the training in how to take care of their babies.''

''Then your understanding of what they want and need from their families is all you have to offer. So tell me what you wanted from your father. You wanted it very badly, or you'd never have done what you're doing now.''

No other parent had asked this of her, but she'd never been this interested in a parent of one of her girls. There was something about this man that forced her to respond to him. She warned herself to be careful. He'd made a fortune persuading people to do things against their wills. Naturally he would use the same skills on her. He already had in persuading her to come with him today, in making her like him even though she disapproved of almost everything about him.

But maybe his question wasn't as unreasonable as it sounded at first. He had taken a great chance when he left his meeting to come home. This was a second day and he hadn't said anything about returning to Geneva. He clearly wanted to help his daughter. She had asked him to jeopardize something he loved, and he had done it without hesitation. Would she have jeopardized the shelter under similar circumstances?

She returned his gaze, searching his face for even the tiniest evidence of insincerity, of game playing, of one-upmanship, of anything that would indicate he wasn't being entirely truthful.

What she found was a tremendously attractive man focusing his attention on her. He was asking about his daughter, but she felt he really did want to know about her, that his interest was sincere, not a vehicle to another objective. And she found she cared more than she wanted about his success. Or was it simply that this man was so attractive, so charismatic, she couldn't help herself?

She hoped the answer wasn't the affirmative. She didn't want to feel even the slightest twinge of interest in a man who had put his career before his family. She didn't want to be attracted to a man who would be more interested in pleasing others than in pleasing her. She had very strict guidelines for any man she considered dating. Not that Ron had asked her for a date, but she refused to be interested, even on a casual basis, in a man who didn't satisfy her list of requirements. Ron Egan would bottom out before she got halfway through.

"Every girl wants something different," she stated.

"I'm asking you to speak for yourself."

"Why?"

"Because you interest me. I want to know what makes you tick."

"A well-balanced diet, sufficient rest and regular exercise."

He laughed. She hadn't expected that. It was a deep, thoroughly masculine sound that reached a receptive place inside the core of her. The tug of attraction grew even stronger, her will to resist weaker. Warning bells went off in her head. *This man is dangerous.*

"Do you always keep men at such a safe distance?" he asked.

"You're not a man. I mean, you're the father of one of my girls. I don't look at you the same as I would other men."

"Why can't you think of me as a man as well as Cynthia's father?"

"Because it's my job to see you as Cynthia's father."

"Does that preclude any other relationship?"

"I don't have *relationships* with the fathers of my girls. It would be highly unprofessional."

"Why? Would it cloud your judgment?"

"No, but—"

"Why not?"

She didn't understand how the ground had shifted so unexpectedly, how she was now on the defensive.

"Are you always professional at any price?" he asked. "Don't your emotions ever overpower your intellect?"

"No."

"I don't believe it."

"I don't require that you believe me."

"But I want to."

"Why?"

"I might be a father, but I like attractive women."

"Mr. Egan, this is not an appropriate conversation."

"Call me Ron. And what's inappropriate about a man telling a woman he finds her attractive?"

"It's the circumstances."

"Tell me what circumstances you find proper, and I'll set them up."

Just like her father. He thought money and power could solve any problem. But her irritation at his assumption didn't smother a desire to answer his question. Nor did it stop her from wondering what it would have been like to have met him under different circumstances.

"I'm sure you've met hundreds of attractive women in the course of your career," Kathryn said, trying hard to sound businesslike, "yet you were able to set that aside and concentrate on your business."

"Sure."

"That's what you have to do now."

"Why?"

He was a very stubborn man, but she guessed he hadn't made it to the top by taking no for an answer. "Why wouldn't you?"

"Because I don't see a conflict. I can find you attractive and still work with you to understand my daughter."

"Yes, but finding me attractive isn't the same as trying to establish a personal relationship between us."

"I didn't say anything about a personal relationship. Did you say that because you find me attractive?"

She was trapped. The only way out was to be completely candid. "You know you're an attractive man. I'm sure you've studied your personal appearance in minute detail, put it together like a well-orchestrated game plan, and use it to every possible advantage.''

He grinned. She wished he wouldn't.

"Of course I do. Everybody prefers to be around attractive people. If they didn't, half the people in movies and TV would disappear tomorrow. But we're not talking business. We're talking personal.''

"I'm not.''

"I am.''

"Mr. Egan—''

"Ron.''

"Mr. Egan—''

"I won't let you finish that sentence unless you call me Ron.''

He had moved closer to her. She wasn't easily intimidated, but she had to consciously stop herself from pulling back. She refused to give ground to this man even if her pulse had started pounding in a very unnerving sort of way, even if her normally logical mind was having difficulty maintaining the thread of her argument. Ron Egan was an absentee father who needed to be made aware of the damage his preoccupation with his career had done to his daughter.

"It's time we went back. I've found your background very helpful, but—''

"We can't leave.''

"Why?''

"You haven't called me Ron.''

"I don't need to.''

"I want to hear it.''

He was leaning on the railing, his weight on his left arm, looking up at her with the ingenuousness of a teenager trying to wheedle his way out of trouble. Only he was trying to wheedle her into it.

"Ron. There, I said it.''

"Don't make it sound like a dose of bad medicine. Make it sound like you might even like me a little."

"Look, I don't—"

"Are you always this resistant with men?"

She didn't understand why she'd let their conversation become so personal. "I don't mix business with pleasure."

"I do my most effective work that way. When we do get down to business, it's usually just working out the details of something we've already decided."

"I'm not a businessperson. I'm a people person, and I find it easier to keep the two separate."

"That's a very interesting concept. Why don't we have lunch and discuss it?"

Chapter Four

"Okay," Ron said, lobster juice dripping from his elbows onto the tablecloth-size napkin tucked into his collar, "we've decided I'm a true pirate of high finance. I give no quarter and expect none. I think everyone should take responsibility for their own actions and not expect outside help. You blame my career, my pursuit of money and power, even my failure to marry again, for my abysmal failure as a father. I think we've covered me. Now I want to hear about you. What did you want from your father that you didn't get?"

She'd known from the moment she agreed to have lunch with him she had to answer his question. She'd ordered lobster salad. He ordered a lobster in the shell. He'd surprised her by taking off his coat and rolling up his sleeves. She understood why when he let the juice run down his arms to his elbows.

"Do you always eat lobster like that?" she asked.

"No. I can ease the little sucker out of his shell without

getting a single drop on a linen tablecloth that costs more than some cars. But you're not going to distract me any longer. You have me at your mercy. I want to become a better father. Tell me about yourself.''

She had tried, without success, to convince him that her experiences had nothing to do with his success or failure as a father, but it appeared the only way to convince him was to tell him what he wanted to know.

''My father was away from home much of the time. When he was home, he was always meeting someone or bringing them to the house. There never seemed to be any time when he belonged to just us, when nobody else could interrupt or call him away. The few times he did find himself alone with us—on a family vacation or for an evening at home—I think he was bored and restless. I don't think he was interested in us.''

''I take it he never played with you as a kid, read you stories, or kissed you good-night.''

''Never.'' She hoped she didn't sound as if she were whining. It was a fact she'd accepted. She didn't think too much about it until he kicked her sister Elizabeth out of the house. She had never forgiven him for that.

''How did you rebuild your relationship? Maybe I can do the same thing with Cynthia.''

''It's not the same. I'm an adult. I don't live at home.''

His gaze seemed to become more intense. ''Are you trying *not* to tell me that you and your father don't have a good relationship?''

She might as well get it over with. Ron Egan seemed to have a genius for finding the weak spots. ''My father I and had a serious disagreement about ten years ago. We don't see each other much.''

''How much is that?''

She stopped playing with the remains of her salad and looked him square in the face. ''Usually once a month.''

''Since when?''

''Since he threw my sister out of the house.''

He took his napkin out of his collar, and carefully wiped his mouth and his hands. Then he sat back. "Tell me about it."

She couldn't believe she was getting ready to tell a man she'd known less than twenty-four hours about one of the most difficult episodes of her life, but for some reason she felt she could share it with him.

"My sister got pregnant when she was in high school. She was seventeen and wildly in love with the boy. My father wouldn't let her marry him. And after she did anyway, he said they couldn't live in his house."

"Why?"

"He said the boy was a shiftless bloodsucker. He said my sister had been stealing stuff from his office. Elizabeth was a little wild, but she wouldn't have done anything like that."

"Did you do anything to help?"

"I wasn't there. I was the good daughter who did everything Mom and Dad wanted. I was at boarding school. Elizabeth got herself kicked out of Country Day so she could go to public school. I dated boys from approved families. Elizabeth chose half her dates just because she knew they'd make my father furious."

"So you dedicated yourself to pregnant teenage girls because you think your sister got a raw deal."

"What would you have done?"

"Locked them in the same room until they came to some solution."

"That may work in business, though I wouldn't have thought so, but it doesn't work with personal relationships. You each have to try to understand where the other is coming from."

"Coddle them and make them think being stupid is an acceptable way to behave."

She folded her napkin. It was time to leave. "That's not what I said."

He put a fifty-dollar bill on the table and rose. "You said

your father and sister should be allowed to stay at odds with each other because you have to honor their feelings. Yet you said I ought to take a leave of absence to repair my relationship with my daughter. Your logic is inconsistent. Either you have a set of principles that work in all situations, or you don't have a workable theory.''

She had preceded him out of the restaurant and she waited to answer him until they were in the car.

''I told you I don't pretend to be a professional, so I don't give advice.''

''You're giving me advice.''

''Only because you insisted.''

Kathryn didn't know how she'd let herself get drawn into helping Ron. All the other parents had been more than willing to meet with the specialists she recommended. Why couldn't she keep her distance from the Egans?

Something had been different about them from the first. Cynthia wasn't like the other girls. Or maybe she had reacted differently to her because Cynthia wasn't panicked or hysterical or even silent and moody. Kathryn felt almost as though they were equals even though Cynthia was only half her age.

She didn't kid herself when it came to Ron Egan. Everything was different because her physical response to him had been immediate and undeniable. It didn't matter that she might disagree with him in every way. As a man, she found him powerfully attractive. She wanted to be around him even though she knew it was a foolish thing to do.

He seemed to be truly interested in learning to communicate with his daughter, but he had no idea how to begin. If she didn't help him, he was liable to treat Cynthia as a hostile takeover. They could end up like her own family.

''From now on you and Cynthia will have to work things out on your own.''

''Good. That means you'll be able to go on a date with me tonight, and you won't have to tell me how I'm doing everything wrong.''

* * *

"Everyone will know what I did. How is that better?" Cynthia asked.

"It will be a lot better if you see your friends," Kathryn said.

They had been talking for nearly half an hour. Rather, Kathryn and Cynthia had been talking. Ron had been mostly listening, putting in a word now and then, responding when addressed directly. He felt as if they were conversing in a foreign tongue. The words were ones he knew, but they seemed to have different meanings from what he expected. He wondered if it was just a woman thing, or if there was some special bonding between them. He couldn't remember Cynthia ever being so open and relaxed with Margaret Norwood or the governess, and they'd known her most of her life.

They'd come back to find that Cynthia's best friend, Leigh Stedman, had come by to see her. After refusing to see her, Cynthia had locked herself in her room, extremely upset anyone at school knew where she was or that she was pregnant. It had taken Kathryn several minutes to convince Cynthia to let her into her room. It had taken more than thirty minutes to convince her to talk with her father.

Pacing up and down the large living room, he'd had plenty of time to rehearse what he meant to say. He'd even edited it to make sure he wasn't too severe. But when Cynthia walked through that door, she didn't look like a confident young woman any longer. She looked like the little girl who used to like to curl up in his lap and go to sleep when he worked late. He'd instinctively held out his arms, and she'd come to him.

For a few minutes everything was the way it used to be. They held each other while she cried. But as soon as her tears dried up, she became stiff, their positions awkward. When he released her, she moved away, ultimately sitting in a chair rather than on the sofa next to him. She looked so small, sitting in that huge overstuffed chair with her feet tucked under her, he could almost think of her as his little girl again. But he would have been fooling himself. At first she'd talked exclusively to Kathryn. It was as though she was embarrassed she'd cried in front of him. He'd wanted to tell her it was all right, that she never had to be afraid to come to him when she was frightened or feeling alone.

"I wouldn't look at it like that," Kathryn said. "You have a friend who knows what happened, and she still wants to be your friend."

"I don't have any real friends," Cynthia said.

"I'll bet you do," Kathryn said. "You've only been here two days, and already you're everybody's favorite. People can't help but want to be your friend."

Ron didn't know if Cynthia believed that, but it seemed to improve her spirits.

Cynthia chewed on her lower lip. "They won't want a friend with a baby," she said.

"All real friendships expand to include other people— boyfriends, husbands, children, even other friends. You'll see if you just give your friends a chance."

"Leigh's parents are just about the most important people in Charlotte," Cynthia said. "They'll never let her have anything to do with an unwed mother."

"I think you ought to give Leigh and her family a chance to make that decision rather than you making it for them. I think you'll find very few people are so narrow-minded, so unwilling to make allowances for mistakes."

Ron knew it must have been difficult for Kathryn to say that when her own parents had turned their backs on their daughter for the same reason.

"Leigh told Lisette she's coming back tomorrow," Kathryn said. "You've got to make up your mind what you're going to do."

"Do you like this girl?" Ron asked.

"Of course I like her," Cynthia said impatiently. "I said she was my best friend, didn't I?"

"Would you still want to be her friend if she got pregnant?" he asked.

Cynthia shifted position in the chair before she answered. "Yes, I would."

"Then I'm sure she feels the same way about you."

"I expect it will hurt Leigh a great deal if you cut her off," Kathryn said

"There's somebody else you need to see," Ron said.

"Who?" Cynthia asked.

"Margaret. She's helped take care of you from the day your mother and I brought you home from the hospital. She's devastated you would run away from her."

"This has nothing to do with her," Cynthia said.

"She loves you. That means everything you do affects her. The same is true for Rose, Rosco and Gretta even though they've known you only half as long. If you don't feel you can go see them, at least talk to them on the telephone."

"I didn't think they'd care."

"Margaret cares a lot. She treated your mother like her own daughter."

Ron didn't know whether making Cynthia think about how her behavior had affected others was the best thing to do, but he did know it would stop her from thinking she was isolated and unloved. Maybe if she could believe other people loved her, she could believe he loved her, too.

"Gretta said Margaret's been so upset she hasn't been able to sleep," Ron said.

Cynthia got up. "I'd better call her now. She feels sick when she can't sleep."

"That went better than I expected," Kathryn said after Cynthia left the room.

"Margaret Norwood has been like a mother to her. Cynthia's been so worried about me, the baby's father and her friends, she's forgotten the woman who's taken care of her since she was born."

"Talking to them and seeing Leigh will help pull her out

of her isolation. I think you've done very well for one day."

"*We've* done well. You're still coaching me, remember?"

"You don't need coaching."

"That's because you think I'm so hopeless I'm hardly worth the trouble."

"No, I don't."

"It's only fair that you give me a chance to change your mind. Have dinner with me."

"Are you asking me for a date?"

"Didn't it sound like that? I haven't done it in a long time, but surely things haven't changed that much."

"I told you earlier I don't go out with clients."

"I'm not your client. Cynthia is."

"You're close enough."

"Then you pick what we do. A movie, dinner, the museum. I'm flying back to Geneva late tonight."

"I wondered how long it would be before you went back."

"I'm coming back right after the meeting. I won't be gone more than a day at a time until we get this thing sorted out."

"You need to stop including me."

"You're my advisor. Forget the professionals," he said when she started to protest. "I'm not going to sue you for practicing without a license. Just consider me a friend who needs your advice."

"Do you?"

"Especially tonight. I haven't dated a beautiful woman since my wife died."

"You'll have to ask someone else."

"When you decide what you want to do, let me know when to pick you up. Now I've got to call Geneva and find out how the meeting went today."

Then he was gone, leaving Kathryn's sputtering protests hanging in the air.

* * *

Kathryn decided she needed a new backbone. The one she had obviously wasn't doing the job. She was annoyed with herself for agreeing to go on this date. She had talked herself out of it at least twice before she picked up the phone to call him. She hadn't realized what a terrible snob she was until tonight. She'd given Ron three choices for the evening. The Charlotte Opera's production of Puccini's *Tosca,* the Mint Museum's exhibit of Tutankhamen, or the latest Harry Potter movie. Rather than accuse her of being exactly the kind of snob he'd suffered from growing up, he discussed her choices as if they were all of equal importance.

He said he'd always want to see *Tosca,* but after hearing the recording of Maria Callas in the role, he didn't think he could stand to hear anyone who wasn't absolutely world-class. He'd already seen the Tutankhamen exhibit, so if she didn't mind, they'd catch an early showing of the movie, have a late dinner, and she could drop him off at the airport.

Snobbery had caused her to pit the movie against *Tosca* and King Tut. Honesty forced her to admit she'd enjoyed it. And being with Ron.

"I realized early that being a success in the business world and being accepted in the social one were two different things," Ron was saying over dinner at one of his private clubs. "I signed up for every art and music class I could fit into my schedule. I even went to a couple of ballets." He made a face. "I can't say I enjoy men in pants so tight it makes me uncomfortable just to watch them, but I like opera. I don't even care if the soprano is twice as big *and* three times as old as the heroine is supposed to be. I just get angry when they go for a high note and can't reach it. You'd think they wouldn't give the part to someone who can't sing the notes."

He'd gone from Harry Potter to sports—the University of North Carolina, her alma mater, had just won the national soccer title—to opera. They'd discussed city planning when he said he wished she could get the city fathers to establish more parks. He said people in the inner city needed places for picnics and family gatherings, not just soccer fields, bike trails and ponds for ducks and geese. He was also in favor of preserving more trees, establishing deeper green belts around lakes and rivers, and improving public transportation.

Two things they didn't discuss were his job and hers.

"I can't believe you studied all those things just so you could talk to rich people at parties."

He laughed as if she'd made a joke. She didn't know more than a dozen men who could talk about anything remotely cultural. Most didn't consider it something a *man* needed to know. Like religion and table manners, culture was left to their wives.

"There's a lot more to business than just knowing how to do your job. Besides, I found I liked learning about all those things. It rounded me off, gave me that finish only a certain kind of education and lifestyle can give you. And as I said, I like the Impressionists, opera and Greek myths. I also like horse racing, but I can't afford that."

The more he talked, the more she realized she'd underestimated him, the more she started to feel he probably knew more about everything than she did.

"What do you do for fun?" she asked.

"Nothing."

"Everybody has something they do when they want to let their hair down."

"I don't have time. In my business if you don't work all the time, somebody passes you."

"You'll go crazy."

"Not if you like your work. The pressure can be intense and the hours long, but I like challenges, pitting myself against the other guy."

"That sounds primitive."

"It is. Instead of doing it with rocks and spears, we do it with computers and leveraged buyouts. But there are some things I don't like. I hate golf. It's a boring game, but every executive in the world seems to play. I find eating endless meals at high-priced restaurants or tedious dinner parties a waste of time. And I have little appreciation for fine wines or aged whiskey.''

Now it was her turn to laugh. ''I'm surprised they haven't thrown you out of the country club.'' She nearly swallowed her words. Did he belong to any country clubs? Some discriminated for the most ridiculous reasons.

''Not yet, but I don't go often enough to offend anyone. Belonging to the right club is part of business in Europe. You've got to be the right sort before they'll touch your money.''

He said it all as if it didn't matter, but she could feel the undertone of resentment. He wasn't accepted by the people who mattered, even though he'd accomplished more than they had. He'd accepted it as a fact of life, but it was something he wouldn't—*couldn't*—accept for his daughter.

''Now tell me something about yourself,'' Ron said. ''I find it hard to understand why a pretty woman like you isn't married with her own children.''

''Is that the only thing you think women are good for, being wives and mothers?'' She hadn't expected that of him, but wasn't it what he'd done in his own life, left his wife home to take care of the baby while he roamed the world? That's what her father thought, and just about every other man she knew.

''I've come up against too many tough women across the board table to think that,'' Ron said. ''You're clearly not interested in a career unless you consider taking care of other people's children a career.''

''I think of it as a vocation.''

''I think of it as an avocation, something so important you'll continue to be involved in it but not your main goal in life.''

That's something else all men seemed to have in common, a certainty they knew what a woman was thinking. She didn't know which male gene made them feel infallible, but she hoped medical science would soon find a way to eradicate it. It was time men realized they were no more talented or gifted than women, only bigger and often stronger. And the need for bigger and stronger had vanished centuries ago.

"What is my main goal?" She was curious to know what he thought.

"I don't know. That's why I asked you. Do you have anything against marriage, or do you just dislike men in general?"

He was clever enough to know he'd taken a wrong step. "I have nothing against marriage or men. I probably would have been married ten years ago if I'd found the right man."

"Then you should be going out every night, leaving those girls to Ruby. She looks more than capable of handling any trouble."

"Ruby is absolutely wonderful, but she likes to go to bed early."

"Then hire one of your experts."

"I do. I not only date, but I enjoy all the ordinary social activities normal for someone my age."

"Like what? You avoid your family."

"Not all the time."

"And you stopped running and playing tennis because you couldn't afford to take the time away from the girls. You stopped going to the opera or the symphony because the men you dated didn't know enough to be able to discuss what they'd heard, and you don't like professional football, basketball, soccer or hockey because they're loud and too violent. I won't even ask about stock car racing. I can't see you with that crowd."

"You make me sound like an unbearable snob."

"No, *you* make yourself look like a woman who's cut herself off from the rest of the world. You're young, beautiful, wealthy, intelligent, good company and you have a sense of humor when you let yourself relax. You've got more going for you than ninety-nine out of a hundred women, so why aren't you out there having the time of your life?''

''You've known me for less than two days. What do you think gives you the right to ask such a question?''

''Nothing gives me the right unless it's that I'm interested in you. I even like you. I sure as hell know you're sexy. I'm surprised you don't have to station Ruby at the door to drive off dates so overcome by your body they forget themselves on the front porch.''

She had dated a lot of men, but never one who could segue so smoothly from fine arts to flattery to sexual attraction.

''I've never been attacked on the front porch or anywhere else.''

''What kind of men do you go out with? They can't have an ounce of red blood in their bodies. Or do you give them an injection that renders them harmless for the next four hours.''

She smiled. ''No. I interview them first. That's why I don't end up with the wrong kind of man.''

He looked at her as if she were crazy. ''You interview them?''

''Yes.''

''And they submit to this?''

She began to feel uncomfortable. Some of the men had reacted very unpleasantly. They had been even more rude about her choice of questions, but she refused to give an inch. She wasn't going to end up like her mother. ''Not all of them, but enough.''

''Holy hell! I can hardly wait to know what you ask them.''

Chapter Five

Kathryn had never been reluctant to ask her questions, yet she found herself searching for a reason to turn the conversation to a different subject. "They're only for men looking for a serious relationship with me."

"Assume I'd like to have a serious relationship with you."

Kathryn had memorized her list long ago, but at that moment every item on it flew out of her head. He was the father of one of her girls. He was everything she'd argued against her entire life. There was no denying the sexual attraction between them—she could feel it even at this moment—but he had to know she wouldn't consider him as a possible candidate for a serious relationship, certainly not one that could result in marriage.

"I don't know why you'd make such a joke, but I don't consider it very funny."

"Who said anything about jokes? I'm no different from any other man. I'm attracted to beautiful, sexy women. You have this sleek, elegant, stylishly cool look, but I get the feeling a cauldron of hot emotions is seething just below the surface.''

"You've been watching too many operas."

"You're rigid in your ideas. This indicates even more strong emotions. People only fight hard about things that are important to them."

"I see you include pop psychology in your repertoire." She was beginning to get irritated.

"I find you extremely interesting. No good reason, I just do. I guess you might call that chemistry."

Now he was telling her he liked her against reason. While he was taking all of those classes to round out his education, he should have taken one to teach him what *not* to say to women.

"In case you're interested, you're failing my preliminary test so badly I wouldn't even consider asking you the questions."

He laughed and looked at his watch. "We've got to go. My plane should be almost ready."

"You go on. I'll catch a cab."

"Not on your life." He put several bills on the table and got up. "Come on. You've got to tell me how to pass your preliminary test. I'm anxious to get to those questions."

They talked about his trip while they waited for his limousine. She was surprised he still meant to fly back to Charlotte after the next meeting. He would be gone for just one day.

"You won't get any time to rest."

She didn't know why she was worried about him getting enough sleep. He was a grown man. He didn't need her to tell him when to go to bed.

"I can sleep on a plane. In a taxi, too. The only thing that bothers me is jet lag. I can't ever seem to adjust to the change in time."

They had started on a meaningless discussion of ways to combat jet lag when they got into the limousine. He slammed the door on the limousine as well as on their conversation.

"Now tell me how to pass this test of yours."

Okay he asked for it. "To begin with, never tell a woman you're interested in her in spite of yourself."

"I didn't say that. I meant I don't know what it is about you that appeals to me so much. But it's early days. I'll figure it out."

"And no woman wants to be told she's so sexy men lose control over themselves."

"Bull. Every woman likes to think she has that effect on men. She may not want it to happen, but she likes to think it could."

"Well I don't."

"Okay, you're an exception. What else?"

"She doesn't want a man to tell her he knows her better than she knows herself."

"I never said that."

"You said I was a mass of seething emotions."

"Hell, everybody's a mass of emotions. If they don't seethe, you might as well be dead."

She was getting uneasy. He was knocking over all her objections. "And we don't like to be told things we do are unimportant."

"You don't like me calling your home for wayward girls an avocation?"

"They're not wayward. They've just made a mistake."

"Okay, I withdraw the wayward part, but I stick to it being your avocation. Lots of people are more devoted to their avocations than their vocations. It just depends on how their life falls out."

"It's more than an avocation."

"If you got married and had children, would you give it up?"

"No."

"If it came to a choice between the shelter and your family, would you give it up?"

"If it comes to a choice between Cynthia and your job, will you give it up?"

"I asked you first. And before you say I'm not playing fair, I'll remind you I've missed two days of crucial meetings."

She didn't know why she had to keep reminding herself he had left his meeting, that he had spent most of the day trying to figure out what he needed to do to reach a better understanding with his daughter. He was leaving for Geneva in an hour, but he was coming back at the end of the meeting. At least he said he was. That's more than she'd expected. And whether she wanted to admit it or not, it had changed her opinion of him. Maybe that's why she'd agreed to come out with him tonight. He was proving he wasn't the kind of man she'd thought.

She wouldn't allow herself to ask if he might turn out to be the kind of man she *wanted* him to be. She wouldn't allow herself to want anything when it came to Ron Egan. He was much too dangerous.

"I can't answer for sure," she said. "I guess I'd give up the shelter, but I'd make sure it stayed open."

"You don't sound very sure. Not a very good recommendation for your feelings about the importance of family."

"It's hard to be convincing about a hypothetical situation."

"You don't think it could still happen?"

Did she? She had become very cynical about men. Most who were too rich were playboys. Those that were too poor were fortune hunters or were so ambitious they felt work and success were more important than family. If she did marry, it would have to be to a man who had the same or very similar values to her own.

Did she think she would find him? She didn't know. Her last dates hadn't encouraged her to be optimistic. She'd enjoyed her time with Ron more than time spent with any man she'd dated in years, and he was the opposite of everything she wanted. At least that's how it had seemed at first, and she was inclined to stick with her first impression, especially since Ron's charm and sexual pull on her were affecting her judgment.

"I believe I'll get married," she said, "and not because I'm so desperate I have to lower my standards."

"Who said you were desperate? I bet you didn't like that very much."

"Would you?"

"I've been desperate and survived, so it wouldn't bother me. You never have. I think it might scare you."

"It made me mad." At first. She'd started to feel afraid later. Was she being too rigid in her standards, too demanding in her expectations? Was she overestimating her own value?

"I expect it did. Who said it?"

"A very successful attorney who thought my family connections were just what he needed to turn his law career into a political success. He decided I'd be a perfect political hostess." She didn't know why she was telling Ron all of this. She hadn't told anyone, not even her sister.

"He was right. He just wasn't smart enough to see you didn't want to be judged on your suitability for his career plans. The right man would want to marry you even if you were exactly the wrong kind of wife for him."

"I wouldn't want anybody to marry me if I was wrong for him."

"You know what I meant."

She did, and she was surprised he would say something like that.

"You didn't expect me to say that, did you?"

She wished the interior of the limousine wasn't so well lit. Nothing in his words or his tone of voice implied it, but she could tell he was disappointed in her.

"No, I didn't, but I should have."

She could tell her answer, or her honesty, caught him by surprise.

"Why?"

"I didn't stop to realize you'd probably been treated like that many times by people who didn't consider you in their class but were willing to work with you because you could be useful to them."

"It's happened a few times, but I was using them just as much as they were using me."

She didn't know if he really believed what he said, but he would never have held on to that rusty trailer if slights and snobbish treatment weren't important to him. He wanted to remember what it felt like to be powerless, to be treated like a nobody, to be passed over for people who were much less capable.

"I never thought of it like that," she said. "I guess we all use people."

"The trick is to be fair about it. Now, I want to hear those questions. You've stalled long enough."

"There's no point. Half of them don't apply to you, or I already know the answers."

"Such as?"

"Have you been married before and how many times? How did your last relationship end? Have you ever gotten a woman pregnant? Do you have any children? How often do you call your mother? You can't answer that because she died years ago."

"I'd probably call her every couple of weeks."

Right in the middle of the acceptable range. "How often do you clean your own bathroom? But that doesn't apply either because you have a maid."

"I didn't always?"

"Okay how often did you clean your bathroom when you were in college?"

"I didn't. I lived in a dorm. And we had a communal bathroom."

"At Harvard and Yale?"

"I was a scholarship student, remember."

"Okay, how often did you clean your room?"

"I cleaned my half every week. My roommate only tackled his when he went home on vacation and had to pack up all his dirty clothes for the maids to wash."

Okay, he probably wouldn't leave his underwear on the bathroom floor, but he wouldn't complain if she dried her panty hose on the towel rack.

"Do you have any vices? What's your favorite one?"

Ron laughed. "I don't have time for vices. I work all the time, but you probably consider that a vice."

"What's your favorite female body part and why?"

"You're kidding."

"No."

"Will you tell me your favorite male body part if I answer?"

"This is my quiz. I get to ask the questions, and you get to answer."

"Okay, in case I answer wrong, I'm warning you, I know karate."

"I know jujitsu."

"Hell, I'm impressed you even know the word. Okay, I like breasts, lips, and eyes, not necessarily in that order."

That confused her. She'd never had an answer quite like that.

"Want to explain?"

"I like breasts because, well, I'm a guy and that's what guys do. I like lips because I love to kiss. I like eyes because if the woman has a sense of humor, they sparkle."

He was doing too well. It was time to throw him a curve. "If you were to dress a woman for a very special occasion, would you have any preferences for the dress and heels she wore?"

"I sure would."

Uh-oh. Danger sign. About the only notice *real* men took of dresses and shoes was to make sure a woman was wearing them.

"If it was a real important occasion I'd want her to wear

something black. That way if anything spilled on her, it wouldn't show."

She nearly choked with laughter. "Do your dates often spill food on themselves?"

"No, but it's best to plan ahead."

"What about heels?"

"They can't be so high she can't stand up for thirty minutes without complaining her shoes are killing her. Why do women put their feet into shoes they know are going to hurt? No man would do a damned fool thing like that. This is fun. We've got time for one more."

"How long do you wait before trying to have sex with a woman?"

"That's too easy. I wait until she wants it as much as I do."

They had arrived at the airport. The limousine came to a halt at the curb. "Save the rest for next time. I've got to run." He reached for his briefcase.

"Is that all you're taking?"

"I left everything in my hotel room. I'll be back the day after tomorrow. I hope you can talk Cynthia into seeing her friend."

"I'll try."

"And plan something for us to do. I love my daughter, but I'd like to spend part of my day with you."

Kathryn didn't know why she should be feeling breathless just because a man said he wanted to spend time with her. It wasn't as if it hadn't happened before. Only everything Ron did felt as if it were happening for the first time. She remembered that was a line from some song and smiled.

"What's funny?" Ron asked.

"I just thought of a line from a song."

"That's a good sign. Music is the soul of romance."

Then he stunned her by pulling her out of the limousine. She started to remind him that security wouldn't let her see him off at the gate, but it was quickly apparent Ron wasn't thinking about boarding gates. He took both her hands in his and drew her close.

"I enjoyed this evening. I'm glad you decided to come with me."

"I didn't think I had a choice. If I declined, you'd have come after me." She knew immediately she'd said the wrong thing. It wasn't what she felt. It wasn't what he deserved. "I didn't mean that. I—"

"You're almost as bad as Cynthia. You don't trust people like me to like you for yourself. I don't blame you for the most part, but I'm going to prove I'm different. Now I've got to run."

Without warning he kissed her soundly, picked up his briefcase, turned and headed toward the terminal at a run. She stood there like a statue, her gaze following him, remaining on the door long after he'd entered and disappeared from her view.

It was foolish to attempt to deny this man had a powerful effect on her. On the surface he appeared to be exactly the kind of man she avoided. On the other hand, he *felt* like the kind of man she was looking for. She'd dated other good-looking men, many more personable, at least initially, but none had affected her as Ron did. She couldn't decide what it was about him that made the difference, but there definitely was a difference.

She wasn't supposed to like him, but she did. Regardless of how well he answered her questions, no woman interested in a family, a husband who would come home to dinner and remain faithful to her, would take him on. There were simply too many challenges, too many hurdles. She should never have become involved with him. She should have limited herself to making sure he didn't force Cynthia to go home against her wishes. She was crazy to have let him talk her into giving him sensitivity training.

She had been so sure it would be a simple matter to convince him he needed professional help. Not only had she overestimated her ability and underestimated his understanding, she hadn't once mentioned professional help. Then she'd let herself get seduced into going out on a date with him. She had to be losing her mind. Maybe something about this man engendered insanity in people around him. Maybe that was the secret of his success.

"We'd better go, miss," the limousine driver said. "The police will give me a ticket if I stay here any longer."

Kathryn's sense of her surroundings came back with a jolt. She was still standing on the sidewalk outside the airport terminal staring at the door as if she expected someone to come through any minute. She turned and got back in the car.

"Do you want to go home?" the driver asked.

"Yes." She gave him the address and settled back in the deep, luxuriously cushioned seat. It seemed almost a metaphor for what was happening to her. She was being virtually swallowed by the deeply seductive personality of Ron Egan, pulled into an intoxicating illusion that was as fleeting as it was unsubstantial. Tomorrow would come, or the day after, and everything would change. Once he got back in Geneva, got swallowed up in the excitement of his work, Ron might forget to come back.

He knew Cynthia would be safe. Kathryn would look after her. Why should he take a leave of absence from the career he loved? Cynthia would soon be off to college, a career or marriage. She would have a life of her own. She wouldn't need him, might not even have a place for him. Telling him he ought to take time off for his daughter was another piece of supreme arrogance on her part. In ten years of running the shelter she'd never done anything like that. She was an administrator, not an advisor.

If Ron Egan did come back in two days, she had to be prepared to send him away. Being around him was too dangerous.

"Are you going to see Leigh?" Kathryn asked Cynthia. The four girls were having breakfast. Ruby was moving around, putting food in front of the girls, making it plain she expected them to eat every bite.

"I don't know," Cynthia said.

"I don't see why not," Lisette said. "You can't stay locked up here forever. Besides, you'll want your old friends around after the baby's born and you're ready to go out again."

Kathryn was certain Lisette never considered letting the fact she was a mother interfere with her social life. She probably didn't see the two as having anything to do with each other.

"I think you ought to see her," Julia said. "I don't see why having a baby should cause you not to be friends anymore."

"What do you think, Betsy?" Kathryn asked.

Betsy was so painfully shy she blushed when anybody spoke to her. Kathryn couldn't imagine what stratagems the father of her child had used to seduce her. Betsy blushed, stammered and stared at her glass of milk before she answered.

"I don't think I could see anybody," she said. "I'd be too ashamed."

"Cynthia's not ashamed, and neither am I," Lisette announced. "Having a baby is proof your boyfriend is crazy about you."

Kathryn hoped Lisette learned some tact one of these days, but she wasn't holding her breath. Kerry had been to see her every day, two and three times on occasion, but it couldn't have escaped her notice that none of the other girls had received visits from their boyfriends.

"That may be true," Kathryn said to Lisette, "but getting pregnant while you're in high school can ruin your life if you're not careful."

"It won't ruin mine," Lisette declared. She swallowed the last of her toast and milk. "I'm going to marry Kerry, and our parents will take care of everything."

And they probably would. After they got over being angry. Her mother was already begging her father to let her come home. And if she was reading things right, Kerry's mother would do anything for her adored son. She just had to talk her husband into going along with it.

"I've got to get dressed before Kerry gets here," Lisette announced. "Come on, Julia. You promised to help me."

The atmosphere in the room seemed to go flat after the two girls left.

"Lisette is right," Kathryn said to Cynthia. "You can't shut yourself away from the world just because you're going to have a baby."

"I don't want to shut myself away. I expect I'll meet other girls who have babies, who'll want to talk about something besides boys, football games and who's dating whom this week."

Kathryn laughed. "I hate to disappoint you, but mothers talk about the same things. Only it's husbands, golf and whose marriage is rocky and possibly headed for divorce."

"I'll never get divorced," Cynthia said. "Betsy and I have decided we don't want to get married."

Betsy turned bright red and excused herself before she could be expected to give her reason for such a decision.

"I can understand why you feel like that now, but you might change your mind in a few years."

"No guy is going to want to marry me. I'm fat, boring and so smart I scare boys silly. On top of that I'll have some other guy's baby."

"Lots of men marry women who already have children. That happened to two of my friends just last year."

"It won't happen to me."

"I wouldn't close any doors just yet."

"Have you closed your doors?"

Kathryn's first impulse was to pretend she didn't understand the question, but she changed her mind. "No, I haven't."

"Are you going to date Daddy again?"

Kathryn nearly choked on her coffee. "What made you think we were on a date? We were talking about you."

Cynthia looked a little unsure but she forged ahead. "You were out with him practically all of yesterday. That must mean you like each other."

"I spent the day trying to help him understand you better."

"What about last night?"

"We talked about a lot of things. I have to learn to understand your father if I'm going to help him understand you."

"He'll never understand me. He doesn't want me."

"You're wrong there. He loves you very much. He just doesn't realize you can't put children in a corner and expect them to wait patiently until you have time to take them out again."

"Margaret says Mama never expected Daddy to do anything with me. She says Mama encouraged him to spend all his time working."

"Did Margaret know your mother well?"

"She came to work for them when Mama got pregnant. Daddy was determined she would have everything other wives had."

"Is your father worried about you doing things other kids your age do?"

Cynthia rolled her eyes. "All the time. I can't get him to understand that fat girls with genius IQs aren't exactly the most popular kids in school. They don't get invited to everything, especially trips and overnights."

She laughed, but Kathryn could tell it was without humor.

"I remember this one ski trip he found out about. He hit the ceiling when he found out I hadn't been invited. It didn't make any difference that I didn't know how to ski and didn't want to go, he was determined I was going to be invited. He even offered to put pressure on one of the parents to invite me." She shuddered. "Can you imagine?

I wouldn't have been able to hold my head up after that. Everybody would know.''

"I don't imagine the parents would tell.''

"Are you kidding? It was the Bensons. They blab everything they know.''

"At least his heart's in the right place.''

"I wish I could make him understand I don't want all these things. I don't enjoy parties. I just stand around watching other people have fun. I certainly don't want to go on overnight trips. I'd have to room with some girl who'd rather be with someone else. Then somebody has to let me tag along with their group even though they don't want me.''

"You father just wants you to be accepted. He doesn't want you to have to go through what he went through as a kid.''

"I know. Mama went through the same stuff. Margaret said it's worse for girls, especially if they're not pretty. Mama was pretty angry about things like that.''

It didn't surprise Kathryn that Ron's wife was acutely aware of any social slights. That was the kind of thing a woman would be more concerned about than a man.

"I think it's natural for a father to want the best for his daughter, especially since you're his only child.''

"He probably wanted a son instead.''

Kathryn supposed that was a big worry for every girl in a family without boys. When you were the only child, it had to be even more troubling. "I don't know if your father misses having a son, but he's never said anything that would indicate he isn't perfectly happy with you.''

"He'd want a son to go into business with him.''

"Women are rising to all levels in business these days. Your father said women had given him some of his hardest fights.''

"He never talks business with me. He only wants to know who my friends are and what parties I've been to.

Thank goodness I won't have to deal with a debutante ball now.''

"There's no reason you can't still make your debut."

"I don't want to."

"Have you told your father?"

"Yes, but he won't listen to me. He says I'm too young to know what's best for me."

"You're not too young to know what you want in this case. I think he ought to consider your wishes."

"Will you talk to him?"

"Sure."

"Do you think he'll come back when he said?"

Kathryn wasn't willing to share her own doubts with Cynthia. "You know your father better than I do."

"Daddy's usually very good about keeping his word—Margaret says you can swear by it—but nobody's ever asked him to miss a meeting."

"Or possibly lose a big deal."

"Yeah," Cynthia added, clearly not encouraged by that thought. "What he needs is something more important to him than this deal."

"What he needs is something that's more important to him than his work. Your baby might be that. Some men are crazy about their grandchildren."

"He's not going to get his hands on my baby," Cynthia cried, suddenly very upset. "This is *my* baby."

All the warning signs Kathryn had observed earlier sprang to mind. There was something wrong here, and she had to find out what it was.

"What he needs is a wife," Cynthia said. "Do you think you can find somebody to marry him?"

Kathryn was certain her laugh sounded forced. "I run a shelter for young women, not a dating service for their fathers."

"He dates all the time. I'm talking about someone who'll marry him. It shouldn't be hard to find somebody. He's good-looking and rich. Leigh says he doesn't even look old.

Don't you know some nice woman would like him well enough to go out with him?''

Kathryn didn't want to tell Cynthia how easy it would be for a woman to like her father very much. Neither did Cynthia need to know Kathryn found her father so attractive she temporarily forgot that though they seemed to have a lot in common they disagreed on most fundamental matters.

Kathryn got up to refill her coffee cup. ''Your father will remarry when he's ready.''

''Not if he never stops working.''

''I'm sure he meets lots of women in his work.''

''Not the kind I'd want him to marry. He needs somebody who'll take care of him, somebody who's not interested in him becoming the most famous businessman in the world. He needs someone like you.''

Kathryn didn't like shocks, especially when she was pouring hot coffee. They were unpleasant and caused her heart to beat uncomfortably fast.

''A woman like me wouldn't know what to do with a man like your father.''

''Why not?''

''Well first of all, he travels all over the world all the time. I prefer to stay close to home. He doesn't seem to need friends and family. I think friends and family are very important.''

''But you don't have any friends and you hardly ever see your family.''

Kathryn looked down at her coffee as she stirred in the artificial creamer. ''I wasn't talking about myself.''

''You said you thought—''

''That was a slip of the tongue.''

''I think you'd be perfect for him. You're beautiful, smart and you know how to meet important people. That's just the kind of wife he needs.''

''That may be, but *I'm* not the wife he needs.'' Kathryn picked up her cup and came back to the table. ''Besides, we have some fundamental disagreements about what things are important in life. Starting with you and your baby.''

''If he got married, he wouldn't have time to worry about me and the baby. Besides, he'd probably say it was something his wife should take care of. And if he married you, it would be perfect because we agree on everything.''

Kathryn settled back in her chair. ''Not everything. For example, I'm very uneasy about why you're having this baby and why you chose to come here.''

It was immediately obvious she'd hit a sensitive spot. Cynthia grabbed her plate and got up to take it to the sink.

''Don't run away,'' Kathryn said. ''If we're going to talk about why I ought to marry your father, then we need to talk about why you decided to have this baby. Did you *decide* to have it?''

Cynthia didn't run away, but she kept her back to Kathryn.

''No. It was an accident.''

''An accident you didn't try very hard to prevent?''

''If you mean I didn't refuse to have sex, then I guess you're right.''

''I was thinking more along the lines of agreeing to have unprotected sex more than once.''

Cynthia didn't answer.

''Was this your first time?''

''Do you think boys line up to have sex with somebody like me?''

''I think you liked the boy, but I don't believe you liked him enough to want to have a baby with him. That would imply you want to marry him like Lisette wants to marry Kerry.''

''He wouldn't marry me even if I wanted him to. He'd probably deny he's the father.''

''You said he doesn't know so you can't know how he would react.''

Cynthia swung around. ''What do you think he'd do?

He's seventeen. This would ruin his chances of a football scholarship. And my father would probably kill him.''

''Your father will certainly be very angry, but I doubt he'll resort to violence. However, that's not the issue. The issue is this is his baby—''

''It's my baby!''

''—as much as it's yours,'' Kathryn said, pushing a point Cynthia obviously didn't want to address. ''You have to let him make his own decision about what to do.''

''I won't tell you his name.''

''I don't want you to. I'm just saying the baby doesn't belong to one parent any more than the other.''

''Mama said men weren't interested in babies. She said babies belong to their mothers.''

''I expect the boy will want to stay as far away as possible, but you've got to give him the chance to decide. Talk to your father about it when he gets back.''

''*If* he gets back.''

''If Margaret says you can swear by what he says, then I'm sure he'll be back. If anybody knows a man better than his wife, it's the housekeeper.''

''Margaret says he ought to get married again. She says it's not good for a young man to be without a wife. She says he'll meet all kinds of women who'll give him diseases.''

''I'm not sure this is something Margaret should talk to you about.''

''I know all about STDs. Everybody does. That's another reason I think you ought to marry him. I know you haven't been—''

''This conversation has gotten entirely off base. Leigh is coming by this afternoon. You don't have to see her if you don't want to. But if you keep putting her off until she gives up, you'll always wonder about her friendship, and that will be doing her a disservice. If you're the kind of friend you'd like her to be, then you owe her that opportunity.''

Cynthia looked mulish.

"Now you have lessons to do if you're going to keep up with your schooling. And I have bills to pay if I'm going to keep this shelter running."

But an hour later Kathryn gave up and pushed her checkbook aside. She couldn't get Ron out of her mind. Or Cynthia's crazy notion that she should marry him. There wasn't a single reason she could think of to recommend the idea, so she didn't understand why she couldn't get it out of her mind. She didn't have many friends and she barely got along with her family. That wasn't a recommendation for becoming the wife of a man like Ron Egan. He needed someone who could understand his need to be the world's greatest overachiever. And achieve social acceptance which she knew he would ultimately find meaningless.

She couldn't understand why she couldn't stop thinking about him. She had to figure out what it was so she could get over her obsession.

It wasn't really an obsession. Maybe it was just fascination. But when she was with him, differences didn't seem to matter. He was a charismatic man. She guessed that's what made him so successful in the business.

But she wasn't with him now, and differences did matter. Still, they didn't seem insuperable. Common sense told her they wouldn't be easy to overcome. They came from different worlds and were poles apart on how they felt about it. He wanted to conquer her world. She wanted to ignore most of it.

She'd never thought of walking into a ready-made family, husband, daughter and grandchild. A man who already had a grandchild might not want more children. And then there were the inevitable differences over how they should handle the situation. She would always be an outsider because Cynthia was *his* daughter, not hers. And this didn't even begin to take into consideration the possibility that Cynthia might be jealous of any children she might have. Children might say they didn't value money, but few things could break up a family more quickly than squabbles over who was going to inherit what.

Kathryn closed her desk and got up. She needed something to take her mind off Ron. Her friends had been begging her to let them take her shopping. They said she never bought anything really nice for herself because she saved all her money for the shelter.

Today she felt like buying a new dress. Maybe even shoes and a bag to go with it. She'd call two of her friends. They'd enjoy it even more if they could share being amazed she had finally broken down and agreed to go shopping. Then once she bought the dress, she'd have to think of somewhere to wear it. She'd let them help her with that, too. They'd try to match her up with some guy they thought would make a perfect husband, but she wouldn't go out with him unless she wanted to. This was really an excuse to see her friends again.

Chapter Six

"We're having a problem with Schmidt and Wasserman," Ted was saying to Ron. "They won't listen to anything we say."

"This isn't a matter of money for them. It's an issue of national pride."

"Do you think you can change their minds?"

"I don't know."

"One of the other men said they wouldn't approve the merger if Schmidt and Wasserman were against it. What are you going to do?"

Ron had arrived at his hotel two hours before the meeting. He'd used that time to shower, change and listen to a report on what had been happening the last two days. It wasn't good. Ted and Ben had done everything he would have done, but two essential men—two government cabinet ministers—continued to argue against the merger. It didn't matter how the other men voted. These two men had the power to block it.

By the end of the day it had become very clear that the merger wouldn't—couldn't—go through without the approval of the government. With an election coming up that was predicted to be close, those men were afraid to do anything that might be unpopular with the voting public. Ron would have to give them something they could offer the people, or they would withhold approval.

"We have to come up with a reason they can't afford to vote against the merger," Ron said. "Hire as many people as you need. Spend as much as you have to, but you've got to find something we can use to persuade them to change their minds."

"Do you think you can keep them negotiating long enough to find it?" Ben asked.

"*You* have to keep them negotiating. I'm flying back to Charlotte tonight." He stuffed the last of the papers into his briefcase. "In fact, if I don't leave soon, I'll be late."

Both assistants reacted with shocked surprise. They'd spent the evening around the conference table in his suite going over every aspect of the merger, preparing arguments to bolster their position, brainstorming where they thought the next day's discussions would lead. Ron looked at his watch. "The chartered jet should be warming up its engines right now. I'll call you before the meeting tomorrow."

"You can't leave now," Ted said.

"I'll be back again in a couple of days, but I have to go home. My daughter needs me."

He couldn't afford to devote all his time to the merger. He had his daughter's life to straighten out. Maybe his own life needed straightening out just as much. He'd never stopped working long enough to think about it. But now he had, and he was beginning to realize something important was missing

"But we've never done a negotiation without you," Ben said.

"They expect you to be here," Ted added.

Ron knew that. He'd always used that as one of his selling points. Once you had his company, you had his undivided personal attention until everything was worked out and the last paper signed. That he never tried to handle more than one job at a time was a signature of his style.

He had sensed the resentment in Schmidt and Wasserman the minute he'd returned to the table that morning. They hadn't displayed any emotion. They simply rejected everything he said with icy politeness. This blanket refusal to listen to anything he said had stymied him until he realized their fear of the election was at the root of their refusal to be swayed by his arguments.

"You have to be so brilliant they won't remember I'm not here," Ron said as he grabbed his coat. "You've got to keep them coming back to the table until we can find the one piece of information that will change their minds."

He was at the doorway when an idea hit him. "Has anybody surveyed the workers?"

"That's their biggest argument," Ted said. "The workers are afraid they'll lose their jobs."

"Has anybody actually asked them? I don't mean the managers. I mean the men who bring their lunches in a pail."

"They say—"

"I could be wrong, but I smell the hand of the Arneholdts here. Maybe they don't want anybody to know what the common man thinks."

"That could take weeks, even months."

"We don't have weeks. We might not even have days. By tomorrow I want people at the gates of plants all over the country. Go into the countryside. Ask a cross section. I want reports every day. If we see a trend developing, we can use it."

"What if everybody's against the merger?"

"Then we have to find out why. That may be even more important."

"We'll have to stay up half the night."

"If you want my job, you'll have to stay up *all* night,"

Ron said as he passed through the door and sprinted for the elevator.

He clutched the bulging briefcase to his side as he settled into the limousine. He was uneasy about leaving the meeting. It wasn't merely that the negotiations might fail. His reputation was at stake. It wasn't written into the contract that he would be present at all negotiations, but that was his reputation. People expected it. And not delivering on an expectation rendered his personal integrity vulnerable. And his personal integrity had been the cornerstone of his success.

He had to weigh that against his daughter's happiness. He knew she could work everything out without him. She might do so more easily, but that wasn't what he wanted. He wanted the improvement of their relationship to be part of the solution. If Kathryn was right, Cynthia's having this baby was a cry for the love and affection he hadn't given her. Cynthia had made the mistake, but it had been his neglect that drove her to it.

The feeling of guilt, or responsibility, weighed heavily on him. He'd always planned everything he did in meticulous detail, worked at it with unremitting effort, had used each success to build even greater success the next time. He'd never failed.

Now he had.

Then there was Kathryn. He didn't know quite what to make of her or of his reaction to her. At first he had felt simply irritated by her assuming control of a situation that was none of her business. Then he felt a need to make her prove he could trust her to take care of Cynthia, even for a short time. Finally he had surprised himself by asking her to teach him how to become more sensitive toward Cynthia and women. Had he expected her to fail? Had he feared he might? Even though any success on her part meant a past failure of his own, he wanted her to prove she had analyzed the situation correctly and knew how to fix it.

But there was something about Kathryn that tugged

strongly at him beyond the situation with Cynthia, beyond even his physical attraction to her. And while this—whatever it was—was intriguing, it was also irritating. He didn't need something else pulling on him right now. Cynthia and the merger were already pushing him into a corner. Still, he couldn't help thinking about Kathryn. She was tough and vulnerable, that rare combination he found most exciting in a woman. Kathryn wouldn't back down when she thought she was right. She didn't pull punches and she wasn't intimidated by him in any way.

It was obvious she was sensitive to people's needs or she wouldn't have made a success of the shelter. Even more telling, the girls wouldn't have confided in her, believed she could keep them safe. Yet she was vulnerable. Beneath her list, hidden behind her toughness and competence, was a vulnerability. Partly what he suspected was a rich feminine tenderness, and partly what he was sure was very real fear. Kathryn Roper was not a happy woman. And for some reason that wasn't okay with him. He didn't know what he'd do when he found out what she feared, what had hurt her so badly, but he meant to find out. Then he meant to see what he could do about it.

Kathryn was about to close her book when the phone rang. She looked at the clock. It was 12:33 a.m. Too late to take the call. She shouldn't even have been up this late, but she was keyed up. Too keyed up to pay real attention to the romance she'd been reading.

That's because you haven't stopped thinking about Ron Egan all day.

She had tried to put him out of her mind, but it seemed everything that happened reminded her of him. There had even been a story on the news about some trouble in the trailer park where he'd grown up. She probably wouldn't have remembered it, but she recognized Ron's trailer as the TV camera panned for a view of the park.

After five rings, her voice came on the answering machine. She hated the sound of her own voice on tape. It sounded too soft and feathery, as if she were some kind of helpless female. Then the message…

"This is Ron Egan. I don't want to wake you up, but I just got back from Geneva. I'm a little tired right now—"

She snatched up the phone. "You didn't wake me. I was reading."

"You shouldn't be up so late. You'll have bags under your eyes tomorrow."

It was probably just polite conversation, but no one had given a thought to her being up late since high school.

"The girls won't care."

"Look, it's too late to talk about it now, but I've got an idea for something that might start those girls and their families talking again. I've got to catch a few hours' sleep or I won't know what I'm saying, but I'll be there at about eight-thirty. Is that too early?"

"No." It was. The girls would just be starting their lessons. Their regular teacher had called in sick. If she couldn't find a substitute in the morning, she'd have to try to supervise their studies.

"Good. Tell Cynthia I missed her. I missed you, too."

Her heart fluttered. She told herself not to be foolish, that this was what she got for reading a romance late at night. "Like a thorn in you finger, I imagine," she said. She heard Ron chuckle softly.

"Not quite that bad. If you're interested, maybe I'll tell you about the two real thorns in my side. I won't keep you up."

"Are you driving?" she asked.

"No. My car is at the house. I had a limousine pick me up."

"Good. I don't imagine you've had much sleep since you left. I wouldn't want you to fall asleep at the wheel."

Why was she babbling on? It was no more than a twenty-minute drive from the airport to the section of town where he lived. Even a man suffering from severe sleep deprivation could stay awake that long.

"I intend to fall asleep as soon as I hang up."

"Won't that make it harder to get to sleep later?"

It might, but talking on the phone with a foolish female who couldn't tell when to hang up probably wouldn't help, either.

"I can sleep any time, any place. Now I'm keeping you up. Go to sleep. I'll be there before you know it."

"You don't have to be here so early. You need to sleep more than you need to talk to me."

"That's what I told myself when I was debating whether to call you this late, but I was wrong."

There was no point in trying to deny it. Ron Egan was interested in her, and whether she wanted to admit it or not, she was pleased. And excited.

"You're tired," she said. "We'll talk tomorrow."

"Eight-thirty."

"Good night."

"Good night."

She fumbled the phone back into its cradle, too preoccupied to care. Ron Egan was interested in her. What was she going to do about it? More to the point, what was she going to do about the fact she liked him, too? They were wrong for each other. Not that she believed he was thinking about marriage. He was unattached at the moment and they had been thrown together by circumstances. It wasn't surprising they would be interested in each other as long as they had a common interest. That sort of thing happened all the time.

But that wasn't really the way things worked for her. She'd never been interested in a man just because of proximity. In fact, being thrown together by random circumstances such as being in the same college classes or working together on a committee normally made her withdraw. She hated the phony kind of intimacy such situations created. It was like being away from reality for a few hours or days, and doing, saying or feeling things you knew you'd never do, say or feel once you went back to your *real* life.

That meant she would never see Ron again. A feeling akin to panic came over her. She tried to deny the feeling. She tried to blame it on being tired, to having eaten a piece of coconut cake at eleven-thirty, but she knew she was fooling herself. She *wanted* him to be interested in her, and she didn't want him to disappear when Cynthia moved back home. She didn't know what she wanted the relationship to mean, but she did know she didn't want to give it up just yet.

She told herself she was being as foolish as her girls had been about the boys that had gotten them in trouble, but that didn't change anything. She knew she would be downstairs long before eight-thirty. And whether she found a substitute teacher or not, she'd be listening for the sound of the doorbell.

The doorbell rang at precisely 8:30 a.m. Kathryn decided Ron must have waited on the porch for the second hand to reach twelve. She told herself she couldn't run to the door. She'd already changed her routine so she could be in the living room. Anything more would be too obvious. She opened the door to find Kerry O'Grady on her porch. He looked as if he were frightened out of his mind.

"I've got to see Lisette," he said.

Kathryn blocked Kerry's path. He knew she didn't allow visits until the girls finished their lessons.

"My dad's back," Kerry said. "He says I can quit school and go to work. He says I can go live with my mother's relatives. He says I can do any damned thing I want, but he's not going to support me and my gold-digging little whore. I've got to see Lisette."

Kathryn struggled to mask her disappointment. "Why aren't you in school?"

"This is more important than school," Kerry nearly shouted.

"I agree, but you can't see Lisette. She would get so upset it would take me a week to calm her down."

"What are we going to do?"

Before Kathryn could answer, a black Bentley pulled into her driveway. Ron Egan got out and waved to her. Instead of coming toward her, he opened the trunk, and began to take out one package after another.

"I think Mr. Egan would appreciate some help with those packages," she said to Kerry.

"I don't want to help anybody with packages," Kerry practically wailed. "I want to see Lisette."

"Help Mr. Egan with the packages, and I'll think about it."

Kerry turned to help Ron. Kathryn thought it might be a good idea if he did have to work for a while. His mother had done her best to keep him her little boy. If he and Lisette did marry, at least one of them should be capable of acting and thinking like an adult.

Kathryn was glad Ron had thought to buy Cynthia something in Geneva. Still, even if he was worth a hundred million dollars, a dozen packages were too many. She couldn't stop him from giving them all to Cynthia, but she would explain that neither his guilt nor Cynthia's anger was likely to be assuaged by such extravagance.

"I brought something for all the girls," Ron said when he reached the porch. "Tell me where I can put them."

It never occurred to Kathryn he would have bought presents for the other girls, too. "You can put them in the back parlor," she said, opening the door for the men to pass inside. "I'll have Ruby take them up later."

"Nothing doing," Ron said. "Presents are no fun unless you get to open them together."

"The girls are studying."

"I can wait," Ron said.

"Yeah," Kerry said. "We can wait."

Ron set his stack of presents in a sofa and settled down next to them. Kerry followed suit on the sofa opposite Ron.

"It won't take them long to open their presents," Ron said. "You could consider it a study break."

Kathryn knew she wouldn't get anything done until Ron had handed out his presents. "I'll tell Ruby to bring the girls down."

"She's got to come, too," Ron said. "I brought something for her."

"Why would you buy Ruby a present?" Kathryn's surprise caused her to ask before she realized it was a rude question.

"Because she answered the phone when I called. Somebody had to tell me the girls' names and help me figure out what to give them. You can stop standing there with your mouth open. You have a beautiful mouth, but I like it better when you smile."

Kathryn closed her mouth, too stunned to smile.

"While you're trying to remember how to smile," Ron said, "you can open your present."

"You shouldn't have bought me anything," Kathryn said. She was afraid her surprise was clear to both Ron and Kerry. Her pleasure was, too.

"I couldn't bring something for Ruby and not for you," Ron said.

Kathryn worried what Kerry was thinking. She'd always remained above gossip. If he started telling people Ron was giving her gifts, they could get the wrong idea.

"They're not terribly imaginative," Ron said. "I didn't have much time, and airport shops never have a good selection."

Kathryn didn't patronize airport shops—they never had anything she wanted and charged twice as much as she'd have paid elsewhere—but she had no doubt Ron would have had them fly anything in that was out of stock.

"I'll get the girls," she said.

It took a little convincing to talk Ruby into leaving her kitchen long enough to accept her gift, but the girls came tumbling down the stairs as if they were responding to a four-alarm fire.

"Don't you say a word about your father," she whispered to Kerry. "We'll figure out something later."

She needn't have worried. The moment Lisette saw Kerry, she started babbling happily. Kerry couldn't have gotten a word in if he'd tried.

"Your father brought something for everybody," Kathryn said to Cynthia. "That was very thoughtful of him."

Cynthia appeared unexcited by the stacks of presents. "Why?"

"Ask him."

"He'll probably say it was rude to give me a present without bringing something for everyone else. Like he would even remember me."

"Leigh remembered you when you didn't think she would. Don't you think your father has an even better reason?"

Kathryn wondered whether Cynthia was afraid to believe her father had truly thought of her. She couldn't be too critical of Cynthia. She had never believed her father had thought of her when he came home from trips bearing presents, even when they came from stores in the cities he'd visited. It was obvious to Kathryn his secretary had ordered them.

"The other girls can't open their presents until you do. If you don't hurry, Lisette will explode."

Julia was pleased, Betsy petrified. Ruby Collias didn't appear able to decide whether to disapprove or just accept her present and go back to her kitchen.

"You have to open your presents, too," Lisette said to Kathryn. "We all want to know what you got."

"You can start with this one," Ron said, handing her a small but rather heavy package. He'd gotten two presents for each of them.

All of the girls received necklaces with their birthstones as pendants. Naturally Lisette's would be a diamond. She squealed with delight, jumped up and gave Ron an impetuous hug and kiss.

"You don't have to hug me," Ron said to the other girls. "Just open your other gift."

"Miss Roper hasn't opened hers," Lisette said.

Kathryn knew she couldn't accept anything as extravagant as a birthstone pendant from Ron. Her birthstone was a ruby. She held her breath as she tore off the paper and opened the box.

"They're little pictures," Lisette said, obviously disappointed.

"They're coasters for the living room," Ron said. "Now I'll have someplace to set my glass of water."

Even as Kathryn breathed a sigh of relief, she felt her internal tension level rise. The pendants were probably handled by someone in his office, but Ron had obviously picked her gift out himself. It didn't matter that it was worth only a few dollars as opposed to a few thousand; it meant more because he'd chosen it.

"Maybe you'll get something better next time," Lisette whispered.

Kathryn knew it would be impossible to explain why her coasters were more valuable to her than a ruby pendant would have been.

The second gift was the same for everyone—very expensive German chocolate. The girls started sampling theirs immediately.

"It was very thoughtful of you to remember us," Kathryn said. Taking the hint, each girl thanked Ron, even Betsy who was so nervous she barely whispered the words. "Now run upstairs and put away your pendants. I'd hate to see you lose them."

Lisette clearly wanted to take Kerry off by herself. "I have to talk to Kerry first," Kathryn said to Lisette. "I'll tell you when you can come back down. You, too, Cynthia. I need your father's help for a few minutes."

Cynthia didn't show any of Lisette's reluctance to leave.

"What can I do?" Ron asked.

"Kerry, tell Mr. Egan what your father said. Maybe he can think of some way to help."

"That's a nice man," Ruby said when Kathryn entered the hall. "You be nice to him." With that, she turned and headed back to the kitchen.

Kathryn very much wanted to know what Ruby meant by her remarks, but she put her presents away and returned to the living room. Kerry had just finished telling Ron what had happened.

"Have you ever held a job?" Ron asked Kerry.

"No."

"Cut the lawn or carried out the trash?"

The boy shook his head.

"Then I suggest you put all thoughts of marrying Lisette out of your head, go home and tell your father you'll do anything he wants as long as he doesn't throw you out."

Kathryn was hardly more surprised than Kerry. "I love Lisette," the boy said. "I want to marry her and take care of our baby."

"You're a baby yourself," Ron said, dismissing him carelessly. "Leave playing house to real men."

Kerry jumped up, uttered a few four-letter words and turned to the door.

Ron grabbed his arm and nearly threw him back onto the sofa.

"It's easy to cuss when you get mad. It's not much harder to get your girlfriend pregnant. What's hard is stepping up to the role of being a man, a husband and a father. It wouldn't be as important if you only had to worry about Lisette. She's got a family to take care of her, but you've helped her create a baby. And no matter what kind of spoiled kid you are, no matter how little you were concerned with anything but your own physical gratification, you're this baby's father. For the rest of your life. It's up to you to determine if the kid will say *That's my dad* with pride or use some of your own four-letter words. You've got to learn to think and act like a man, learn how to support a family.''

Kerry looked as if he'd been hit in the face with a fish. Kathryn didn't feel much different. Ron's actions had taken her by surprise, but it was the emotion behind his words that riveted her attention. He was white about the mouth. She hadn't seen him look this intense, so tightly wound.

''I want to take care of my kid,'' Kerry said, his voice barely more than a whisper. ''I love Lisette.''

Kathryn was afraid Ron was going to tell the boy he had no concept of what love was, but instead he released Kerry and settled back into his own seat. ''Tell me why she ought to marry you instead of waiting for someone else.''

''Because nobody else will ever love her like I do,'' Kerry said.

''What do you love about her?''

Kathryn listened as Ron guided Kerry into giving a more intelligent answer than she would have expected from him.

''Have you thought of the changes getting married and having a baby will make in your life?'' Ron asked.

''I haven't thought of anything else since we found out.''

''Do you have any idea what you want to do? It'll be hard to finish your education and work enough hours to support a wife and child. And there's Lisette's education.''

''I've thought about all of that,'' Kerry said. ''I know what I want to do.''

''Good. Go discuss it with your family.''

''My father won't listen.''

''Make him. If you're going to be the head of your own family, you've got to stop thinking of yourself as a kid whose parents will take care of everything. Your decision forced you into the role of a man whether you're ready or not. Now it's time to step up to the plate.''

Kerry didn't look completely confident, but neither did he look like the panicked boy Kathryn had found on her porch.

''Now you need to talk to Lisette.''

"You can use the TV room," Kathryn said. "Mrs. Collias will call her for you."

"You're not going to sit with us?" he asked Kathryn.

Kerry seemed to have matured in the last half hour. "I think this is something you need to discuss in private."

"Thanks."

"You were a little rough on him," she said to Ron.

"Not half as rough as life is going to be."

"I'm sure of that, but I don't approve of being so hard on kids. They need understanding, not criticism."

"Is that why you're still angry at your father, because he criticized your sister instead of understood her?"

"This has nothing to do with me or my sister."

"It has everything to do with you understanding the responsibility these kids have taken on. It's good to give them support when the shock hits, but they've got to understand the rules have changed. They've created a new life. It doesn't matter how innocently. Somebody's got to make them realize they're not kids anymore. I expect both Kerry and Lisette's parents will come around sooner or later, but Kerry needs to start thinking like a man now. Lisette's not ready to carry her part of the load."

She was sure of that. No matter what they worked out, Kerry would need all the love and patience he could muster to help Lisette adjust to the life ahead of her.

"No kid is ready to be a father at seventeen," Ron said. "He ought to be dating a different girl every night and sneaking beers with his buddies."

"Is that what you did?"

"I didn't have buddies or money for beer, but guys need a period of pretty much limitless freedom before they're ready to settle down for good."

She wasn't sure any of the men she knew were ready to settle down, even the ones who weren't driven to be wealthy enough to retire by forty. They all seemed to want a relationship that was more like an extended honeymoon.

"Thank you for the presents. It was very thoughtful to think of the girls and me."

"Think nothing of it. Did Leigh come back to see Cynthia?"

"Yes. She spent nearly an hour here yesterday. Cynthia was a little unsure at first, but it wasn't long before they had their heads together, whispering and giggling about everything that's happened in the last few days."

"Has it only been a few days? It seems like weeks."

"Things aren't going well in Geneva?"

"This one is tough." He suddenly grinned. "That's why I charge so much."

It was a grin to forestall further questions rather than one of amusement. He was just as bad as his daughter about not wanting to share, not wanting to depend on anyone else. She guessed that came from the years of his lonely struggle to lift himself out of a background of poverty, but that didn't make it any easier. Nobody should have to go through life feeling alone. It was always easier to carry the load when you had someone to share it with.

Not that she had a lot of room to talk. She never discussed the situation between her and her parents with anyone, not even her brothers. She didn't mention it to Elizabeth because Elizabeth mentioned it enough for both of them. But that wasn't sharing. It was more like replenishing the feeling of blame, culpability, or renewing her anger when it showed signs of wearing thin. Anger and guilt. She didn't know how it happened, but every time she saw her sister, she ended up feeling guilty she hadn't been the one thrown out of their parents' house.

"Got anything planned for this afternoon?" Ron asked.

"The usual. The girls visit with friends. Sometimes they go out with their families. We rent movies to watch in the evening."

"Then you don't have to be here."

"No, but I usually am."

"I need to talk to Cynthia a little while. That will give

you time to tell Mrs. Collias I'm taking you out for a drive
and lunch. I wish you'd told me about the movies. I'd have
rented a theater. The girls need to get out once in a while.''

Kathryn had never been poor, but she didn't think in
terms of renting a whole theater for half a dozen people.
Apparently Ron Egan did, which made it even harder to
understand why he should want to spend his afternoon with
her.

''I have an idea how to get these kids and their parents
together long enough to really talk to each other.''

''We can talk about that here.''

''This isn't something to talk about. You have to see it.''

''I don't know why I let you talk me into this,'' Kathryn
said. ''It'll be a disaster.'' She'd known Ron for two weeks,
long enough to know his boundless energy could convince
her he was right when she *knew* he was wrong. Yet she'd
let him talk her into this harebrained scheme which, during
the course of the last week, she'd become more and more
certain would never work.

''It may not achieve everything we want, but at least it's
a step in the right direction. The girls and their parents
won't see anybody but themselves. They'll have to talk to
each other.''

''No, they won't. They can leave.''

''I'll lock the gates.''

''They'll stare at each other in stony silence.''

''That's what I'm here for.''

They were headed to a private corporate retreat in the
Blue Ridge Mountains near Asheville. Ron had hired the
entire complex and invited the girls and their families to
spend the weekend together. He'd even convinced Kerry's
parents to come along. Kathryn didn't know what kind of
pressure Ron had brought to bear on Kerry's father, but the
man had left a message saying there'd be hell to pay.

''You need to spend time with Cynthia,'' she said.

"I will, but I've got to make sure everyone else is making some progress. That's why I had Cynthia invite Leigh."

Leigh had visited Cynthia every day for the last week. Once Cynthia started to believe Leigh's friendship was strong enough to survive the stigma of Cynthia having an illegitimate child, she had started to look forward to her friend's visits. Leigh's presence had gone a long way toward helping Cynthia begin to bridge the gap between her and her father. Leigh liked Ron. She said she wished her own father were as attentive and understanding.

"I'm counting on you, too," Ron said to Kathryn.

"I don't mediate family fights. I still think you should have let me bring—"

"They can talk to your psychologists and family counselors next week. This weekend I don't want anybody telling them what to do."

"I hire professionals because they can't figure that out on their own."

"Go with me on this thing," Ron said. "It may not be the answer, but we've got to try everything."

Kathryn didn't know when her *I* had become Ron's *we*, but sometime during the last week he'd invented a role for himself and stepped into it with all the enthusiasm of a new convert. He'd been to Geneva twice, but had returned the next day both times. He'd contacted the parents of the kids, convinced them to take part in this weekend. She looked forward to it with fear and trembling. Ron seemed excited.

Kathryn looked out the window at the tree-covered hills and the low mountains in the distance. The Blue Ridge didn't have the grandeur of the Rockies or the Sierra Nevadas, but they were more welcoming. The air wasn't so thin, the trails were grassy and tree-covered, and temperatures were moderate. It could be an idyllic location for a close-knit family's weekend getaway. She didn't know how it would work as a backdrop for real-life versions of a family feud.

They had left the paved road a mile back. The mountain fell off at a near-forty-five-degree slant.

"I hope it doesn't rain this weekend," she continued.

"The forecast is for sunny days and cool nights," Ron said. "I ordered it especially for you."

Kathryn laughed. She wasn't entirely sure he hadn't. He'd already managed several things she had thought impossible, getting Kerry's father to agree to come to the retreat being at the top of the list. She was relieved when they reached the paved drive that curved around the base of the hill on which the retreat had been built. The arching limbs of some ancient maple and hickory trees kept the glare of sunlight from their eyes. They rounded a stone wall that encompassed a flower-filled garden, and Ron pulled the Bentley to a stop in the parking lot in the middle of the complex. A quick count showed Kathryn four buildings, the two largest with two stories. One had a huge front porch and the other an even larger deck. The stone-paved court-yard between them offered a view out over the mountains. The view of the evening sunsets would be fantastic.

"I hadn't realized the complex was so large," she said.

"It was built to handle up to sixty executives and their wives."

"Do you think it's big enough to handle Shamus O'Grady?"

"I once had the senior executives of the big three automakers here. I think it can handle Shamus."

Kathryn wasn't sure. Even now she saw Shamus approaching their car, a glass in his hand. Probably his famous Irish whiskey to fuel his even more famous temper. Kerry was only a step behind his father, his face a mask of anger. "You'll get your chance to find out sooner than you thought."

Ron popped the trunk and got out of the car. "Glad to see you had no trouble finding the place," he said to Shamus. "Kerry, how about giving us a hand here?"

"My son's not a bellhop," Shamus grumbled. "He doesn't carry luggage."

"We can handle the luggage. I want Kerry to help with the food. You can lend a hand though if you want."

"I thought you said this place was first-class," Shamus groused. "I didn't know we had to bring our own food."

"Mrs. Collias wouldn't let us leave without her chicken salad. She said you never know what strangers will put in it."

"You promised this place had a gourmet kitchen," Shamus said.

"That doesn't mean they know how to fix Mrs. Collias's chicken salad," Kathryn said. "The girls love it. Not to mention her rum cake, her special cheese bread, and roasted pecans no one else in the whole world knows how to make."

"I thought we were supposed to be *getting in touch with ourselves*," Shamus said, "not eating ourselves into an early grave."

"This is for the picnic tomorrow."

"I'm not going on any damned picnic," Shamus said. "I didn't give up a weekend at the club to pick ants out of my food."

"Take it easy, Dad," Kerry said. "You said you weren't going to jump to any conclusions. What do you want me to carry?" he asked Kathryn.

"Has it ever occurred to you that you'd have more business if you weren't so hard to get along with?" Ron said.

"I have all the business I want because I'm the best," Shamus shouted. "People stand in line to get me to build their house."

"But not the really big houses," Ron said. "Have you noticed that?"

"I have," Kerry said as he lifted the cooler from the trunk. "I heard one of the boys at school talking about it."

"You never said anything to me," Shamus shouted at his son.

"That's because you never listen to me," Kerry replied. "Where does this go?"

"In the recreation room downstairs," Ron said. "There's a refrigerator and freezer in the closet."

"I don't do those big houses because I can't deal with those women," Shamus said. "They don't know what they want. One of them had me rip out a kitchen twice."

"You got paid, didn't you?"

"Yeah, but—"

"She paid for the privilege of being able to change her mind. She wanted the house of her dreams, Shamus, not the house *you* thought she ought to have. Does the rum cake go in the refrigerator?" he asked Kathryn.

"I've got the best reputation of any builder in Charlotte," Shamus shouted.

"And the worst reputation as a person," Ron replied. "Do you think it would be all right to cut the cake before dinner? Rum cake is one of my favorites."

"Don't you dare," Kathryn said. "Ruby will chop off your fingers if she hears."

"Did you have anything to do with my losing the Harris contract?" Shamus asked.

"No," Kathryn said. "I did. When Naomi told me her contractor was driving her nuts and they hadn't even started the house, I told her she didn't have to work with anybody that made her miserable."

"Dammit!" Shamus shouted, his face turning purple. "I worked a damned year to get that contract."

"Then you've got Kathryn to thank for the fact Naomi Harris is willing to give you another chance," Ron said. "After the last time you talked to her, she said she would live in a tent before she'd let you build her house."

It was almost comical to see the air go out of Shamus.

"There's a catch somewhere," Shamus said. "What is it?"

"Naomi can't stand people yelling, even when they

aren't yelling at her," Kathryn said. "She believes everybody in the world ought to get along together."

"Save the sweetness and light for Sunday. What's the catch?"

"The *catch* is you have to find a way to incorporate a little sweetness and light into your personality, or Naomi will give the job to your biggest competitor."

"And when is she going to see if I've got this sweetness and light?"

"She's not going to unless I tell her you've improved. I told her I was spending the weekend with your family in the mountains."

"I suppose you had to nose it around that Kerry knocked up some chick and now he wants me to support them."

"You've got to learn to express yourself a little better, Shamus," Ron said. "Talking like that can make you unpopular."

"Especially in this case," Kathryn said. "Naomi and Lisette's mother are friends."

"That whole damned crowd sticks together," Shamus said. "I didn't want Kerry to go to school with them, but his mother wouldn't let me rest until we got him enrolled. Now look what's happened? He's got some *young lady* pregnant, and I'm stuck in the woods trying to make nice when I rather bash their heads in."

"Bashing heads is Dad's solution to every problem," Kerry said. "Got anything else that needs to be carried in?"

Kathryn couldn't believe the difference in the boy. He'd had several long talks with Ron in between Ron's visits to Geneva. She didn't know what they discussed, but Kerry had developed a backbone. She hoped his father would be proud of him, but she supposed he would more likely see Kerry's new maturity as some kind of challenge.

In a way she felt sorry for Shamus. He'd come from Ireland as a boy, pulled himself up from poverty without anybody's help. Ron said Shamus interpreted Kerry's acceptance by his friends as a rejection of himself. It was ironic everything he'd worked for was to give Kerry the chance to move into the very society that he now saw as a barrier between them.

"Did you know about any of this?" Shamus asked his son.

"Yeah. I talked Robbie Harris into getting his mother to offer you the job, but he was really ticked when you treated his mom like you did. I tried to tell you about his mom, but you never listen to anybody. You have all the answers. And if anybody argues with you, you shout a little louder until they give up and go away. Well, you've shouted everybody away but Mom and me. Give me the pecans," he said to Kathryn. "Lisette's crazy about them, but Ruby says it's not good for the baby for her to eat too many." He turned to Kathryn. "Don't tell Lisette." He winked. "I want to surprise her."

"She's a child," Shamus said. "You can't marry a child."

"She's old enough to have a baby," Ron said. "That qualifies her as a woman, even if she's not as mature as we might wish."

"Don't try and come the high-and-mighty with me," Shamus roared. "You've got a kid in the same condition. What are you doing about its father?"

Kathryn knew it hurt Ron to have his daughter's situation flung at him like that, but she was proud of the way he responded. He didn't raise his voice. If anything, he sounded more patient than ever.

"I don't know who he is yet," Ron said. "When I do, I'll decide what to do about it."

"Well I've already decided what *I'm* going to do."

Kerry was halfway to the lodge, but he turned around at his father's words.

"Kerry's not going to marry that girl. He's going to finish high school and go to college like his mother wants. He's going to be a doctor or a lawyer and be so damned respectable he can look down his nose at anybody he wants.''

''You know I don't want to go to college,'' Kerry said. He didn't retrace his steps, just stood there, halfway across the parking lot, facing his father with a maturity Kathryn knew would have been impossible a week before. ''I don't need to go to college to build houses. I want to go into the business with you as soon as I graduate.''

''I'm not letting you build houses,'' Shamus said. ''You're going to college.''

''No, I'm not.''

''What are you going to do to support that girl and your kid? I'm not paying your bills.''

''I'll start my own company,'' Kerry said.

Shamus uttered a derisive laugh. ''And how the hell are you going to do that? It takes a hell of a lot of money to get started these days.''

''I know. That's why I've talked to Mr. Egan about being my partner.''

Chapter Seven

Shamus turned a royal purple. "You did this!" he screamed at Ron. "You encouraged him to defy me."

"No. I just told him since he was about to become a father, he had to start acting like an adult."

"He's a kid!" Shamus shouted. "He ought to act like a kid."

"I wish both our children hadn't made the decisions they did, but it's too late for that. Your grandchild will arrive in a little more than six months. That's a fact that can't be ignored."

"I can ignore it," Shamus said.

"Maybe, but I don't think you will. Come on, Kathryn. If we don't get settled soon, they'll start the party without us."

Ron had arranged for the families to be grouped together in large suites with several bedrooms. He and Kathryn were in a suite with Cynthia and Leigh. The two girls had driven down an hour earlier. As they approached their building, Leigh leaned out the window.

"Hurry up," she called down. "Wait until you see this setup."

Kathryn was only slightly more prepared than Leigh for the luxury she found. Their suite was made up of four huge bedrooms, each with a private bath, and opening onto a common room big enough to contain a conference table, an entertainment center, a business center, an area for socializing around a large stone fireplace and a wet bar.

"I wish Daddy could build us a beach house like this," Leigh said. "That way all of us could stay there at the same time. My grandparents have a place like this. It's loads of fun when all the cousins get together."

"I wouldn't know," Cynthia said. "I don't have any cousins."

"Well you can hardly blame your parents for that," Kathryn said. "I imagine they would have liked some brothers and sisters."

"Your mother especially wanted a sister," Ron said to his daughter. "She was delighted you were girl."

"Didn't you want a son?" Cynthia asked her father.

"I wanted several children," Ron said. "But I never regretted having you, not even when we found out your mother couldn't have any more kids."

"You must have wanted a boy to carry on the business."

"I was more interested in having boys to play football with. I never got to do that as a kid. I was looking forward to it."

"So instead you got a fat daughter."

"I got a tiny thing—you only weighed five and a quarter pounds—with no hair at all and huge blue eyes. For the first week you stared at me like I was something out of a fantasy movie. After that you seemed to decide I was safe and would even let me hold you without screaming for your mother."

"Mom says I did that, too," Leigh said, laughing. "It

used to scare Dad to death. To this day he swears girls come into the world yelling at men.''

"The smart ones know to check them out carefully," Kathryn said. "Are you girls settled in your rooms?"

"I'm practically lost in mine," Leigh said, "but I love it. Even my parents' bedroom isn't so big as this one. I can't wait to tell Mom about the king-size bed."

"But your family is one of the most famous in Charlotte," Cynthia said.

"That's because everybody's in politics. That doesn't mean we have a lot of money. We don't have anybody as smart as your father. I used to tell my brother he ought to marry you and get your father to give him a job."

"But I thought…" Cynthia let the sentence fade.

"We had some ancestors a couple hundred years ago who were in the right place at the right time," Leigh said. "We've had a few more since then who have done fairly well, but it takes smart people like your Dad to keep thinking of new ways to make money. You don't have to be smart to know how to spend it. My dad says the dumber you are, the more you spend. Now I'd better stop chattering. Mom says I never know when to shut up."

Kathryn thought her mother was probably right, but maybe she had given Cynthia something to think about. Having her best friend openly admire her father wasn't a bad thing.

"We're all gathering for hors d'oeuvres at six," Kathryn said. "If your father and I don't hurry, we'll never be ready."

"We can help," Leigh said.

"Thanks, but I'll probably go faster by myself."

"Yeah. I'll probably ooh and aah over everything you brought. Mom says you have the best taste of any woman in Charlotte."

"Of course she does," Ron said. "She chose to spend her weekend with us."

"Not that she had much choice after you railroaded her into it," Cynthia said.

"I admit I was doubtful at first, but after the way your father handled Mr. O'Grady in the parking lot, I think it may turn out okay."

"That man scares me," Leigh said. "He always looks like he wants to hit somebody. I think you were very brave to face him."

Ron laughed. "I don't think he considered hitting me."

"I don't know. You ought to hear some of the things Kerry says about him."

Ron gave her a conspiratorial look. "Could I enlist you two girls to help me this weekend?"

"Sure," Leigh said. "What do you want us to do?"

"Tell me something about the kids and their parents?"

Kathryn opened her mouth to object, but Ron forestalled her.

"I'm not talking about gossip. Everybody has a reason for feeling the way they do about something. It may be completely crazy, but to them it's valid. If I can understand what it is, maybe I can figure out a way to bring them around to my point of view."

"You mean force them to do what you want," Cynthia said.

"I know what he means," Leigh said. "Sometimes people are afraid of things they don't need to be afraid of. But they'll never tell you, so you don't know what to say."

Cynthia looked to Kathryn for confirmation. "I'm not sure I like the idea of prying into people's private lives," she said. "I wouldn't want people doing that to me."

"It's not prying exactly," Ron said. "It's pretty much what a psychologist does when you go to him."

"He's a professional. Besides, you know he won't use it to try to get you to do something you don't want to do."

"Everybody knows why they're here," Ron said. "I take that as a sign they want the same thing."

"Shamus said you forced him," Kathryn reminded him.

"He'd already thrown away the Harris contract. I'm only offering him the possibility of getting it back. He has plenty of other work."

"But he wants the Harris contract very badly," Kathryn said. "I think you're taking unfair advantage of him."

"He wants his son back even more," Ron said.

The more she learned about Ron, the more she realized how he had become so powerful. It was odd he could see other people so clearly, could analyze their position in detail, yet he had no idea how he was perceived by the people around him. He only saw himself as an extension of his work, not as a man whose work was only part of his life.

"Will you agree to help me?" Ron asked all three.

Leigh agreed enthusiastically. Kathryn hesitated a moment.

"I'll go along for the time being. But if you do something I think is wrong—"

"Don't hesitate to stop me. Cynthia can tell you I don't always get it right."

Cynthia didn't appear to like being put on the spot. "You're not very good with ordinary people," she said.

"I know," Ron said, "but I'm trying to learn. Will you help?"

Cynthia appeared undecided.

"Of course she will," Leigh said. "She wants things to turn out right for everybody."

"I didn't tell you they'd be better off with their parents," Cynthia said, apparently peeved her friend had shared what she clearly thought was confidential.

"But you said it would be better if they *could* go home," Leigh said. "Miss Roper thinks the same thing, don't you?"

"Yes," Kathryn said. "I consider my shelter a last resort."

"You were my first choice," Cynthia said.

Kathryn knew what Cynthia meant, but she doubted the girl realized how much the remark hurt her father.

"I think it would be best if we mingled before dinner," Ron said. "I want to make everybody feel as comfortable as possible."

"I'm not the hostess type," Cynthia said.

"It's like playing a game," Leigh said. "Pretend you're somebody like the president's wife. I know," she said delighted with her idea, "Queen Elizabeth."

"In that case, I guess I should curtsy." Kathryn made an elaborate but not very graceful curtsy. "I'm out of practice." But she had achieved her goal. Cynthia smiled. It was only a small concession, but maybe she'd stop fighting her father. Kathryn didn't know whether she thought his being successful would undermine her decision to leave home, or whether she resented that he hadn't done any of these things for her first.

"I'll let Leigh be Queen Elizabeth," Cynthia said. "I'll be Princess Anne."

"I'll be some duchess or other," Kathryn said. "Who're you going to be?" she asked Ron.

"I think I'd better be the head of the United Nations," he said, grinning broadly. "It's the only way I can outrank all this royalty. Now let's get ready. We don't have much time."

He picked up his suitcase and disappeared into his room.

"Do you really think this is going to work?" Cynthia asked Kathryn.

"I don't know. A lot depends on your father's powers of persuasion."

"He can talk anybody into anything," Cynthia said.

"In that case I suggest we back him to the fullest so we can share his glory when everybody ends up living happily ever after."

"Everybody except his daughter," Cynthia said.

"I expect he'll try his hardest to make sure you're happiest of all."

"He never has before."

"I think he has. He just didn't realize he was doing it the wrong way."

"Daddy always thinks he knows the answer."

"Not any more."

Cynthia didn't look convinced.

"All he's asking is that you give him the same chance to show he's changed the other kids are giving their parents. Remember, he's the one who organized this weekend. Don't you think that's a good sign?"

"Of course she does," Leigh said. "I've offered to trade fathers any time she's ready."

"It's not just that," Cynthia said. "There's the baby and everything else."

"We can't fix everything at once," Kathryn said. "For the weekend, concentrate on restoring communication, getting to be friends again, learning to trust each other. Don't you want things to work out between you and your father?" she asked when Cynthia vacillated.

"Yes."

Kathryn feared Cynthia had planned how she thought everything should go and wasn't sure she wanted to risk this new development. Kathryn couldn't be sure whether Cynthia was afraid to try for fear she'd be hurt again or fear she'd lose control over the situation.

"Then you'll really do your best to help him this weekend. And not just with the others. He wants to help them, but it's you he's really concerned about."

"Okay," Cynthia said, "but I'm not going to believe things just because he says them. He's going to have to show me."

"Fair enough," Kathryn said. "Now I'd better go, or I won't be ready on time. I have a feeling your father wouldn't appreciate that."

"Yes, he will," Cynthia said. "Dad always says a person's appearance tells more about him than the words that come out of his mouth. Greg, that's his secretary, says he can spend hours deciding what to wear for an important first meeting with a client or the first time he comes to the negotiating table. We might end up waiting on him.''

"Wouldn't they listen to anything you said?" Ron asked Ted.

"Nothing," Ted replied.

"You showed them the results of the poll?"

"They said they had more scientific polls that said just the opposite."

"Have you seen their polls? Do you know how they gathered the information?"

"Yes. They're skewed in the directions they thought the government wanted."

"Did you tell them?"

"Yes, but they didn't believe me. They said Americans will do or say anything for the sake of money."

"The Arneholdts are behind this."

"How do you know?"

"It's not cheap to convince a respected polling company to falsify its results. You've got to find proof. Hire investigators if you have to."

"That's not the only reason they're still refusing the merger," Ted said.

"What is it?"

"You've always conducted merger negotiations personally no matter how long it takes. They say your being in America shows you don't think it'll succeed so there's no point in wasting your time."

"I've been back three times since we started."

"Apparently that's not enough."

"Did you tell them I have personal business I can't ignore?"

"I don't think they believed me. Everybody knows this is the first time you haven't conducted all the negotiations yourself."

Ron was painfully aware of this. He could only assume none of them would have allowed a family crisis to keep them away from their work. He was also aware his absence was injuring the negotiations to the point the merger might fail.

"Tell them I'll be back on Monday," he said. "In the meantime, see what you can dig up on the Arneholdts. If it comes out the government is being manipulated by this family, they'll be falling over themselves to vote for the merger to save their political necks. You can do this without my being there. I'll call you early tomorrow."

Ron turned off his cell phone. He'd reached a crossroads, a moment of decision he'd never expected to face. His whole life had been directed toward stockpiling so much success it would force others to acknowledge his achievements. Most important of all, it would force people at the highest levels of society to accept him and his daughter as peers.

That goal had never changed, *could* never change, as long as he remembered the years when he was ignored, looked down on, pitied, even despised merely because he didn't have money, the proper background and social experiences. He felt as if he'd spent his entire life being invisible, performing herculean tasks without anybody noticing. He realized it wasn't an admirable goal, not the kind of thing you would want the world to know about you. It wasn't even something he was especially proud of, but it was something he couldn't get rid of, something that continued to drive him.

But that wasn't the only reason to pull off this merger. He needed this one major triumph to position his company securely in the upper ranks. He especially had to make it work if he was going to assume a less conspicuous role in the company, a company that up until now had prospered primarily because of his personal reputation.

And he was endangering all of this by staying in Charlotte. But he risked losing Cynthia if he went back to Geneva.

Before Kathryn broke in on his meeting, he'd never

thought that could be possible. He was certain the tie between him and his daughter was strong and unbreakable because it was strong and unbreakable for him. No matter how few hours he spent with Cynthia, she'd never been far from his thoughts. She was the center of his world. Everything he did was for her. No matter what happened in their lives, he'd assumed each held first place in the other's heart, that nothing could threaten—much less sever—their tie.

But he'd been wrong. All that he had worked so hard to achieve seemed to come his way easily. All the things he'd taken for granted seemed about to slip away. He was faced with the decision of risking something he understood and wanted—his career—for something he didn't understand yet found essential—the love and understanding of his daughter.

But he couldn't give up one for the other. He understood enough to know he had to have them both. He didn't know how he was going to manage that, but maybe Kathryn could help him figure it out.

That was still another problem. He was beginning to feel he wanted Kathryn, too. He didn't see how he could have all three. But it seemed like all three were essential for his happiness. He was beginning to realize he'd never really been happy before. He'd been so busy chasing success, he'd forgotten to pay attention to himself.

Just weeks ago he'd been certain his life was on track, about to achieve the success he'd worked toward since he was ten. Now he was in danger of losing everything at once. How could he have been so blind?

The important question was, what was he going to do about it? He didn't know, but he had a strong feeling he would have to depend on Kathryn to help him find the answers.

He decided she was the best part of being in the worst mess of his life.

Kathryn backed away from the door. She doubted Ron was saying anything he wouldn't want her to hear, but she didn't want him to think she was eavesdropping. Besides, she didn't want to know what he was saying. Just the thought of a business conversation reminded her of the times her father was too busy to be involved with his own family. And remembering that always made her angry. He thought his family should behave with the same logic as his business. When they didn't, he didn't attempt to understand them. Kathryn had tried to be a dutiful, obedient daughter, but Elizabeth had been spoiled. She was beautiful from the moment she was born, vivacious, able to charm anything in pants. She became adroit at using the attention and indulgence of her mother and older siblings to protect her from her father's strictures. When the break came over her pregnancy, their father had put his foot down. Much to Kathryn's astonishment, her mother had supported him.

Kathryn had taken her sister's side, and the argument ballooned out of control, everyone saying things they later regretted.

Now here was Ron, unable to go even a few hours without calling Geneva. He had a pregnant daughter who was estranged from him, a retreat full of angry parents, and he still couldn't keep his mind off his work. She guessed she shouldn't have expected anything different. People all over the world sought his help and advice. It was hard for a daughter to compete. A thirty-year-old woman who ran a shelter for unwed mothers didn't stand a chance.

As soon as that thought ran through her mind, Kathryn knew she was in danger of becoming enamored of a man who represented everything she abhorred. Over the past two weeks he'd spent nearly every moment he was in Charlotte with Cynthia or with her. She'd given up pretending they weren't dating, but she'd held fast to the belief that it was only a temporary circumstance. Apparently her heart had decided it liked Ron—liked his genuineness, his readiness to admit his mistakes and his resolve to correct them—and didn't care about anything else. She didn't know what her brain had been doing while her heart was cooking up this disaster. Whatever it was, it had been a strategic error. She had to run while she had a chance.

Yet for the next few days it would be impossible to keep her distance from Ron. Regardless of any personal danger, her primary responsibility was to start the girls and their families talking. From the moment she accepted them into her shelter, she had become *in loco parentis*. She owed it to everyone not to let this opportunity slip away.

Then there were Ron and Cynthia. Cynthia depended on her. Ron depended on her. She shouldn't have assumed such obligations if she had any doubts about being able to carry through to the end. By accepting his help with her shelter, she'd tied herself to him in additional ways. She not only couldn't ignore him, she had to pay close attention to everything he did. If he was successful, she had to know how to do it again.

After he was no longer here.

Ron looked at the people in the room and felt adrenaline start to flow. They had huddled together in distinctly separate groups in the recreation room, some around the pool table, others near the TV, one group at a large window facing a distant mountain, and still another backed up against the bar where they'd put the ice and soft drinks. Everyone seemed to be avoiding the food in the middle of the room. This was a challenge to Ron's skill, and that always brought with it an eagerness to prove himself equal to the job. He decided to start with the most difficult task.

"Remember to keep moving," he said to Kathryn, Cynthia and Leigh. "Don't let anyone get you in a corner. Get people talking. That's the first step in getting them relaxed."

"They look like they're afraid somebody's going to attack them," Leigh said.

"Somebody is," Cynthia said. "My dad."

She acted as if it were a terrible thing, but Ron heard a

trace of pride in her voice. She might not like him right now, but she was proud of his abilities. He wondered if Kathryn felt the same way. She'd been mighty cool since she came out of her room. It was almost as though they were back to that very first night, her distrusting him and disliking him.

"I'll start with Kerry's parents," Ron said.

"Do you think you should after the way he acted in the parking lot?" Kathryn asked.

"He's got to know I'm not trying to undermine his relationship with his son. Until then, he's not going to cooperate with anything we do."

"I'll take Betsy," Cynthia said. "She's scared of almost everybody else."

"I'll take Lisette's parents," Leigh said.

"I guess that leaves me with Julia," Kathryn said.

"Battle stations everyone," Ron said.

"This is not a war."

"It is to Shamus."

Ron headed over to the O'Gradys who were standing together by the door to the courtyard. It was obvious Kerry wanted to be with Lisette. It was equally obvious his father was standing in his way.

"Is your suite okay?" Ron asked.

Shamus's looked angry, but his wife looked nervous. She kept glancing back and forth between her husband and her son.

"It's very nice," she said. "Very luxurious."

"You can't buy me with a fancy suite," Shamus said.

"I'm not trying to. I only want you to be comfortable. The rest of the weekend won't be easy."

"It will be for me," Shamus said. "I'm not staying. We're leaving right after dinner."

"You can't," Ron said. "The gate is locked, and I'm the only one with a key."

Ron thought Shamus would explode. His wife looked as though she didn't know what to do. Kerry smiled. "I guess that answers that question."

"You can't make us stay here. That's kidnapping."

Kerry laughed. "I can see the headlines now. *Crazy Irishman accuses internationally famous businessman of kidnapping him in a luxurious mountain retreat along with several other families. Police didn't understand the charge since the Irishman admitted he'd gone there willingly.*"

"Don't talk to your father like that, Kerry," his mother said. "It makes him angry."

"I can't make him angry, but it's okay if he makes me angry and you miserable."

"Don't say that."

"Why not? It's true."

"Neither of you should be trying to make the other angry," Ron said. "I'd hoped you'd use this opportunity to come to an understanding of what's important to each of you."

"And you've made that so easy, telling Kerry you'd bankroll him."

"I asked him," Kerry said, "but he said you'd want me to go into business with you."

"He's giving you ideas, making you feel too big for your britches."

Kerry mumbled a couple of oaths under his breath. "I'm going to sit with Lisette. There's no point in staying here. You won't listen to anybody but yourself."

"Kerry, come back here," his father shouted. "If you don't, you can find some other place else to live."

"Shamus!" his wife exclaimed.

Kerry turned around. His expression had lost the anger of a moment ago. He looked tired. "I already asked Uncle Mike. He said I could stay with him until you came to your senses."

"You call him back right this minute," Mrs. O'Grady said to her husband. "If you don't, you can live in that house by yourself." When Shamus hesitated, she turned and walked off after her son.

"See what you've done!" Shamus said, turning to Ron. "You with your big promises."

"Nobody could have done anything if you hadn't driven Kerry away first."

"I'm not driving him away, you daft fool. I'm trying to save him."

"By denying him what he wants? Would you have listened to your father if he'd told you you couldn't become a contractor?"

"He did tell me," Shamus said, his voice slightly less belligerent, "but I knew it was my way out of poverty."

"Then why should you expect your son to be any different?"

"Because I've done all of this for him. He won't have to fight his way up the way I did."

"I said something very much like that a few days ago. I didn't understand when my daughter didn't instantly throw her arms around my neck and thank me."

"What did she do?" Shamus asked.

"Pretty much what Kerry just did. Those were my goals, my reasons—not hers. I never asked her what her goals were. I still don't know. She doesn't trust me enough to tell me."

Shamus was quiet a moment. "Do you think she'll tell you?"

"I don't know. I didn't exactly ignore her, but I saw what I wanted to see, and ignored all the warnings along the way. Now I find myself estranged from my daughter and my professional career in danger of collapsing. It strikes me you're in pretty much the same situation."

Shamus was quiet for another moment. "What are you going to do?"

"First I have to decide what is more important. Even if I manage to save both, everything I do in the future has to be guided by that decision, or I'll find myself in the same predicament before long."

"You trying to tell me something?"

"You've got to decide which is more important to you, your pride or your family. I think your wife and son have already made up their minds." Mrs. O'Grady had joined her son. "I've got to circulate. Can't have my guests saying the host didn't make an effort to speak to everyone. Bad manners."

"Like you care."

"I'm discovering I care for quite a number of unexpected things."

Like Kathryn Roper. He saw her talking to Julia Mingenmeer's parents while Julia stood by looking uncomfortable. He wondered all over again what could have induced a young woman with Kathryn's advantages to devote so much of her time and resources to these girls. He now knew it was Kathryn's sister's pregnancy, rather than her own, that was the reason Kathryn established her shelter, but there was something else that bothered Kathryn, something that caused her to divert all her maternal feelings to the daughters of other women. Ron was determined to find out what it was. Kathryn deserved the chance to have her own family.

Ron wanted more family. He hadn't known it until he'd started talking to Kerry and the families of the girls. He and Erin—both only children—had wanted at least three children. Maybe more.

He wondered how Kathryn felt about large families.

Such thoughts were premature, but he already knew he wanted her to be part of his life *after* he and Cynthia were back home. He hadn't dated much since Erin's death. People constantly offered to fix him up with a *perfect* woman, but Ron preferred working late—even all weekend—to blind dates.

But his feelings for Kathryn had been different from the start. He always kept the parts of his life carefully separated. Physical attraction in one corner, business in another, family in still another. Kathryn had managed to spill over into all three. He hadn't thought much of it at first. He was too busy dealing with the immediate problems facing him. When he did get a few moments to think about it, he realized how special Kathryn had been to him.

He'd been of two minds about her from the start. He hadn't want to get involved with a woman who had abetted Cynthia in running away from home. He'd wanted to bring the whammy down on her good and proper, but a few hours' consideration—maybe it had taken only a few minutes—had convinced him he was strongly attracted to Kathryn. No red-blooded man could be around her and not be attracted. She was just too pretty, too vital, too... He wasn't sure what word to use, but it was impossible for him to be indifferent to her.

But it hadn't taken him long to realize that behind that facade she was as unhappy as the rest of them. Every time they had come close to talking about her family, she changed the subject, a dead giveaway something was seriously wrong. He intended to fix it. That was the least he could do after what she'd done for Cynthia and the rest of these girls.

He looked around the room. Cynthia and Leigh were talking to Betsy's family. It was a shame the girl was so shy and nervous...or just plain scared.

Maybe the boy had given her the feeling he understood her, that he would stand up for her. He could see how she would reach out to anyone who gave her the sense of importance her family didn't. He'd have to have a long talk with them. Now that she'd gotten the courage to break away, Betsy wouldn't go back unless things changed radically.

He couldn't help but wonder if Cynthia had felt that way about him. He'd done everything he could to make sure she felt loved and cared for, but he was learning things that mattered to him didn't necessarily matter the same way to other people.

He wondered what was at the bottom of Julia's disaffection from her family. Her parents seemed exactly what you'd expect in professional and social circles, and genuinely interested in their children.

They said they would do anything that might bring Julia home, yet both parents were in earnest conversation with Kathryn while Julia shifted her weight from foot to foot looking bored and angry. They needed to learn to talk *with* their daughter rather than just *about* her.

Could the same be said of him? He thought he'd tried to talk to Cynthia during the last few years, but had he *really* talked to her, really *listened* to her, or had he just thought he had? Whatever the case, he'd have to do better. It was hard watching her be so animated, so open, talking to Betsy's family, when she was so closed and withdrawn when he tried to talk to her. He would have to count on Leigh and Kathryn to help convince Cynthia he'd changed, that he really did love her and want to learn to make her happy.

It was hard to stand back and wait for someone else to do the work for him. All his life he'd taken the initiative, sometimes despite active opposition from people who should have been helping him. He was aggressive, decisive, hardheaded, confident, consistent and knew exactly what he wanted. He'd have to learn to make these attributes appear positive in Cynthia's eyes.

In Kathryn's, too.

In the meantime he'd better make sure his brilliant idea of a weekend retreat was a success. Lisette's family was next. Lisette was a pretty girl with a very engaging personality, but he didn't understand how a boy like Kerry could have fallen so desperately in love with her. He would have thought they'd drive each other nuts. He was relieved to see the Saunders family actually appeared to welcome his approach.

"This is an absolutely beautiful place," Mrs. Saunders said when he reached the group. "Thank you for inviting us." She looked uneasily at Lisette, who was snuggled up against Kerry. She appeared to be using him as a barrier against her parents. "It's been good to be able to spend a few minutes with Lisette."

"I hope you'll have more than a few minutes together before the weekend is over." He'd have to remember to tell Kerry not to monopolize Lisette.

"It's important we find out something about the boy," Mr. Saunders said, casting a harsh look in the direction of Shamus O'Grady who stood by himself across the room. "I hope he's nothing like his father."

"Paul, don't talk like that in front of his wife," Mrs. Saunders said.

"Shamus has a lot of good qualities," Ron said.

"Then he's kept them hidden," Paul replied, not intimidated by his wife's strictures.

"You're both right," Mrs. O'Grady said. "Shamus is a good man, even a wonderful man sometimes, but he came up so hard he can't understand not everybody else is like him."

"We did everything parents are supposed to do," Mr. Saunders said, "but she runs to Kerry every chance she gets. Everything he says is right. Everything we say is wrong."

Ron wasn't sure what had gone wrong here, but it was clear Lisette had put her future in Kerry's hands.

"She's only sixteen," Mr. Saunders said. "How's she going to go to college and take care of a baby?"

"We had such plans for her," Mrs. Saunders said. "I know she's my daughter and I'm prejudiced, but she's so smart and talented. You should see her dance. Classical ballet. There there's her music. She's taken piano since she was four. She plays Chopin beautifully. Just last year we discovered she has a remarkable voice." She sighed in disappointment. "Her grandmother is convinced that with all her talents she could become Miss America."

Ron was getting the picture of a young woman who likely saw herself not as a person but as a collection of talents and attributes to win honors and bring glory to the family. She probably didn't think anybody could love her unless she was winning some kind of trophy.

"I'll tell you what I've been telling myself and everyone here this weekend," Ron said. "Ask Lisette what she wants for herself. Don't take her first answer because she's going to tell you what she thinks you want to hear. Keep after her until she tells you the truth."

"We know what she wants," Mrs. Saunders said. "She has wanted the same things all her life."

"At least one thing has changed," Mrs. O'Grady said. "She wants to marry my son and have his baby."

"And ruin her life," the Saunders said in unison.

"It won't ruin my life," Lisette said. "It's what I want more than anything."

"There's nothing wrong with a husband and a baby," her mother said in a wheedling tone of voice. "I'd love to be a grandmother, but there's so much you had hoped to accomplish."

For the first time since Ron had known her, Lisette looked miserable rather than confident and cheerful.

"I thought I wanted all those things, but I want Kerry and the baby more."

"But you've worked so hard for so long," her father said.

"Right now we need to focus on Lisette, Kerry and the baby," Ron said. "It'll be here in less than six months. It would be best if you'd figured out what you want to do before then."

"We know what we want to do," Kerry said. "We want to get married."

"That's crazy," Mr. Saunders said. "You're too young."

"They're obviously not too young to become parents," Mrs. O'Grady said. "I think that makes them old enough to be married."

"I don't know what you can hope to get out of this," Mr. Saunders said to Mrs. O'Grady. "We don't have any money. Not the kind you have."

"This has nothing to do with money," Mrs. O'Grady said.

"It has to do with wasted opportunity," Mr. Saunders said.

"There are a couple of facts you can't ignore," Ron said, hoping to keep the argument from escalating. "Lisette is pregnant, and she and Kerry want to get married."

"We're *going* to get married," Kerry said.

"You have to start from there," Ron said to the three angry parents. "Your old plans won't work anymore. And I think you ought to include Mr. O'Grady in that discussion," Ron said. "He's just as concerned about Kerry's future as you are about Lisette's."

"Then what's he doing standing across the room by himself?"

"Trying, just as you are, to come to grips with the new reality."

A waiter came in to announce dinner. Ron was relieved. He hoped it was too soon to tell, but so far he hadn't been very successful. He not only hadn't brought about any kind of reconciliation or understanding, only dinner had prevented what threatened to be a heated, probably rancorous, fight. He had to find a way to get these two families over the disappointment in the failure of their plans for their children and move on to coming up with new plans that took into account the present situation and their children's needs and wishes.

"I shouldn't be there with you," Kathryn said to Cynthia. "Your father wants to talk to you alone."

"I don't want to be alone with him."

They were leaning against a railing on the flagstone patio between the two meeting buildings. The mountain fell away abruptly in front them. It had turned cool enough to need a sweater for bare arms, but the half moon was brilliant and the night air crisp and dry. Kathryn had always preferred the mountains to the beach in the summer, something else the men she dated didn't understand.

"Are you afraid?"

"No."

"Then what's the problem? He wants to talk about the things he doesn't understand."

"No, he doesn't. He wants to tell me what to think. He gets paid millions to do that with people who're just as strong-minded as he is. I haven't got a chance."

"Of course you do. You decided to come to my shelter, didn't you?"

"I did that while he was away. If he'd been here, he'd have found a way to talk me out of it. He always does."

"What do you mean?"

"We're always having these discussions where I tell him what I think. Then he tells me what I ought to think. I tell him again what I think, and he begins to dismantle my argument piece by piece. When he's done, I have no choice but to agree with him even though I know I don't agree with him.''

''Have you told him that?''

''No.''

''Then I think you should. Say it very nicely, but make it clear you won't be argued out of your position.''

Cynthia turned away and looked out over the mountain. ''It won't work.''

''You have to try. Otherwise, this whole weekend will be a waste. Your father has worked very hard to make it a success.''

''Of course he has. This is what he does. He couldn't stop himself. It's how he thinks.'' She wrapped her arms around herself and turned back to Kathryn. ''Ron Egan *never* fails. He can't afford to. It could ruin his reputation.''

''That may be true in his business, but this is very different. He wants to help the others, but his real objective is to make things right with you.''

''Then why did he stay away from me all evening then spend most of dinner talking to you?''

''Probably because you were sullen and refused to speak to him. Leigh told you as much.'' Kathryn reached out, took Cynthia's hand. ''I know you're angry with your father, but I'm sure he's genuine in his desire to try to understand what *you* want. You know how helpful he's been to Kerry.''

Kathryn's sympathy had gone out to Ron. She didn't know what it was like to face powerful men across the board table, but it couldn't be any worse than facing four sets of angry, resentful, bullheaded parents who'd already alienated their children and weren't the least bit reluctant to turn their anger on Ron.

She had tried to warn Ron he had set himself an impossible task, but she had to admit it was better to try and fail than not try at all. If nothing else, Cynthia would have a better notion of how difficult her father's work could be. It would be good for Cynthia to think of someone else besides herself.

Maybe he had used strong-arm tactics to get everybody here, but she was proud of him for having the courage to tackle a nearly impossible task. He kept up a brave front, but he couldn't hide his disappointment from her. She wanted to put her arms around him and tell him not to try so hard, that nobody could make people listen when they didn't want to.

That last thought showed Kathryn just how far her mind had changed with respect to Ron. She still believed he valued his career too much and his daughter too little, but he was proving he could learn from his mistakes.

"Your father thought if he gave you some space, maybe you'd lighten up and cut him a little slack."

Cynthia pulled away from Kathryn. "Daddy would never use a phrase like *lighten up and cut him a little slack.*"

"Okay, so I paraphrased it. Another reason he stayed away was to help the other girls. He'd committed himself to coming up with solutions for everyone this weekend. He was just doing his best to make that happen."

"But don't you see, that's exactly what he's always doing, putting everybody ahead of me. Just once I want to come first."

Kathryn supposed it came from being young, of having no perspective, of being frightened, but it was obvious Cynthia couldn't understand that nearly everything Ron had done since he appeared out of the night that first evening had proved she was very much in the forefront of what mattered to him. Ron would have to handle the rapprochement with his daughter himself, but it would be up to Kathryn to help Cynthia see that though her father might be employing old skills and using old ways, he was using them to achieve new ends. He was attempting to win his daughter back.

"I don't think you understand exactly what your father is doing and why, but that can wait," Kathryn said. "The important thing right now is to go in there and listen to him, to give him the benefit of the doubt, to trust him."

"Maybe I should lick his hand like an old dog."

Kathryn's optimism flagged. "It's time to see if you've inherited your father's skills of negotiation. If so, this ought to be an interesting evening."

Chapter Eight

Ron knew what he said during the next half hour would probably be the most important words of his life. But for a man who made his living by choosing the right words and knowing when to use them, he was at a loss for where to begin. It was only the first night, but so far his idea of a weekend retreat hadn't worked out very well. The O'Gradys and Saunders were barely civil to each other while Lisette and Kerry wouldn't listen to either set of their parents. Betsy and Julia didn't appear to have made any more progress with their families than he had with Cynthia.

He set the empty cola can on the bar and walked over to a window that looked out over the courtyard below. He swirled the ice in his glass. He'd stood here and watched Kathryn and Cynthia talk, wondering what they were saying, wondering what he should say. Now Cynthia was coming to talk with him. The suite, so big and impersonal, seemed to say nothing warm and comforting could happen here.

He felt himself tense when he heard the door handle turn. He looked up as his daughter entered. She looked as if she were facing a grim task, one she'd love to avoid but knew she had to endure before she could be free again. Ron felt his hopes sink.

Ron barely kept himself from breathing a sigh of relief when Kathryn followed Cynthia into the room. He hadn't asked her to come—the whole point of the weekend was to throw the families together without outside influences—but he was glad she had. They didn't agree on lots of things, but she wanted him to be successful with Cynthia. And she liked him. He wondered if Cynthia did.

Ron wasn't sure he wanted Cynthia to see him as her confidante, but he did want her to feel she could come to him when she was in trouble. At the very least, he didn't want to be closed out of her life just when she needed him most. He was relieved when Cynthia chose to sit directly across from him. Kathryn chose a seat across the room, much as she had the first night back in Charlotte. Could it truly have been only two weeks ago? It seemed like years.

"Did you and Leigh had a good time?" Ron asked. How did you start a conversation when anything you said could be taken the wrong way? "Thanks for all your help with the parents."

"We didn't do anything but talk," Cynthia said.

"That's exactly what I wanted you to do. Everybody was nervous when they got here. They won't be able to make any progress if they feel tense and defensive."

"Do you feel tense and defensive?"

He hadn't expected such a question from his daughter. He glanced at Kathryn, but she shook her head. No help from that quarter. "Yes," he replied. "Now that you mention it, I do."

"Why?"

He'd planned to do the interrogating, but Cynthia had struck first. "Because you and I don't seem to be making any progress. It seems like every time we talk, things are worse. Tonight you didn't even want to talk to me. Why?''

Cynthia squirmed in her chair, but she didn't back down. "You haven't told me why you're defensive."

"I guess it's because everybody thinks I did something wrong, something I *knew* was wrong, and didn't do anything about it because I didn't care, but it's not true."

Cynthia turned to Kathryn. "Do you believe that?"

"What I think doesn't matter. This is between you and your father."

"But it does matter," Cynthia said.

"Why?" Ron asked. "Are you saying you can't believe anything I say unless Kathryn agrees with me?"

Cynthia met his gaze for a moment, then dropped hers to her lap. "I'm not a good judge of people. Sometimes I believe what I want to believe whether it's true or not. Other times I'm scared to believe things. Then there are the times I don't know enough to be able to tell what's the truth. I feel a lot better when Miss Roper agrees with me."

Ron swung his gaze to Kathryn. "It looks like the ball is in your court."

Kathryn looked at Cynthia. "I don't know what your father might have done to prevent this situation from arising, but I'm sure he didn't realize what was happening. I'm equally certain if he had known what was happening, he'd have done everything in his power to stop it." Kathryn directed her gaze to Ron. "I've always thought he devoted too much of his time to his career and too little to his daughter, but I feel certain he loves you very much and will do anything he can to restore a relationship he realizes is very important to him."

Ron hadn't expected such generous support from Kathryn. While he thought she had come to like him personally, she continued to make it clear she disagreed with the importance of his career in his life.

"Do you believe me now?" Ron asked his daughter.

She squirmed under his scrutiny. "I don't know."

"Why not?"

"Because I don't feel it's true."

Ron fought against letting his irritation show. A logical person didn't make decisions based on feelings. Any consultant worth his salt knew that you could have six very intelligent people in the same room participating in the same conversation, and all six would come away with a different interpretation of what people meant by what they said. You dealt with facts, observable actions, concrete outcomes. Depending on feelings could send you into a miasma of supposition at variance with the facts. But he restrained himself.

"What do you feel?" he asked.

She clearly didn't want to answer him. She clasped her hands tightly in her lap, bit her lip. That reminded him so much of what she did when she was a little girl that most of his irritation melted. He wanted to reach out, take her in his arms and assure her everything would be all right, but he knew they had a long way to go before she would let him do that.

"It's hard to say how I feel," Cynthia said. She was backing away, looking for a way out of telling him something she thought he wouldn't like.

"You said you would be candid with your father," Kathryn said. "You said you wouldn't let him argue you out of your position."

"I know," Cynthia said.

"What's holding you back?" Ron asked.

"I don't like saying mean things about you," Cynthia flung at him. "After all, you are my father."

"If my being your father is to mean anything beyond a biological fact, you've got to tell me what you're feeling. I really don't know what it is. If I'd known, I'd never have let things get this bad."

"What do you see as bad?" Cynthia asked.

"Your being pregnant at sixteen. Your not wanting to talk to me about that or anything else."

"Is that all?"

"It's enough."

"It's not even the beginning," Cynthia said, her anger apparently enabling her to push past her reluctance to hurt her father's feelings. "I don't feel like you care about me, about what I want, what I feel, what makes me happy, what makes me sad, my friends, anything. I'm just some teenager who lives in your house, someone you check on once in a while to make sure somebody is taking care of her."

"That's not true. I love you."

"You love your daughter, whoever that might be, but you can't love me because you don't know who I am. You haven't asked my opinion on the war on terrorism, whether the Tar Heels will make the Final Four, or whether I think North Carolina ought to allow nude beaches. You don't know whether I want to stay at Country Day or transfer to Latin. You don't know who my friends are, who I've been dating, if I'd like to go out for cheerleading."

"If you wanted to discuss any of those things, all you had to do was bring them up."

"You made me feel that next to your work they were frivolous, that you had more important things to do."

He couldn't dispute that. He couldn't think of anything that interested him less than whether she wanted to go out for cheerleading. She'd never indicated a desire to change schools, he knew better than to interfere with her friendships, and he'd damned well have met every date at the door with a shotgun if he'd had any idea his daughter would end up pregnant.

"I have a lot of deadlines," Ron said. "Some things can't wait."

"Everybody told me not to bother you, that you had important work to do. They didn't say what I did was unimportant, but that's what they implied."

"Margaret wouldn't say that."

"Why not? Mama did. When I wanted to sit on your lap or ask you to read me a story, she'd tell me not to bother you, that you had important work to do. Everybody acts like what I do isn't important compared to you."

Ron hadn't suspected the problem extended beyond him and his daughter. He was at a loss to know what had been said and what he could do about it.

"You don't have to ask me," Cynthia said, resentment filling her voice. "You can ask Miss Roper."

"I can't help you there," Kathryn said. "All I know is the article in the newspaper was very flattering. Then when the second article came out in *Time*, he became a minor celebrity."

"That's all I heard about for months," Cynthia said. "Everybody wanted to know what you were doing and how much money you were making. Why did you let them interview you? Didn't you know it would make my life miserable?"

"I thought you'd be proud of me." *The Charlotte Observer* wanting to do an in-depth article on him pleased him more than the *Time* article because it meant he was finally getting some recognition in his hometown. He was no longer the upstart from the trailer court who'd managed to wheedle a few scholarships out of some nice schools. He was that brilliant young businessman who'd distinguished himself at some of the finest schools in America and was making a name for himself on the international business scene. "It never occurred to me that it would be a problem for you. You should have told me."

"And have half the world saying I was an ungrateful brat or that I was just jealous of your success?"

"Nobody would say that. There's no comparison between the two."

"That's just it," Cynthia cried, pouncing on his words before he could understand the way she'd taken them. "Everything you do is important. Nothing I do is."

So it wasn't just that he'd failed to be aware of the changes in his daughter as she grew up. Everything around her had conspired to make her feel unimportant, that other people—strangers—had more of a right to her father's time than she did. And her own mother had begun the process.

"The world doesn't value feelings when they're set against large sums of money," Kathryn said. "It's not fair, but that's the way it is."

"The world might not value your feelings, but I do," Ron said. "I know I've let myself get overly preoccupied with my job. There have been times when I've almost forgotten I had a family. It may not seem like it, but everything I did was as much for you as it was for me."

"Yeah, right!"

Complete disbelief. How did he explain that a father could love his family so much he would work himself to exhaustion for them? Just because this wasn't a case of a poor man with a backbreaking job working to support a large family living below the poverty level didn't mean it couldn't be the case. Kathryn had said Cynthia might not want the same things he wanted. If that was so, she wouldn't see his work the same way he did.

"Both your mother and I came from poor backgrounds. We only got ahead by constant hard work."

"Mama told me that all the time. I suppose she did it to make me understand why hard work and success were so important to both of you, but if you're doing it for me, how come I got left out, forgotten, ignored?"

"Because I forgot you weren't your mother or me," Ron said. "I forgot you'd grown up under circumstances that made it impossible for you to understand how your mother and I felt."

"That's like what happened to Kathryn," Cynthia said. "Nothing changed her father. I don't see why I should expect you to change."

"I'm not going to change completely," Ron said. "I'll always be driven to succeed. It's bred in me. What I can change is the way I relate to you and the other people I care about."

"How do you propose to do that?"

She didn't believe a word he said.

"I'm depending on you to tell me," Ron said. "We wouldn't be in this mess if I'd known what to do. You can't imagine how guilty I feel that something I didn't do caused you to want to go out and get pregnant."

Immediately Cynthia went from looking angry to defensive. "I never said I got pregnant because of you."

"Then what was it? You're intelligent. You knew what could happen if you had unprotected sex. No teenager wants her life turned upside down, her education put on hold, her friends drifting away because they have nothing in common, her time consumed in caring for a baby who requires her attention twenty-four hours a day. You had to have a reason. And that reason had something to do with my failure to provide what you needed."

"Is that how you see a baby? Is that how you saw me?"

"Your mother was twenty-two, not sixteen. I had been working for two years. We were ready for children. We had the time to devote to them."

"I want this baby," Cynthia said. "I don't consider becoming a mother ruining my life."

Ron had no doubt Cynthia *did* want the baby. But whatever her reasons might be for wanting it, he was convinced they were the wrong ones.

"Tell me why you want this baby, why you don't want to share it with its father."

Cynthia's reaction told Ron he'd made a wrong move. She appeared to stiffen, flinch and draw back.

"You've wandered away from the point," Kathryn said. "You said you hadn't provided Cynthia with something she needed and you wanted to know what it was. That doesn't necessarily have anything to do with the baby."

"Okay," he said, trying to sound unflustered, "what did I do wrong? What do I need to change?"

Cynthia seemed to relax a little.

"I never said you did anything wrong," she said.

She'd implied he'd done *everything* wrong, but he wasn't

about to contradict her. He just wanted her to talk. And keep talking until she said something he could understand.

He wondered if his parents had ever had this much trouble communicating with him. He didn't think they'd tried very hard, wasn't even sure they'd wanted to, but he was certain once he'd made up his mind what he wanted for his future, he'd stopped listening. They simply didn't have the same goals. What worked for them didn't work for him. Once he'd figured that out, he didn't see any need listen to them.

Had that happened with Cynthia? He couldn't understand how that could have been the case. They wanted too many of the same things—education, a career with marriage and family to follow, as well as being a fully accepted part of society. The big things were all in place. Why didn't the little things follow?

"I must have done something wrong. You've got to tell me."

Now that he was giving her permission to say anything she wanted, Cynthia's anger seemed to have disappeared.

"I'm trying, baby, but I need some help. You know I wouldn't have knowingly hurt you."

"You didn't do anything terrible," Cynthia said. "I just felt left out. Like what I wanted didn't matter."

"But what you want has always mattered. Why do you think I work so hard?"

"For yourself."

There was no hesitation this time. No gaze sliding left or right. Her words reflected a deeply held conviction.

"Of course it was for me. I love my work. I love being successful and making a lot of money. But it was for you, too. I wanted you to have all the things I never had, the things I had to sacrifice for. I didn't want you to have to go through what your mom and I endured."

"I know all that," Cynthia said, "but I always felt like I was part of the career, part of the success, that I came in a package with everything else."

Ron couldn't understand how she could feel like that. He had done everything he could to make sure she didn't want for anything. That's why he had a staff of four just to take care of her. That's why he'd bought a house in the Eastover neighborhood, why he'd put her on the list to attend Charlotte Country Day School the day she was born. That's why he paid for any private lessons she wanted, why he sent her on vacations with friends to places he didn't have time to take her.

"I don't understand," he said. "When have you ever wanted something that I didn't get you?"

"I don't think you understand what she's saying," Kathryn said.

"No, I don't." Ron hadn't meant for his voice to be quite so sharp. He paused, leaned back in his chair, took a deep breath. "I'm trying, but I don't understand."

Kathryn looked to Cynthia, but the girl shook her head, unable or unwilling to explain further.

"Let me tell you what I think Cynthia is trying to say," Kathryn said. "Cynthia, stop me if I'm wrong."

Cynthia nodded.

"I think she's trying to say she feels you did all of this for her because you thought you were supposed to, that it was your idea of what she wanted. But you never asked what she wanted, never did anything just for her."

"Of course I did. Who else could I have been doing it for?" He was trying to contain his frustration, but this didn't make any sense. He couldn't understand. What in the hell was she talking about?

"For you," Cynthia said, some of the anger she'd bottled up coming out. "And for Mama. Margaret tells me all the time what Mama planned for me and all the other children she hoped to have. I know it all by heart. But you never once asked me if I wanted something different."

"Did you?"

Her anger and the energy it produced disappeared. She looked almost apologetic. "No, but you never asked me."

He could feel control slipping away, the pressure of his frustration on the verge of breaking out of his restraint.

"Are you sure I never asked you?" he asked.

She nodded.

"Not even once?"

She shook her head.

"I asked you about going to Exeter," Ron said. "You said you'd rather stay with your friends."

"And you never forgave me for it, either."

"Of course I did."

"You haven't been home once since that you haven't mentioned some connection you made through somebody you went to boarding school with. You've told me at least a dozen times you'd never have known what a brilliant tactician Ben Archer could be if you hadn't been on the debate team with him."

"Ben's a tiger. I couldn't be here right now if he wasn't in Geneva."

"That's something else. I feel like I'm forcing you to sacrifice all the work you and everybody else has done because I got pregnant."

"I'm not sacrificing all the work we've done just to be with you. But if that's what I had to do, I'd do it. There's nothing in Geneva that's as important to me as you."

He'd always known that, but he'd probably never acted like that because he'd never been forced to put the two up against each other. "You don't believe me, do you?"

She dropped her gaze, wouldn't look at him. "It's what you say."

"But it's not what I do? Is that what you're saying?"

"I think you try, but your heart isn't in it."

"What do you mean?"

"When you're away, you always call when it's a good time for you. I usually have to wake up out of a sound sleep to talk to you. When you're home, you're in the office or on the phone."

"But we go lots of places together."

She lifted her head. "And you spend the whole time talking about business. You talked about this meeting all through the homecoming football game. You called Greg on the cell phone four times. Leigh's mother asked me why you even bothered to come to the game."

"I have to make sure Greg writes down my ideas when they occur to me. If I don't, I might forget them."

"I'm sure that's good business, but it makes me feel like I'm in the way."

"You aren't."

"It feels like that."

"Is that how you'd feel?" he asked, turning to Kathryn.

"I walked out on a date just a few weeks ago who insisted upon talking on his cell phone during dinner."

"Sometimes you have no choice but to take care of business."

"He initiated the calls," Kathryn said.

Ron felt the heat of embarrassment in his face. He'd initiated the calls, too. "So you're saying when I'm with family, or out with you, I should never allow business to intrude."

"I didn't say that," Cynthia answered though he'd addressed the question to Kathryn. "I just don't want to feel I'm in the way."

"I refuse to go out with a man unless he leaves his cell phone or pager at home," Kathryn said. "If he doesn't have the time to concentrate on me, then I don't have the time to concentrate on him."

"What if there's an emergency?" Ron asked. "Something could happen at the shelter."

"I always tell Ruby where I'm going."

"There are still times when you couldn't be reached. Having a phone just in case an emergency comes up would remove all worry."

"No Palm Pilots, either," Kathryn said. "One date tried to outline a presentation he was giving the next day."

"I don't care about any of that stuff," Cynthia said, beginning to sound impatient. "I just want to feel even if you have to talk on the phone you'd *rather* be talking to me."

"Did you tell me I was paying too much attention to work and not enough to you?"

"Lots of times. You'd stop for a little while, but soon you'd be doing it all over again. After a while I gave up."

For Ron, there never seemed to be any time constraints on doing things with his family. If he didn't do it today, he could do it tomorrow. Or the day after that. That wasn't true in business. Things had to be taken care of the moment they came up—opportunities had to be grasped, or they would disappear. Erin had understood that and encouraged him to pursue every opportunity that presented itself.

After she died, he'd doubled his efforts because of the promises he'd made to her. Cynthia had been too small to tell him she didn't feel the same way her mother had. And if he was honest with himself, he'd have said she was too small for him to think she had an opinion he ought to consider. It would never have occurred to him that she could really want him. He thought girls wanted their mothers. They only wanted their fathers when it was time to go to the debutante ball or host the big summer party at the beach. It was only boys who wanted their fathers to do things with, to ask questions, to talk with about making plans for the future, what they wanted out of life.

Maybe he'd been wrong. Maybe some girls wanted that same kind of relationship with their fathers.

The idea pleased him. He'd always felt like an adjunct to Cynthia's life. From the moment she was born, he'd loved her dearly, but Erin had said children were a woman's job. Nothing had come along to change that picture. Or if it had, he hadn't paid attention to it. He'd always thought of himself as the provider, the parent who made Cynthia's life possible, not a participant in it. For the first time he realized how much he had missed out on. Cynthia's problem was his problem, too.

"If I could do it all over again, what would you want me to do?" he asked Cynthia.

"Think of me first."

That sounded so simple, but Ron wondered if he'd ever thought of anybody before his career, including himself. Since he was ten, he'd thought of nothing but the kind of life he wanted and what he had to do to get it. Thinking back, he couldn't remember what he was like back then, what he wanted out of life before that fateful day when he realized not all children were like him. Had he been happy? Had he been content with his toys, the clothes he wore, his parents, his trailer? Did he have friends he enjoyed playing with? What had happened to that little boy? Was there anything of him left?

Erin never talked about the years before they met. Maybe there was a little girl she had forgotten, a little girl who wasn't driven by dreams of a life different from the one she had, a little girl who wanted more from people and less from things.

Maybe that's where both he and Erin had changed. Their parents failed to give them that sense of security, of safety, of being loved and valued that all children wanted and needed. In its place, they'd reached for something else. But Cynthia had never felt insecure, unsafe, or ignored the way they had. She couldn't understand their needs because she'd never experienced them. He and Erin had been successful in giving their daughter what they themselves had missed. But that very success had formed a barrier between them, a barrier he must now learn how to dismantle.

"I do think of you first," Ron said, "but obviously not in the way you need me to think about you. You have to lead me until I learn enough to know how to do it by myself. I want to, baby, I really do, but I don't know where to begin. Do you believe me? Will you help me?"

Without warning, Cynthia jumped up from her chair and flung herself into his arms, her words made indecipherable by her sobs. After practically running from a room when he entered, his daughter's sudden change of attitude shocked Ron. But the biggest shock of all was the strangeness he felt holding his daughter in his arms. Had it been so long he'd forgotten what it felt like? Had it been so long he'd forgotten he missed it?

He no longer needed to be convinced of what Cynthia said. He *felt* it in his bones, his muscles, his heart. This child was what he'd worked for all those years, but he'd lost sight of her. He'd felt alone after Erin died with no one to share his dream. He'd turned to his career, concentrating on it so much he'd lost sight of everything else. He meant to change that starting right now. He didn't know what he had to do or how long it would take, but he would succeed.

Chapter Nine

"It was a brilliant idea to invite Mr. Egan to be part of this weekend," Mrs. O'Grady said to Kathryn as they got ready to leave. "I don't think anyone else could have made Shamus admit he'd made a mistake."

"I can't take credit for this weekend," Kathryn said for what had to be the twentieth time. "It was Mr. Egan's idea. He made all the arrangements."

"Then it was brilliant of you to talk him into coming up with the idea," Mrs. O'Grady said, apparently determined a man couldn't be responsible for the success of the weekend. "I wouldn't have thought such a famous man would have taken the time for people like us. Shamus says he has a really important meeting going on in Geneva right now."

Ron had been on the phone several times over the weekend. He hadn't said anything to Kathryn, but she could tell from his expression things weren't going well. She'd half expected him to leave for Geneva at any moment, but he had held to his commitment to remain for the entire weekend.

"All I know is his firm has been handling negotiations for a merger."

"He must love his daughter very much to stay with her instead of getting back to Geneva. Shamus says it looks like things are falling apart."

"I wouldn't know anything about that. I've got all I can do to keep track of these girls," she added, hoping she didn't sound rude. It had been made very clear during the weekend that everyone thought there was something going on between her and Ron. She had realized too late it had been a mistake to share the same suite with Ron and his daughter, even though she'd made it abundantly clear from the beginning she was acting as a chaperon for Leigh. It didn't do any good to say they'd met because of his daughter. The other fathers weren't single. Too, none of them were as handsome, as rich or as famous as Ron. That made him an even more interesting subject of gossip.

"I think he's interested in you," Mrs. O'Grady said.

"He's a very busy man who travels all over the world. I don't think he'd be interested in a woman who's basically a homebody."

"Who's saddled herself with a bunch of runaway unwed mothers."

"That, too. His daughter is the only reason we know each other."

"That might have been true at first," Mrs. O'Grady said with a conspiratorial wink, "but he's very well aware of you now. He's a nice man. I wouldn't turn my back on him if I were you."

Shamus and Kerry came out of the bungalow carrying the last of the luggage. Ron had managed to negotiate a shaky peace between father and son. As far as Kathryn knew, they hadn't come to any decisions, but they were talking. That was progress.

"I wish Mr. Egan was riding back with us," Mrs.

O'Grady said. "He's the only person who can keep Shamus and Kerry from shouting at each other. Maybe I could ride with you and he could take my place."

"You can ask him if you like, but it's time your husband and son learned to talk to each other without a peacemaker. If they're more interested in fighting than in making decision that will affect the rest of their lives, we might as well learn that now and save everybody a lot of time and effort."

Kathryn wouldn't have done anything to dissuade Ron from exchanging places with Mrs. O'Grady, but she had been looking forward to riding back with Ron. She'd hardly had a chance to talk to him all weekend. When he wasn't closeted with Cynthia, he was talking to one of the families, mediating arguments, calming troubled waters, and coming up with alternative solutions to their problems.

"They're the two most important people in my life," Mrs. O'Grady said. "I couldn't live without either one of them."

"Tell them," Kathryn said. "Lay down the law. Tell them you won't put up with this nonsense any longer. If they can't start to act like sensible adults, you'll leave."

"I couldn't do that!"

"Sure you can. Go visit your sister. Your mother. Or treat yourself to a nice vacation at a really expensive spa. You'll feel much better afterward."

"But what would they do without me?"

"Let them find out. It might make a difference."

Mrs. O'Grady promised to give the idea some thought.

"Is this everything?" Shamus asked Kerry as he struggled to arrange the luggage in the trunk of his Mercedes.

"Everything except Mom's overnight bag. She wants that up front with her."

"You ready to go?" Shamus asked his wife.

"I was just thanking Miss Roper for the lovely weekend," she said to her husband.

"I hope we'll see you again soon," Kathryn said.

"You will," Mrs. O'Grady and Kerry replied in unison.

Shamus looked disgruntled. "There's a lot more to talk about," he said.

"That's true for everyone," Kathryn said.

"I'm surprised Egan stayed," Shamus said. "It's going to cost him the merger."

"He hasn't said anything to me about that."

"He wouldn't, not with you hating men in business."

"I don't hate men in business," Kathryn said, shocked anyone would make such an accusation.

"Seems pretty widely accepted," Shamus said.

"Don't listen to him," Mrs. O'Grady said. "He doesn't understand why a woman would ever want to question a man." She winked. "I've been a right trial to him over the years."

Kathryn waved goodbye to the O'Gradys then saw off the other families. Betsy and Julia seemed more unhappy than when they arrived. Their parents were willing to talk, but she didn't think they understood Julia and Betsy any better than when they arrived.

She waited while Ron said goodbye to Cynthia. She'd offered to ride with Leigh so Cynthia could be with her father, but both wanted to stick to the original arrangement. Kathryn suspected Cynthia wanted to go over everything in detail with her friend.

Ron and Cynthia were the success of the weekend. They had a lot to work out before they could rebuild their trust, but they were talking.

"Where's your luggage?" Ron asked as he walked toward his car, waving to his daughter as Leigh's car disappeared around the curve of the stone wall.

"In the car. I'm packed and ready to go."

"I should have helped you with the luggage and seen everybody off."

"It was more important that you spend the time with Cynthia. You've already given a lot of time to the other families."

They got in the car and Ron started the ignition and backed out of the parking place. "I don't know how much good I did. I was hoping for more."

"If you hadn't done anything except jump-start your relationship with Cynthia, this would have been a successful weekend."

Ron smiled. "We're not there yet, but the roughest part is over."

They were silent as they drove through the woods to the road down the mountain. The weekend had been tiring and strenuous, but Kathryn had enjoyed it. She felt invigorated. Maybe it was the fact she and girls had gotten out of their routine. Whatever it was, she wouldn't have minded doing it all over again.

"I had hoped bringing everybody together would show them what they were missing," Ron said.

"I think it worked for Kerry and Lisette, but I'm not so sure about Betsy and Julia."

"I'll have to think of something else."

"You don't have to do this. Your only responsibility is your daughter."

"You got me interested," Ron said. "I figured if you thought it was important enough to devote your life to, I could give it a weekend now and then. Maybe even more somewhere down the road."

"What do you mean?"

"Nothing yet. Just that I never thought about boys and girls in situations like this. Their families, either. I don't imagine there's a lot being done to help them. This weekend's started me thinking about it."

"I don't know how you had time with all that was going on here and in Geneva."

She wasn't sure she should have mentioned Geneva. She thought Ron ought not put his business before his family. She thought that healing his relationship with Cynthia was unquestionably more important than any business meeting. But she couldn't help wondering if her telling him he ought to stay with Cynthia until everything was worked out could be partially responsible for his merger going bad.

"I'm used to working on more than one thing at a time," he said. "Business deals never come one at a time. It's usually feast or famine."

"If this was a feast, you don't appear to have been enjoying it."

Ron gave her a quick glance before turning his gaze back to the road. "Shamus has been talking, hasn't he?"

"When he was leaving, he said the merger was in trouble."

They had reached the end of the private drive through the woods. Ron waited until he'd pulled out on the twisting mountain road before he replied.

"There's a tricky political situation involved. The politicians are afraid to move until they know how things are going to settle out."

"Would things have gone better if you'd been able to stay in Geneva?"

He sent her a sharp look. "Do you want the truth?"

"Why wouldn't I?"

"Some people don't want to hear answers that don't fit their notions of how things ought to be."

"Do you think I'm like that?"

"I don't know. You seem so set against nearly everything I do."

"Then I've given you the wrong impression. I'm not against business. I realize men must have careers if they're to support their families. What I am against is men ignoring their family responsibilities for their careers."

"And you think I've done that."

"You know I do, but that's not what I asked."

"I have a reputation for handling negotiations personally. The political situation is the real stumbling block, but I may lose the whole deal because I'm not there to keep the people coming back to the table until that's resolved. Is that what you wanted to know?"

"Yes."

"Then you should also know I don't regret my decision. My career will always be important to me, but my daughter is more important. I hadn't realized how close I was to losing her. I'm going to work very hard to make sure we grow close again. I'm also going to try to be a damned good grandfather, but I'm not going to give up my work. It's not just a way to make money. It's not just a barometer of my success or social acceptance. It's my work, my career, something I do better than almost anyone else. I can't give it up any more than you can give up your shelter. It's part of who I am."

Kathryn hadn't realized she'd grown so tense. She'd certainly gotten more than she'd asked for.

"Will you have dinner with me when we get back to town?" Ron asked. "I've got a few hours before my flight leaves."

His request was unexpected, but not nearly so unexpected as her reaction to it was unwelcome. Her pulse started beating almost as rapidly as it had when she was a young girl acting silly over a handsome boy who'd paid attention to her.

"Why would you want me to have dinner with you?" she asked. "You just said you had no intention of giving up your career."

"What has that got to do with dinner? We both have to eat."

Now he was being a humanitarian. Somehow that didn't appeal to her.

"You know I like being with you," he said. "I tried all weekend to find some time for us to sneak away and misbehave in the moonlight, but either you had gone to bed or I got nabbed by somebody wanting to talk my ear off without listening to a word I had to say."

Kathryn couldn't keep up. Surely there was something she was missing. "But we don't agree on anything."

"Of course, we do. We agree that family's important,

that I have to get things straight with Cynthia. We also agree we like other, that we find each other attractive.''

She hadn't been willing to state that out loud. It was even more uncomfortable to have Ron do it.

''Besides, I've been thinking about kissing you for three days. I can't very well do it while I'm unloading suitcases and the girls are watching. It wouldn't be the least bit romantic.''

''I wouldn't have thought you were the romantic type.''

''Dreamers are always romantic, and I've been a dreamer since I was ten.''

''I thought you were a schemer.''

''How do you think I managed to make my dreams come true?''

''I need to talk to the girls, see how they feel about what happened over the weekend.''

''The girls are spending the night with their families. Cynthia is staying over with Leigh. You have nothing to do all evening but have dinner with me and see me off at the airport.''

''I didn't know I was seeing you off at the airport.''

''That'll give us plenty of time to kiss in the limousine.''

He had to be teasing her. ''This may be your idea of a joke, but—''

''What do you mean?''

''This abrupt change, talking about kissing me.''

''No man in his right mind jokes about kissing a beautiful woman. Either he means what he says, or he's a fool. I happen to find you extremely attractive. It's been damned hard to keep my hands off you all weekend. Hell, I would give my right arm to crawl into bed with you right now, and I haven't said that to any woman since Erin died.''

Kathryn was in a state of shock. She knew Ron liked her. She liked him, but she hadn't taken her feelings seriously because she knew the barriers between them were too high, too strong.

At least that's what she'd thought until now. She

couldn't believe she was reacting like this, but she couldn't deny it any more than she could stop it. She was excited about kissing Ron Egan—his remark about misbehaving in the moonlight made that particularly easy to visualize—but it was his comment about getting into bed with her that had caused her limbs to tremble.

Or should she say shake with desire.

Surely this couldn't be happening to her. She wasn't a girl anymore. She wasn't so inexperienced with men that the mere thought of physical intimacy caused her to become a quivering mass of nerves. Yet that's exactly how she was feeling. And why should Ron be the one man to cause her to feel this kind of excitement? She had been prepared to dislike him from the moment she saw him. She *had* disliked him when he forced his way into her house. What had happened to cause her feelings to change so dramatically?

"I didn't mean to offend you," Ron said.

"Why did you think you had?"

"Your silence. That's a weapon a lot of women use when a man has done something wrong."

"I'm not silent because I'm offended. I'm silent because I wasn't prepared for what you said. I had no idea your feelings were so strong."

"You're probably upset because I was so blunt."

"No. I—"

"I know I'm too direct. I never learned how to say things to please a woman. I've spent most of my life studying men—business men—trying to take their minds apart, to know exactly how they think and why. I never did that with women. Erin and I understood each other from the start. After she died, I forgot what little I knew. Since then I haven't been interested enough in any woman to learn how to please her. At least not the way I'm interested in pleasing you."

It was on the tip of her tongue to ask what way was that. Fortunately, Ron continued.

"I never can think of romantic things to say. I just come right out and say what I want. And I want you."

She didn't think anything he could have said, no matter how romantically phrased, could have affected her any more strongly than that bald statement. There was no pretense, no attempt to disguise or blunt the power of his words. He had laid it right out there without any hesitation, without any equivocation.

"Have I frightened you?"

"No, but you have surprised me."

"Why? I haven't attempted to hide that I'm strongly attracted to you. I was that first night."

"I haven't been thinking about you like that."

"Why not? Don't you find me attractive?"

"You know I do. I'm sure every woman you've ever met has felt the same way."

"I'm not interested in every woman. I'm interested in you." He turned toward her for so long she had to stop herself from telling him to watch the road.

"I like you and find you attractive, but the purpose of our relationship is to find a way to bring you and your daughter back together."

"That may have been true for two or three minutes. Probably not even that long."

"Do you always make up your mind that quickly?"

"No. I'm usually extremely deliberate. I think through the situation from every possible angle, weigh all outcomes very carefully, then step back and start the process all over again."

"What made it so different with me?"

He grinned, something he did too often for her comfort.

"There was nothing to weigh. You were the enemy. You disapproved of everything about me. So it was safe to be attracted to you."

"Did anybody ever tell you that you're a strange man? What man in his right mind would think like that?"

"It depends on what you consider a right mind. A pragmatist would say I was a fool and needed mental help."

"So would I."

"But a romantic—and remember all dreamers are romantics at heart—would feel Fate had intervened and shown him the one woman in the world who was destined to make him supremely happy."

"Not even a romantic could be that harebrained. Besides, you're not looking for some woman to make you supremely happy, at least not beyond a night or a weekend. You're married to your work. You're having trouble making room in your life for your daughter."

"If I take a leave of absence from my career—your advice by the way—I'll have all kinds of room."

"You just said you wouldn't give up your work."

"I said I couldn't give up my career. I said nothing about my *work*."

"I don't see the difference."

"Have dinner with me and I'll explain."

Kathryn could give herself all the advice and warnings she wanted, but she knew she was going to have dinner with Ron. She knew she was going to see him off at the airport. And she knew she was going to lie awake half the night thinking about him. He'd already invaded her dreams, but his saying he wanted her had raised the stakes to a new level.

She wanted him.

She could hardly believe it. She couldn't understand it. She could barely muster the will to admit it, but there was no question in her mind. She wanted Ron, too.

She had dated several attractive and eligible men over the last twelve years. She'd even developed a relationship with two of them, but no one had ever had such a powerful effect on her. And for the life of her she couldn't understand why. Ron was attractive, but he wasn't stunning. He was manly and aggressive, but she wasn't fond of aggressive males. He was rich and successful. That was practically a strike against him. He had screwed up his personal life in pursuit of success and recognition. In the past that would have removed him from consideration before he'd had a chance to ask her for a date.

So what was it about this man that had enabled him to leap all the barriers, avoid consequences of his actions, and render all handicaps ineffectual?

"You're taking a long time to make up your mind."

"I'm trying to decide where all this is going."

"Where do you want it to go?"

"Nowhere. That's why I don't understand why I'm even considering having dinner with you."

"And seeing me off at the airport."

"Especially that. That's what a wife does. Or a steady girlfriend. Or maybe even a mistress."

"And you don't want to be any one of those?"

"I didn't know you were looking for one."

"I wasn't."

"But you are now?"

"I don't know. I just know I'm interested in looking."

"I have no intention of being any man's mistress. You'd better look somewhere else."

"I like where I am."

"Why?"

"That's what I want to find out."

"You can't expect to find out over dinner."

"It's a beginning."

"Dinner's where you find out if you can stand to be around each other for four or five hours straight. We've already spent a weekend together."

"We were only in the same place. We hardly saw each other."

"Having dinner will add up to even fewer hours."

"You're right. We need a lot more time together. Why don't you come to Geneva with me?"

Chapter Ten

Kathryn had completely lost her mind. There couldn't be any other explanation for the fact she was about to board a private jet to spend the next thirty hours with a man she'd known just two weeks. There couldn't possibly be any other reason for her risking the gossip that would be the inevitable result of such a junket. Or the damage to her peace of mind. She didn't fool herself. She wasn't going on this trip with Ron because she was curious about the way supermoguls worked. She was going because she had fallen for him. More important than that, she was going because she hoped something would come of it.

That's the part that convinced her she was insane.

"Is this *your* private jet?" she asked.

"It belongs to the company, but I guess you could say it's mine."

It looked like the inside of an office or a conference room. There was a table with enough space for half a dozen people. There was a bar as well as deeply cushioned chairs that reclined for people who wanted to relax or take a nap. Televisions, computers, phones, just about every kind of machine you could need were placed around the interior.

"All you need is a kitchen and a bedroom, and you could live here instead of bother with a hotel."

"I have both, but we don't use the bedroom because it's too inconvenient to commute from the airport."

"We?" The kitchen didn't surprise her. *We* in the same sentence with *bedroom* did.

"My assistants fly with me most of the time. It gives us time to make last-minute preparations. We usually eat at least one meal on the plane."

Apparently no female companionship was wanted. She wondered if it was significant that he'd made an exception in her case. "How do you decide who cooks?"

"We have a chef."

She knew that. She was just trying to make a joke. Her nerves were getting to her. She'd never done this before, but she was going to take it as far as it would go. She didn't know why she thought anything could come of it, but something deep inside kept telling her she'd never find out if she didn't try. And if life was a gamble, maybe this was part of the game.

"Do you want something to eat? Something to drink?"

"After that dinner? I won't be hungry for a week." He'd taken her to his private club for dinner. Everything had been prepared by his chef, wines chosen from his private cellar.

"Do you want to relax? Watch TV? Watch a movie? We've got dozens of tapes and DVDs. We can take off as soon as your luggage arrives."

She'd called Ruby and asked her to pack a bag for her. She'd felt like a child talking to her mother, embarrassed about what she was doing, angry she was embarrassed. She was an adult and should be able to make her own decisions without feeling anyone had to approve them.

"You didn't tell me what you would need," Ruby had

said, "so I packed something for every occasion." She had packed three bags.

She had been too mortified to admit she'd probably need very little. Ron would be tied up with his meeting, so she'd spend most of the day by herself.

"You're not sorry you came, are you?" Ron asked.

She smiled, hoping to mask her nervousness. "No, but I don't know what to do without feeling in the way."

"Do exactly what you want," Ron said. "I'm going to be a terrible host because I have to work."

"When are you going to sleep? We're getting there just in time for the meeting."

"I'll sleep tomorrow, or the day after. You might want to go to bed early. It's only eight o'clock here, but it's two in the morning in Geneva. We'll land in seven hours. It'll be 3:00 a.m. here, nine o'clock there."

Great. Not only was she acting crazy, she was going to be sleep deprived as well. No telling what she'd do and not even remember. A porter went by with her luggage.

"Let me show you the bedroom," Ron said.

It wasn't large, but what it lacked in size it made up for in elegance. "Did you design this?" she asked.

Ron smiled. It was a wicked kind of grin, the kind she was certain could have gotten him in all kinds of trouble had he been willing.

"The plane belonged to a movie star with a taste for luxury. I had the rest of it redone, but I didn't change this room since I never use it."

Kathryn loved it. It was beautiful.

"I'll leave you to unpack."

"Do you mind if I watch a movie while you work?" she asked. She wasn't used to going to bed at eight o'clock. There was a TV in the bedroom, but she didn't want to stay in the room.

"Maybe I'll watch it with you."

"Does that mean I have to watch some movie where the body count exceeds my age?"

He laughed. "I don't know what you'll find. The guys picked them out."

"Surely at least one person who works for you is a beta male."

"Only alphas allowed. We're operating in a world of sharks, remember? It's eat or be eaten."

He laughed, but it was probably true. The competition must be even more fierce for him than it was for her father. "Do I dare ask if you have a decent book on this plane?"

"Not unless you like secret agents, espionage, or really bad guys. I think one of the guys likes Stephen King."

"I'd be up all night."

"I should have thought to ask the staff to send something else."

She didn't mind. It was pretty good proof her being invited on the plane was an exception. It would be foolish on her part to think Ron had been celibate since his wife's death, but it was important to her that she wasn't just another in a long line of women to satisfy his physical needs while he devoted most of his time to his career. She was taking a huge gamble, doing something completely unlike herself. She wanted to feel Ron was doing the same. This had to be extremely important to him, or she'd lost her gamble already.

"It's okay," she said. "I'm sure I'll find something."

Ron surprised her by stepping up close, taking her in his arms and kissing her very thoroughly. "I'm glad you came," he said, his voice husky. He stepped back just as abruptly. "Now I'd better leave you to unpack."

He left the room and she sank down on the bed. She could see herself in a full-length mirror on the door to the bathroom. It was almost like looking at a stranger. Even her features seemed unfamiliar. What was wrong? Why didn't she look or even feel like herself?

Fear.

She'd stepped out of her safe haven, opened herself up to a man who was practically everything she didn't want in her life. She hadn't merely allowed herself to become attracted to him, she wanted Ron more deeply than she'd ever wanted any man. What other reason could she have for such a desperate gamble?

Did she think by coming on this trip she could transform him into the kind of man she wanted?

No.

Did she think it would make any significant changes in what she looked for in a man?

No.

Was she hoping for a husband, or would she settle for something more temporary? She didn't know. Everything had happened too fast. Her feelings had changed even when she was certain her feelings would never change. The chances she was willing to take had increased. Was she so desperate? Or so foolish?

She couldn't decide. She only knew she wanted and needed Ron Egan. She didn't yet know *how* she needed him. Maybe she would find the answer in Geneva.

The question was, would she be able to live with the answer?

Ron paused just outside the bedroom door, shook his head in bewilderment and told himself he was crazy. Why on earth had he asked Kathryn to go with him to Geneva? Moreover, why had she agreed? He felt the plane vibrate as the pilot warmed up the engines. They'd be in the air soon. Too late to change his mind, too late for Kathryn to change hers.

He headed toward the bar, took a bottle of cold spring water from the fridge, and took a swallow. Didn't he have enough to worry about? His merger was going south, threatening to take a good bit of his business and professional reputation with it. He had very few hours to figure out how to keep the two government flunkies coming to the table, and he couldn't stop thinking about Kathryn.

He had a teenage daughter who was pregnant and who

had just begun to talk to him. He had to start from the ground up to rebuild their relationship. It would take all the time and concentration he could muster to keep from screwing things up again. And he had to help Cynthia figure out how to continue with her education, be a good mother to her child, and somehow have the life of a normal teenager and college student, a practically insoluble problem. That would become more difficult when, sooner or later, the father of the baby turned up, and he had to deal with that.

And into this turbulent mess he called his life he had just introduced a woman who didn't like very much about him and none of what he did. He had to be deranged. If they hadn't been thrown together by Cynthia's running way, he'd never have given her five minutes of his time. Yet now he couldn't stop thinking about her.

He'd dated women with more spectacular bodies, more beautiful faces, more sophisticated senses of style, yet he'd felt a strong physical attraction for Kathryn from the moment he set eyes on her. She was pretty, had plenty of style, and thinking about her body caused his temperature to rise. Maybe the simplicity of the way everything about her came together in a way that said there was nothing fabricated about her, nothing pretentious, nothing to hide, was the key. She was exactly what you saw, and that's the way she intended to remain.

He liked her intensity. Or maybe he meant her strength of character. She knew what she wanted, what she didn't, and she didn't equivocate. And she'd managed to tell him she disapproved of just about everything about him without making him feel she thought less of him as a man. She conceded to him the right to make his own choices at the same time she made it clear she didn't agree with them.

But he was most impressed she cared enough about the girls to devote her time and financial resources to make sure their mistakes did as little damage to their lives as possible. The emotional strain of dealing with teenagers under those circumstances must be tremendous. And then she had to deal with the parents as well. Even with the help of the experts she hired, he didn't see how she managed it.

He kept his temper with his clients because he was well paid to do it. She voluntarily put herself in the way of the anger of a lot of people because she wanted to help girls she'd never seen before they walked into her shelter. He had more money and more resources, but he'd never thought of doing anything like that. It ought to make him feel ashamed.

But all of this brought him back to the original question. Why had he asked her to go to Geneva with him? What did he expect—no, what did he *hope* to get out of it? He knew it wasn't just a thoroughly satisfying tumble in the bed. He wanted that and had told her so. He wouldn't turn it down if she offered, but there was something else.

She was vulnerable, but she had learned to cover it up. Maybe even deny it. Yet he could sense it lurking somewhere way down deep, maybe so deep she didn't realize it was there. At some level she still ached, yearned for what she couldn't have, couldn't find, maybe couldn't even identify. He'd promised himself he'd find it and fix it—just as he'd promised he'd fix his relationship with Cynthia—but he hadn't come close to figuring out what it might be.

He had figured out one thing: Kathryn had made him realize he was lonely, that he needed more than his work to feel fulfilled. Even more than his daughter and his future grandchild. He was a man with the physical and emotional needs of any other man. He'd ignored those needs far too long.

"Are you sure you don't mind watching this movie?" Ron asked her for the tenth time.

"I can't say I would have chosen *Chariots of Fire* if I could have found *A Room with a View* or *Shakespeare in Love,* but it's better than a clutch of Terminators or any of those action-adventure movies. Besides, it's kind of romantic in its own way."

If she was completely honest she wouldn't have cared if they'd watched one of the sweaty-muscles epics. She'd spent the last hour wrapped in Ron's embrace. Every so often he would whisper something, an excuse apparently to kiss her ear. She'd asked him once if he shouldn't be working. He'd said he still had time, so she didn't mention it again. She was hoping he wanted to kiss more than her ears.

"Are you glad you decided to come with me?" Ron asked.

That was a little more direct than she wanted to be. "I still can't believe I'm here. I don't want to think about what people are going to say when they find out."

"You're an adult. You can make your own decisions."

"That sounds exactly like what a man would say when he's trying to talk a woman into doing something she knows she shouldn't."

"Is that how you feel?"

Yes, but she couldn't put any of the blame on him. "A little bit. We haven't known each other very long, and you have to admit this could be seen as rather suggestive."

His grin turned positively brilliant. "You want to give them something to talk about?"

"No. This is something I did for myself. I wouldn't want to share it, even without the threat of gossip." That was true, but it exposed her feelings a little more than she wanted at the moment.

"Why did you come?"

"Let me ask you first. Why did you invite me?"

"No big secret there. I like you. I enjoy your company, and I wanted a chance to get to know you better. That didn't look likely as long as that shelter was standing between us. Besides, in Charlotte you saw me only as Cynthia's dad, a man who'd screwed up and didn't know how to straighten things out. I wanted you to see me as myself."

"How could I think of you as a screwup? You're famous the world over."

"Only in certain circles. Tell me why you decided to come with me."

Kathryn felt as if she were about to tell him things she wasn't even sure about herself. "Can I come back to that later?"

He sat up, looked at her with curiosity and surprise. "This isn't like you. You always know exactly what you think. I can only assume you don't want to tell me."

"I don't, but I'm also not sure. This was something I did on impulse. I'm still trying to figure out why."

"I'm a firm believer in impulses. They tell us what we really want."

"You don't seem very impulsive."

"I'm not. Inviting you along was the first impulsive thing I've done in years. It felt so good I'm looking for something else impulsive to do."

"You'd better be careful. You might scare those people you're trying to convince to accept the merger."

"I don't want to think about them. Let's think about us. What would you like to do?"

"I don't know yet. I don't know anything about Geneva."

"I can show you anything you want."

"You'll be in the meeting all day. Maybe we can save that for next time."

"Is there going to be a next time?"

"That's up for negotiation." She thought she was making a little joke, a least a play on words, but he took her quite seriously.

"What can I do to convince you that there ought to be a next time?"

"Let's concentrate on this time first."

"Fine with me, but the movie is disturbing me. Mind if I turn it down?"

He muted the TV before she had time to answer. Reaching out and placing his hand on her cheek, he turned her head to face him. "Now I can concentrate on you."

She smiled at him, happy he hadn't waited for her to make the decision. "I didn't realize you had a problem."

"Not that kind," he said, grinning back. "I just have a one-track mind, and right now I want that track focused on you."

"What about me is so interesting?" She wasn't trying to put him off. She really wondered what a man like him could see in a woman like her.

"You're a damned good-looking woman. I don't know which of your parents is responsible for the way you're put together, but I have to compliment them on a job well done."

"You sound like all the men I know. Body first, everything else so far up the track you can't see it."

"I'm not quite that bad, but yeah, I'm a body man." He brushed her lips with his. "Don't you have even a tiny bit of interest in my body?"

She kept remembering how Ron looked this past weekend in his cutoffs and T-shirt. He hadn't mentioned going to a gym or working out, but he must have done something besides sit around conference tables to be in such great shape. Lisette's mother said he looked too young and attractive to be a business tycoon. Mrs. O'Grady was more direct. She said it was a shame to hide all that male virility beneath business suits. Betsy and Julia's mothers wondered how such an attractive man could still be single after nine years. Kathryn had concentrated on keeping everybody from realizing she was just as impressed by Ron's body as they were. Having the women mention it to her several times a day had made it very hard to keep her mind on helping the girls and their families.

"No self-respecting woman could make an admission like that," she said.

"Why not? Don't tell me women drool over Brad Pitt and Mel Gibson because of their minds."

It was hard to carry on a conversation when he kept

covering her mouth with tiny kisses. "No self-respecting woman will admit she drools over movie stars."

"How about Prince William?"

"He's too young for me."

"How about me? I'm just the right age."

"I'd never make such an admission."

"Why not? I admit I drool over you."

"Men are allowed. Women aren't."

"That doesn't seem fair." He sat back and flashed that wicked grin again. "In the interest of fair play, I'm giving you permission to drool over me. And any other man you like," he added, "but I hope you won't like too many more. I have a fragile ego."

She laughed. "Your ego could withstand an atomic blast." But no sooner had she said it than she realized she was wrong and should have known it. "You don't have that kind of ego, do you? I know I shouldn't talk about it—it's bad manners—but you don't, or you wouldn't care about social acceptance."

The smile seemed to freeze on his face. She imagined he'd learned to do that to shield his feelings when he was growing up.

"How disconcerting to have my tawdry ambitions exposed when I'm trying to make love to a beautiful woman. Sort of takes the steam out of things."

"I'm sorry. I didn't mean—"

"It's not something I'm proud of, but I can't deny it." He picked up the clicker and unmuted the movie. "If you'd rather watch—"

She took the clicker from him, muted the movie again.

"I'd rather go back to what we were doing before I destroyed the mood. There's nothing socially unacceptable about you. And if other people don't see that, it's their loss."

"You remind me of Erin. She was fierce about my feelings of inferiority."

Kathryn wasn't sure how she felt about being compared

to his dead wife, but she didn't intend to let that destroy the mood, either. "Good. I hope she said all the things I would have said."

The grin was back. "Tell me what you'd have said. I have this inferiority complex, remember, so make it really good."

"Are you fishing for compliments?"

"Got any floating around?"

"Maybe I could think of a few if you don't start kissing me again and mess up my concentration."

"Can I do that?"

"You know you can." She wondered if she was blushing. She ought to be. She sounded as if she were *asking* him to kiss her.

"Hmmm," he said. He cocked his head to one side and pretended to be in deep thought. "Do I prefer you talking or silent?"

"I thought every man's secret wish was for a silent woman." Only after she'd spoken did she realize the significance of what she'd said.

"Who am I to go against the wisdom of the entire male species? I'll opt for silence, too. You'll have all day tomorrow to think of compliments."

Then he kissed her. Again and again and again. There was nothing shy or hesitant about his kisses. Just as in business, it seemed that in his personal affairs, Ron Egan believed in being very direct. Kathryn couldn't have resisted him if she'd wanted to.

And she didn't want to.

She threw herself in his kisses with an abandon none of her previous dates or companions would have recognized. Cool, controlled and demanding Kathryn Roper had turned into a woman hungry for what this man could give her, needing what this man could give her, wanting more than anything what this man could give her. In the past she'd waited for her companion to come to her, to make the advance, to set the tempo. She'd responded enthusiastically on occasion, but never had she felt as if she wanted to set the agenda, control the tempo, adjust the heat upward.

Somewhere in the back of her head a howling genie screamed that she was lowering her standards, that she couldn't behave in such an abandoned manner with a man who stood for virtually everything she despised.

A second genie popped up to say she wasn't entirely sure Kathryn despised all that much about Ron. Besides, she didn't fully understand him or his business. Maybe she'd applied strictures that didn't fit.

A third genie interrupted to say the whole discussion was nonsense. She didn't have to be thinking about marrying a man to enjoy his company. Ron Egan was attractive, intelligent, fascinating, as well as having a body men ten years younger would envy. On top of that, he was the most interesting man she had met in years. It would be foolish for Kathryn to waste this opportunity to enjoy his company because of philosophical differences.

Kathryn happily awarded the victory to the third genie, complimented the second on her perspicacity and ruthlessly banished the first. Now unencumbered by doubt, she devoted her full attention to Ron's kisses. It didn't bother her in the least that she was gradually sliding down in the sofa. It was much easier to kiss lying down. Especially if she abandoned all restraint.

Kisses on her eyebrows and temples were tantalizing. Kisses on her neck or collarbone were titillating. Kisses on her ears turned up the heat. But nothing excited her as much as a big, hungry, ruthless kiss on her mouth. She wasn't a passive partner. She didn't like lying there while Ron had all the fun. She wanted to participate.

When his tongue invaded her mouth, she countered with an equal energy. Her tongue pressed back against every attack. They had slid down in the sofa until their bodies were in contact from shoulder to knee making the feeling all the more intense.

Somewhere in the midst of this intensity Kathryn realized she hadn't had a necking session like this since her college days. Nor had she enjoyed one half as much. Her two serious relationships had been just that—all too serious. They had none of the unrestrained excitement, the sheer abandon, the crackle of electric energy, the chemistry that existed between Ron and her. It was a sheer visceral reaction, all the more powerful because it was unencumbered by rational thought.

The last shred of control vanished when Ron's hand cupped her breast. Even through her blouse and bra, the feeling was electric. She heard herself gasp for breath, felt her body arch, push her breast more firmly against his hand. The feeling that swept over her was so strong, so overwhelming, she felt dizzy. She hadn't realized how long it had been since she'd allowed any man to touch her. To have someone like Ron, a man whose effect on her was out of all proportion caused her to react much more strongly than she could have imagined.

Hungers she thought buried, or at least forced into slumber by the strength of reason and resolve, gnawed at her with the voracious appetite of a starving beast. Her body trembled when Ron began to unbutton her blouse. Her breathing stopped when he unhooked her bra. It came in uneven gasps when his hands touched the superheated skin of her breast. Her skin had never felt so sensitive to the touch. She was certain all her senses were at least a dozen times more acute than normal. When his fingertips touched her engorged nipple, she felt she was ready to jump out of her skin.

She had to get herself under control. At this rate she would be a mindless mass of jelly in a matter of minutes. She hadn't guessed at the tension that had built up over the years since she'd practically cut herself off from all but the most formal dates with carefully chosen men. She had no suspicion of the need that had gone unfulfilled or the strain it had put on her. She had no idea she was capable of being so strongly attracted to a man or so strongly affected by him. She had foolishly concluded she was beyond any sort of youthful temptation to throw out reason for emotion.

But she was wrong. Ron's attentions to her body proved she was dangerously close to losing control. She didn't know what would happen if she crossed that barrier, but she resolved not to find out.

Then Ron touched her breast with his lips, and her resolve when up in smoke.

Kathryn couldn't remember when, or if, anything had ever affected her so dramatically. There was no question of her being able to think, reason, or make choices, no matter how basic. She could only remain where she was as Ron treated her breast to a profusion of sensations, each seemingly more intense and pervasive than the last. Every part of her body reacted to his touch as if he had a hundred hands and was able to touch her in a hundred places all at once. She felt besieged. Assaulted. Reduced to helplessness.

Despite the feeling that she was losing what little control she had over the situation, she wouldn't have changed anything. She couldn't remember when—if ever—she'd felt so wonderfully alive. The lethargy which had threatened to engulf her a few weeks ago was completely forgotten. The pessimism about her future evaporated. The fear that her chances for love had vanished haunted her no longer. She didn't know what lay ahead, but as long as Ron Egan was in her future, it would be exciting.

She tried to pull his lips away from her breast. When she couldn't, she gripped his left hand and covered it with kisses, finger by finger. The more feverish his attention to her breast, the more frenetic her kisses. She kissed the palm of his hand, pressed it to her face, then started kissing it again. All the kisses she wanted to give to the rest of him she showered on this single hand.

Until she realized his other hand had moved down her

side, under her skirt, and was proceeding up her thigh. Action preceded thought. She pushed his lips from her breast and sat bolt upright.

"Stop!"

Chapter Eleven

The limousine moved slowly through the heavy morning traffic. Geneva wasn't any different from the rest of the world. It seemed everybody worked in the same part of the city and had to get to work at the same time.

Kathryn felt very much on edge. Ron had asked her to attend the first hour of his meeting with him. He wanted her to see what he did. He didn't anticipate being through until six at the earliest, so he put the limousine at her disposal for the rest of the day. His discussion with his assistants hadn't been encouraging. If Ron couldn't come up with something today, the government representatives would probably walk out of the meeting. If that happened, the negotiations were effectively over.

But while Kathryn was acutely aware of the importance of this meeting, of the tension in Ron's body, of the harried expressions of his two associates who sat directly across from her, her thoughts were centered almost entirely on the events of the previous evening. In a moment of unreasoning panic, she had stopped Ron in the midst of what could only be described as a passionate encounter. She knew enough of men to know what she'd done was taboo. No woman would encourage a man in such a fashion then, without warning, scream at him to stop.

She hadn't actually screamed, but she might as well have. She thought Ron would have a heart attack.

She didn't know what had gotten into her. Shock? Ron had said he wanted to climb into bed with her *before* he invited her on the trip. If she hadn't wanted that to happen, she should have stayed home.

But despite her confusion, she was sure if she had it to do over again, she still would accept the invitation to come to Geneva, but she would have taken the time to figure out exactly what she wanted out of the trip. Then she could have made sure Ron didn't believe she was promising more than she was willing to give. It was only fair.

Ron had been shocked at her response—even a man trained to keep his feelings from showing could only control so much—but he'd behaved admirably. He had every right to accuse her of being a tease, of leading him on. Instead, he apologized for letting his feelings get out of control. He said he'd never do anything to hurt her. Then he'd proceeded to act as if nothing out of the ordinary had happened. Putting his arm around her and cuddling up against her as he had just moments before he put the TV back on and they finished watching the movie.

Kathryn didn't know how he did it. She was so mortified, so hugely embarrassed, she was practically tongue-tied for the rest of the evening. She would have given anything to be able to run into the bedroom, close the door and cry. But if he could behave with such class, then the least she could do was try to behave just as well.

By the time the movie was over and it was time to go to bed, she was too exhausted to spend the night, as she had intended, scrutinizing her actions and motives until she knew what had prompted her to behave so outrageously.

She fell into bed, thankful for Ron's tender kiss as he told her good-night and wished her sweet dreams.

Her nightmares were probably just reward for her behavior.

Next morning Ron had continued to behave as though nothing untoward had happened. The chef who came on board immediately after the plane landed had breakfast ready as soon as she was out of the shower and dressed. Ron had already showered, dressed and was conferring with his assistants. Kathryn could guess what the men thought when she came out of the bedroom, but they acted with punctilious decorum. And were so caught up in their work they soon seemed to forget her presence. Even when they'd all gotten into the limousine and headed into the city, they seemed unaware of her presence.

But when they finished discussing business, their sudden awareness of her caused them to fall silent. With the men occupied with their own thoughts, she was left to stare out the window at the city. But it looked like so many other European cities she'd visited her thoughts went back to Ron and the night before. She practically sighed with relief when Ron said they were close to the hotel where they held the meetings.

He looked at his watch. "If this traffic doesn't ease up, we'll be late."

"Schmidt and Wasserman are never late," Ted said. "They spend the night in a nearby hotel and walk over."

Ted and Ben stayed in a similar hotel, but they had been waiting at the airport to talk with Ron when he landed. It hadn't taken more than a few minutes to tell Ron the government representatives hadn't responded to any of the information or poll results they'd provided. "It's like they don't mean to accept the merger, no matter how much information we provide," Ted had said.

Ron had run through every offer they'd made, every compromise, every piece of information they'd provided—economic and well as political—to show the merger would be good for the country. He wanted to know their exact word-for-word response to each, even asking about inflection of speech, expression, body posture. Ron wanted to know what was happening in their homes and offices, whether things were going well or if they were under some kind of pressure. Kathryn had never realized negotiating a merger required such complete knowledge.

The limousine driver pulled the car to a stop in front of a modern, nondescript building.

Once out of the car, he ushered Kathryn through an impersonal lobby, up a utilitarian escalator, down a hall decorated with modern art in stainless steel frames, and into a conference room that looked like the set of a futuristic movie. Everything—walls, furniture, curtains—were shades of grey, the room made up of straight lines and sharp angles. She found the visual image jarring.

"What a ghastly room," she said in a soft voice.

"Imagine spending every day for the last three weeks in it," Ted said.

"I'm surprised no one's been murdered."

She had never seen a more grimly sober, depressing, austere group of men in her life.

"I see you are back," one man spoke in heavily accented English.

Kathryn didn't have to be told this man was one of the government representatives. No one else would have spoken with such disdain.

"You are late as well," a man on his left said. "I can guess the reason for your tardiness."

Kathryn didn't need to be told she was the *reason* the man referred to, but she was more aware of Ron's reaction. He stiffened, and his expression hardened.

"I'm late because the flight took longer than expected and the traffic was worse than usual." He remained standing behind his chair, his hand at Kathryn's elbow.

One of the men opened his mouth to speak, but Ron cut him off. "But despite my tardiness, I have had time to confer with my assistants. They've assured me they've provided you with all the information we've been able to gather, both by research and by conducting opinion polls. They've also assured me they've explained in great detail how to interpret this information and how it applies to the merger we're discussing.''

The man opened his mouth. Again Ron cut him off. ''They've informed me that despite all the evidence our research can provide, you still hold to your original positions. Is that true?''

''Yes. We—''

''Even though the data we've presented has shown the situation has changed substantially in the last half year?''

''We do not believe—''

''Yes, or no.''

The man looked slightly startled, then miffed. ''I had started to explain—''

''We've heard enough of your explanations. I want a straight answer. Yes or no.''

''Yes.'' The man's tone and expression indicated he was mortally offended by such abrupt and ungentlemanly behavior.

''In that case I see no reason to waste mine or my assistants' time in further discussion. As of this moment, these negotiations are over.''

The two government representatives, coldly impassive up until now, couldn't hide their surprise. The other twenty men in the room stared at Ron in disbelief.

''I have instructed my assistants that as soon as we leave this building, they are to make available to the news media all the data we have gathered and presented to you during these past weeks. As for your comments on the reason for my tardiness, you do your government a great disservice by the tastelessness of your remarks.''

With that Ron turned and escorted Kathryn out of the conference room. Ted and Ben followed. No one spoke as they left the building nor as they walked the short distance to the hotel where Ron's team stayed.

"Did you really mean that?" Ted asked after they got in the elevator.

"I thought Wasserman was going to have a coronary," Ben said. "I hate to think what losing this deal will mean to the firm, but it was worth it to see his face."

"The data will crucify him," Ted said.

"It might even bring down the government," Ben said.

"That's what I hope they'll realize," Ron said.

The elevator opened into the foyer of a suite that occupied a whole floor of the hotel. Kathryn saw several people at work, heard conversations from others coming through open doors. Ron had turned the suite into an office away from home.

"Then you don't want us to turn everything over to the media?"

"Give them twenty-four hours."

"You think they'll come around?"

"If they don't now, they will afterward."

Kathryn had expected Ron to send her off to the limousine and settle down to work, but he remained standing in the foyer.

"It may take a little longer than twenty-four hours. Play it by ear but have everything ready. This isn't a bluff."

"What are you going to do?" Ted asked.

"I'm going home. Make it clear to Schmidt and Wasserman I have no intention of coming back. If they want to negotiate, they have to negotiate with you. I can't be wasting my time on those two."

Kathryn felt as stunned as the two assistants looked.

"Don't you think you can handle it?" Ron asked.

"Sure, but you always handled everything yourself."

"I've decided to change management style. I'm going to delegate more. If you two bring this off, you're in for one hell of a bonus."

"And if we don't?"

Both men were tense.

"You're still the best two merger negotiators around, after me, of course. We'll have other deals to work on. Now Miss Roper has never been to Geneva. I'm going to show her around before we head back to Charlotte."

"When did you decide to do that?" Kathryn asked when they were once again in the limousine.

Ron put his arm around her and drew her close. "I said inviting you was the first spontaneous thing I'd done in years and it felt wonderful. Well, that was the second and it felt just as good."

"But what made you do it?"

"When I walked in and saw their faces set in the same implacable mold, I knew there was no point in talking. I also knew I'd rather spend the day with you. So I said to hell with it. I'd given it my best shot. You can't win every time."

"But this is important to your career. Shamus said losing this deal could break you."

"It won't break me, but it will delay my being able to take a less active role in the company."

"But you don't mind losing the deal?"

"Of course I mind. I've worked toward something like this for twenty years. Maybe I could pull it off by staying here and giving in, but I'd be selling my clients short. I also realized I wanted to be in Charlotte with Cynthia more than I wanted to be here, that I wanted to spend the day with you more than with them." He pulled back so he could face her. "I looked down the road and saw myself missing the chance to do so much—all for the glory of convincing big companies to become still bigger companies. I decided it wasn't worth it."

Kathryn realized she hadn't breathed. She gulped down air and forced herself to relax. It wasn't business as usual. Ron had really looked at his life and decided what he wanted most couldn't be had through his career. She didn't know exactly how that would translate in real life—she was certain he didn't, either—but the change in him made their relationship take on a whole new meaning.

But she refused to let her mind go that far. She'd let things progress beyond what she was ready to handle once already. She wouldn't do that again. For the time being they were just two very good friends who really enjoyed each other's company.

"What do you want to do today?" Ron asked. "The limousine and I are at your disposal."

"Are you sure you don't want to fly back by yourself? I can lease another plane."

Ron had asked the same question several times, and each time she'd tried to assure him she didn't want to return alone. They were taxiing down the runway, both strapped in until the pilot felt it was safe for them to get up and move around. Ron had offered to bring the chef and a couple of flight attendants, but she had refused. They'd eaten dinner at a wonderful restaurant with a view of the mountains. She wasn't hungry, and she didn't need anyone to wait on her.

"I've apologized for my behavior last night every way I know how. I don't know what got into me."

"I shouldn't have forced you."

"You didn't do anything I didn't enjoy." The plane was in the steep climb that comes immediately after takeoff. She felt glued to her seat. "Letting you make love to me seemed like a very big step when I wasn't sure what you wanted."

"What do you want?"

"Lifelong commitment. A husband and a family."

"Isn't that what you've always wanted?"

"Yes, but for a while I thought I might be willing to settle for something less." She hooked his gaze with her own. "I'm not any longer."

"I get the feeling it's my turn to say what I want."

"It's the only way I'll know what kind of future our relationship has."

She didn't know what she'd do if he said he only wanted a temporary relationship, something he could conveniently slip into and out of when he happened to be in town and had a free evening. Well, she did know what she'd *do*. She just didn't know how she'd survive doing it. She was gradually falling in love with him, might be in love with him already. It was stupid, but there was little point in denying her feelings were very strongly engaged.

"My wants are more complicated," Ron began. "Regardless of what I might want for myself, I have to consider Cynthia, the baby and their future first. I can't let anything I want interfere with that."

"What would you want if you didn't have them to consider?" Kathryn asked.

"Nothing extravagant. Just a woman who could love me."

"Why would that be so difficult to find?"

"Because she'd have to love me for who I am, not for my money or the power and position she thinks I could give her. I told you before I was after social success, that I needed to have people accept me because I'd been denied acceptance before and because their acceptance signified my success.

"Looking back, it seems ironic that for you and Cynthia it was my success that got in the way. When I walked into that boardroom today and faced those two men, I realized I *felt* successful. I could turn my back on them and survive. Once I knew that, I could see what I really needed."

Kathryn was glad he didn't have that pressure on him any longer. She'd seen the struggles and anguish of people who felt they couldn't be happy unless they achieved social acceptance.

"I don't think you'll have any trouble finding a woman who can love you for yourself if you'll just give her a chance," Kathryn said. "Though you don't seem to realize it, you're quite a catch. And I'm not referring to your money or prestige. You're caring and sensitive. I know, men don't like it when you say things like that about them, but it's important to women.''

''I didn't say I didn't like it. I'm just surprised. You didn't used to feel like that.''

''I made assumptions based on other men I'd known, but I know better now. You wouldn't have arranged the weekend in the mountains if you didn't care about people. And you wouldn't have understood Kerry just needed somebody to believe in him, to be willing to support him, before he could stand up to his Dad. I've known him ever since Lisette came to the shelter, and I didn't figure that out.''

''It's hard for women to understand men. We don't think like they do.''

''And when did you have that earthshaking realization? The news media are going to want to know.''

''You know, you've got a sharp tongue when you want to use it.''

Those words struck deep. Her father had said pretty much the same thing the last time they'd attempted to talk. ''So I've been told. Getting back to telling you how wonderful you are—''

''Don't let me stop you. It doesn't happen all that often.''

She ignored his smile. It was messing up her concentration. ''I believe you're loyal and supportive once you've committed yourself. You don't always understand women very well, but a wife could help you there.''

''If she could put up with my not understanding her long enough to help me understand her.''

''If you found this paragon, what would she have to do to fit into your life?''

''She'd have to love my daughter and her baby as much as she loved me. She'd have to become an integral part of our family. That wouldn't be easy.''

''It's being done every day.''

''And then there's my career.''

Kathryn had been waiting for the other shoe to drop.

"I love my work, and I'm good at it. I wouldn't be happy sitting around living on my money. I have to be doing something I enjoy and feel is important. Any woman who wanted to join my family would have to be a part of that, too."

Kathryn felt the bottom drop out of her hopes. She couldn't live with a man who valued his career over his family. And to be a successful negotiator on an international basis, Ron's family would have to come second.

"I don't know what I want to do," Ron said, "but if we managed to salvage the Geneva negotiations, I'll hand that part of the business over to Ben and Ted. I really can't do the kind work I expect of myself when I'm no longer willing to stay on the job until it gets done."

Kathryn tried to keep her hopes from soaring too quickly.

"I want to spend more time in Charlotte," Ron said. "Or at least close enough I can come home often. I don't ever again intend to lose sight of the needs of my family."

"Have you any idea what you'd like to do?"

"Not yet, but I've already had a few people asking if I'm going to be in Charlotte more in the future."

"Are you doing this because of what I said?"

It was stupid to be worried about that, but after telling him he should devote more time to his family, she was feeling guilty something she said could have caused him to make this decision. What if he failed? She didn't want to feel responsible for Ron's decision in case it didn't work out.

"Yes, and no, but mostly no."

Now she felt slightly irked. Why did being involved with Ron cause her to behave so unlike herself?

"Cynthia's getting into trouble jolted me out of my old rut, but you jerked the chain that made me stop and think. Without you, I'd probably have ended up shouting and making things even worse. You were a protective barrier between me and Cynthia until I could get over my shock and anger enough to see shock and anger weren't going to help the situation. You also pointed me in the right direction. I probably would have gone off looking for the boy instead of turning the spotlight on myself. But once I cooled down, once I understood the issues and what was at stake, I knew what I had to do. What I *wanted* to do."

She felt better. She was glad she had been able to help, but she was even more pleased Ron had been able to see the problems and make the right decisions on his own.

"Does that answer your question?" he asked.

The plane had leveled off, but the pilot hadn't yet said they could unstrap themselves from the seats.

"Yes."

"Does it fit close enough for you to want to see if this relationship can go further?"

"I'd like that."

Ron unbuckled himself and got out of his seat. He unbuckled Kathryn and pulled her to her feet. He pulled her close to him and put his arms around her. "I don't have to prepare for a meeting. Want to watch one of those movies you bought?"

She'd bought *Emma* and *Bridget Jones's Diary.* "Are you sure you can stand a chick flick?"

Just then the plane banked and began a turn. Kathryn fell against Ron, who had to grab hold of the seat to keep both of them from falling. She ended up in a tight embrace, not a bad place to be.

"It looks like we should have waited for the pilot to let us know when it was safe to get out of our seats," she said.

"I was willing to risk some minor bodily harm to get you in my arms."

"Maybe I'm not."

"I'll protect you. I'd like doing that very much."

Kathryn liked the drift of this conversation but found it hard to concentrate when the angle of the floor under her feet was at variance with the way gravity was acting on her body. "I think we'd better sit down."

"The couch would be more comfortable."

"If we can get there without killing ourselves."

They stumbled across the plane, holding on to each other to keep from falling. By the time they dropped onto the sofa, they were laughing so hard they couldn't speak.

"I feel like I've turned into Lisette," Kathryn said when she finally stopped laughing enough to catch her breath.

"You're prettier."

"Nobody is prettier than Lisette."

"Beauty is in the eye of the beholder. Since my eyes are doing the beholding, I have the right to think you're prettier."

"I guess I'll have to agree with you," Kathryn, smirking like her sister used to do when making fun of somebody important. "My mama always said it was unbecoming for a young lady to argue with an important man."

"And did you listen to your mama?"

"Of course. I was the perfect daughter."

A voice from the past suddenly burst into her conscious, shouting that phrase in bitter anger. The memory caused her to flinch.

"Is something wrong?" Ron asked, concern replacing amusement.

"No." She settled closer to him. "But let's not talk about perfect daughters. Which movie do you want to watch?"

"Die Hard."

She punched him. "No sweaty muscles. *Emma* or *Bridget Jones's Diary.*"

"Which would I like better?"

"Probably *Emma.* It's got Gwyneth Paltrow and the guy is always telling her she's doing everything wrong. Men love to tell women they're doing stuff wrong."

"Only the bossy ones."

"I'm bossy."

"Why says?"

"Everybody."

"Do you always listen to rumors?"

She laughed. "No rumors. They tell me to my face."

"You must have been dating some weak sisters."

"Are you saying you're so strong you'd have no trouble controlling me?"

Ron must not have flashed that entrancing grin much since his wife died. If he had, any one of a thousand women would have dragged him to a preacher.

"You're not catching me in that one," he said. "I want you to do whatever makes you happy."

"Very well said *and* politically correct."

"Hey, that's why they pay me the big bucks." He sobered abruptly. "I *do* want you to do what makes you happy. I have a feeling you haven't been really happy in a long time."

Kathryn refused to go where Ron's statement led. She didn't want to lose her buoyant mood. "Then let's not think about anything but the present."

"And the future."

"Let's take care of the present first."

Ron pulled her close and kissed her. "Like that?"

"Is that the best you can do?"

"Is that a challenge?"

"Could be."

Ron's grin turned truly wicked. "Lady, get ready to be thoroughly kissed."

She grinned back. "I'm willing to let you try."

With a ferocious growl, he pounced on her, covering every available part of her face and head with loud, smacking kisses.

"Has anybody ever talked to you about your technique?" She was laughing so hard she could hardly talk.

He growled louder and redoubled his efforts.

"Why don't you go fly the plane and let me see if the pilot can do better? I remember thinking he was kinda cute."

"Faithless hussy," Ron growled. "I'll make you regret you ever looked at another man."

By now she was backed up in the corner of the sofa with Ron practically on top of her. "Whatcha gonna do, big boy?" she teased.

"I'm gonna kiss you till you're breathless," he said, imitating her. "Then I'm gonna kiss you some more."

"Oh well," she said, trying to sound bored and blasé, "if ya feel like ya gotta."

Ron changed tactics. He kissed her on the mouth. What had begun in fun as a challenge quickly changed to a kiss charged with so much heat all thoughts of humor evaporated. Kathryn felt practically absorbed by Ron's energy, his intensity, the sheer force of his feeling for her. She was so overwhelmed she hadn't regained her equilibrium by the time he broke the kiss.

"How's that?" he said. He was grinning, but it wasn't devilish any longer. It was pure hunger. "Breath coming a little harder now?"

"Definitely," Kathryn said, truly breathless. "So much so I think we ought to move this into the bedroom."

"Are you sure?" Ron asked.

"Very sure," Kathryn replied. "I think I knew when I agreed to come on this trip. I just hadn't admitted it to myself. I was probably afraid it would make me too vulnerable to a man I was certain couldn't be part of my future."

"And now?"

"I'm still not certain you'll be part of my future, but if that's what both of us really want, I think we have a chance."

Ron stood and extended his hand. Kathryn took it and let him help her up from the couch. They walked to the bedroom together. Kathryn kicked off her shoes and climbed on the bed. She patted the spot next to her. "Lie next to me and tell me why you're certain I'll make some man a wonderful wife.'' Ron removed his shoes before getting on the bed.

"Do I get equal time?"

"Only if you do a bad job. Otherwise, I'll be too besotted with you to care."

"What a choice, to bewitch you or have you tell me how wonderful I am."

Kathryn leaned back against a mound of pillows. "I vote for bewitched."

"I'll see what I can do." Ron lay down next to her and took her hands into his. "Do you know that I've been dreaming of doing this for at least two weeks?"

"How could I? You didn't tell me."

"I didn't want to scare you off."

"You might have. You're a famous man."

Ron made a semirude noise. "I'm a man like any other man. The fact that a few people know my name doesn't affect that."

"Well, I think you're special."

He kissed her fingertips. "I hoped you would. Do you mind if we skip the compliments and get right to the kissing part? I really like kissing you."

"It's a great sacrifice, but if you really want—"

Ron leaned over, scooped her up in his arms, and gave her a kiss that was a twin of the one they'd shared moments earlier. By the time he released her, Kathryn was certain she wouldn't have a coherent thought for at least a week.

"I really like the kissing part, too," she managed to say.

"Then let's not waste time with compliments."

Proving that he was a man of action rather than words, Ron readjusted his hold on her, and set to work once more reducing her brain to mush.

None of the men Kathryn had dated had been as forceful as Ron. She had screened them carefully to make certain of that, so she was surprised when she found she didn't mind being overwhelmed by his physical strength as well as the intensity of his lovemaking. For the first time in years she wasn't in control, and she was pleased to find she wasn't the least bit frightened. Whatever happened, she trusted Ron. She felt he would be as concerned about her feelings and emotions as he was about her body.

Deciding she enjoyed her newfound feeling too much to waste time thinking about it, Kathryn threw herself into the kiss determined to equal Ron's in every way. It had been years since she had truly enjoyed kissing a man. It seemed she had become less enchanted with them as the years went by, but Ron made up for all the uninspired kisses she'd endured.

Kathryn couldn't recall that she'd ever felt quite so alive, couldn't recall when her body had been so sensitive to the feel of her clothes they almost irritated her. The day spent with Ron had heightened all her senses. Each time he had touched her, whether helping her into a car or up steps or simply holding her hand as they walked together, seemed to increase the sensitivity of her nerve endings. Her awareness of his physical presence had increased so much she didn't have to see him to know he was near. Each hour, each minute, built on an invisible connection between them.

She had become part of him, he part of her.

That feeling frightened her and excited her at the same time. She was losing some of herself while she gained some of him. This had never happened and she didn't really understand or trust it, but it seemed to be happening on its own without any permission from her.

"Did anybody ever tell you that you have very kissable lips?" Ron asked.

"Nobody has ever made me enjoy being kissed as much as you," she replied.

"Not what I asked, but it'll do," Ron said as he nuzzled her neck. "I don't know what it is about a woman's skin that makes it feel like velvet."

"Very expensive creams, a careful diet and a good masseuse. I can give you her name if you'd like."

He chuckled. "How about a pot of the very expensive cream?"

She hit him playfully.

"You can rub it on me," he said, "all over, anywhere you want."

"Men don't want velvety skin."

"I'll bet you could convince me if you tried."

"You're impossible."

"I'm easy. You just have to know how to tickle me."

She tried, but he obviously wasn't ticklish.

"That's just a euphemism," he said. "You know, tickle my—"

"I get it, you wretched man," she said, laughing despite herself. "I should tell you to leave this very moment."

"It's my bedroom."

"Then I should leave."

She started to get up. He put his hand out to restrain her. "I'd rather you stay."

"So would I." She leaned back and smiled at him. "You'd have to throw me out to get me to leave."

"You're out of luck, babe. The only thing I'm throwing out is my self-control."

If any other man had called her *babe,* she'd have been furious. When Ron said it, it sounded like an endearment. "You'd have a hard time convincing me of that. We both have too many clothes on."

Ron wasn't a man who needed a lot of hints. Her blouse closed in the back, but he had it undone in seconds.

"Hmmm," he murmured as he placed kisses along her shoulder. "I always knew your shoulders would be even more fun to kiss than your neck."

Kathryn didn't understand why men liked kissing her shoulders. She guessed it was just one of those differences that defied explanation. She enjoyed it, so she didn't intend to complain. Ron liked kissing her, she liked holding him close. She put her arms around his neck and drew his head down to her breasts. When he started to knead them, she put her hand over his.

"Let's be still for a moment," she said.

He allowed her to slide her hands over his shoulders as she held him close. Just the feel of his body next to hers was comforting. It was a shame men didn't know how to appreciate the nearness of a woman without frenetic activity. They all seemed to think that unless they were *doing something* they weren't doing anything. For a woman, *being there* was one of the best things a man could do.

Ron allowed himself to be held quietly. She could feel the tension building in him, but she was enjoying holding him too much to let go just yet. She didn't think of Ron as being a big man—she'd once dated a man who played football for the Carolina Panthers—but she could barely get her arms around his shoulders. Apparently his exquisitely tailored suits hid more than she'd expected.

That wasn't a bad thing.

While he rested his head against her breasts, Ron's hand had been moving up and down her arm. Then it slipped behind her back to unsnap her bra. He couldn't remain still any longer. His hand cupped one breast while he nuzzled the other.

"Take off your shirt," Kathryn said. While he did, she removed her bra and tossed it and her blouse from the bed.

"Did anybody ever tell you you have beautiful breasts?" Ron asked.

"Not lately."

"What's wrong with the men in North Carolina?"

"They never tried to make love to me on a plane thirty thousand feet above France."

Ron chuckled. "Then it's a good thing I have my own plane."

Kathryn didn't like kissing a man's chest and shoulders, but she certainly liked running her hands over them. There was something about the size, the hardness and all those muscles that excited her. Kathryn was glad Ron was concerned enough about his health to keep himself in good condition. No fat or flab, just firm, muscled flesh. Lisette often said she liked Kerry because he was big, handsome and had muscles. Kathryn decided Lisette wasn't as silly as she seemed.

But Ron had begun to make love to her breasts, and that made it hard for her to think of Lisette or how much she enjoyed exploring Ron's body. She became increasingly focused on her own body and what was happening to it. When Ron's attention to her breasts intensified, her hands began to move over his back and shoulders with increasing speed, stopping to squeeze when Ron's tongue or teeth caused a particularly strong reaction that caused her body to shudder. She ran her hands through his hair and pressed his head against her breast until he warned her she was about to suffocate him.

She slipped down in the bed until she could kiss him on the mouth. She liked having his mouth on her breasts, but she still liked kissing him the best. She could participate equally in a kiss, feeling she was giving as much pleasure as she was getting. She could even be the aggressor if she wanted. And right now she did want to.

She pushed Ron over on his back.

"A liberated woman," Ron chuckled.

"Just greedy," she said, kissing him as if she wanted to swallow him whole.

"Take me, I'm yours," Ron said, when he got his breath.

"I plan to," she growled. She wondered if his nipples were as sensitive as hers. Her wandering fingers had found his nipple. On impulse she gave it a tiny tweak.

The rumbling sound in Ron's throat turned into a muted roar. In a flash she was on her back.

"What did you do to me?" he asked a moment later.

"Nothing you haven't done to me," she replied.

"Did you like it as much as I did?"

She smiled what she was certain was a goofy, brainless smile. "Yeah, I did."

"Let's do it again."

They wrestled all over the bed, each one trying to gain the advantage over the other. Kathryn knew Ron didn't exert his full strength, and she loved him all the more for it. It enabled her to feel as if she were an equal participant, not just someone who was to receive all the pleasure. But it wasn't long before she was too breathless to continue. Maybe she ought to start working out.

"Stop!" she said. "I'm dying."

"Don't you dare, not when you've got me stirred up like this."

"And how is that?"

"Like I'm about to jump out of my skin. I want you so much I want to take all of you at once. I want to absorb you, make you part of me."

"That sounds like something out of science fiction. I prefer old-fashioned sex."

"Can do," he said, producing that wicked grin she found so hard to resist. "But I think we've still got way too many clothes on for that."

She helped him off with his pants then he helped her out of her skirt. Unexpectedly, she felt a little self-conscious. Maybe it was nervousness. Or maybe cold feet. She wondered if Ron felt he was about to make love to her or if he was just having sex. The distinction made all the difference in the world. She'd never gone to bed with a man so soon after she met him. But then no man had ever made such an awesome effect on her. She'd always controlled her relationships.

She wasn't in control now. She didn't think Ron was, either.

Ron let his fingertips trail down her side. He moved up and across her abdomen before it started to tickle. Laughing would be the wrong thing to do just now even though she almost couldn't help it. She'd have to warn him about that in the future.

In the future. So she'd already made up her mind that

there would be a future for them. She hoped he felt the same way. She was falling more in love with him every moment. Before long she'd be in too deeply to pull back.

But she didn't mean to think about this now. This was the moment to let go, to throw off all fetters, to forget all restraints, to ignore warnings from the nagging little voice in the back of her head that had been picking on her for at least ten years.

Ron was planting kisses on her abdomen, teasing her belly button with this tongue, at the same time trailing his fingers down the top of one thigh and up the other one. Neither of her lovers had ever kissed her belly button. She found it wonderfully erotic. She ran her fingers through Ron's hair and groaned softly as he increased his assault on her senses. It ratchetted up another notch when he removed her panties.

"You, too," she managed to say.

She didn't know if he did as she asked. His attentions to her body didn't wane and her interest in anything but what he was doing to her went from marginal to nonexistent. He was turning her into a self-absorbed being. She tried to fight back by thinking of ways to give him pleasure, to think of allowing herself to take pleasure in enjoying his body, but his finger had moved inside her and found the spot that drove everything else from her thought.

Her self-absorption became total.

Kathryn's body began to tremble from head to toe. Exquisitely pleasurable sensations rocketed through her body, turning every nerve ending into a pinprick of bright sensation. She felt as if she were burning up even though chills raced down her spine. Ron's hand continued to increase the tension until she thought she would explode. Her breath came faster and more shallow leaving her feeling giddy and about to faint. She dug her fingers into Ron's hair, mindless of whether she was scratching his scalp or snatching him bald.

Then when she thought she would have to say something

to stop him from torturing her any longer, the tension broke and flowed from her like water from a tipped vessel.

But she didn't have a chance to come down from the giddy heights. The moment Ron withdrew his finger, he moved above her—it took no more than a moment for him to slip on a condom—and she felt him enter her, stretching and filling her until she felt she couldn't possibly contain him. Her body, exhausted and limp from her climax, tensed against his entry, but his slow movement within her quickly replaced the tension of fear with the tension of ecstasy.

Ron pulled her into his arms and kissed her deeply while he filled her, making her feel as though they were joined both in body and spirit. She threw her arms around him and pulled him close as her body responded to him, thrust for thrust. It wasn't long before all she could think of was her body's need to be closer to Ron, to pull him inside her until he could become part of her, until he could reach the need that seemed buried deep inside, a need no one had been able to reach before.

"Hurry!" She didn't know why she said that. The word just came out on its own. Yet her body seemed to understand. It picked up the tempo, forcing Ron to move faster to match her. She could hear herself breathe, occasionally moan softly, but that only served to make her more determined to reach that undefined goal her body strained toward.

But as the tension increased, her muscles lost their elasticity, and she felt as if she had to struggle against the tightening bands that threatened to lock her body into immobility. Ron's movements had become slightly erratic and he was breathing harder. Then just as she felt her muscles clamp down and lock her body into place, Ron stiffened and paused. Then simultaneously their tensions broke, and blessed, sweet release washed over them.

Chapter Twelve

Ron watched Kathryn as she slept. She looked so beautiful, so peaceful. He didn't know if he loved her. He hadn't been looking for love when he met her. Nor when he asked her for that first date. Not even when he asked her to go with him to Geneva. But he had found something that was mighty close.

Despite being miles apart in so many ways, Cynthia's situation had created a little island where they could meet that had nothing to do with the worlds they lived in. His one attempt to show her his world had had startling results. He still wasn't sure what had made him decide to walk out on the negotiations. He was satisfied he'd made the right decision, but would he have done it if Kathryn hadn't been with him, if he hadn't been anxious to spend the day with her? And if he wouldn't have done it without her, what did that mean?

As he watched her sleep and marveled at the feeling of calm that filled him, he realized that for the first time since

Erin died he was thinking of sharing his life with a woman. He hadn't intended to remarry. For one thing, he didn't have time to look for the right woman. For another, any future wife would have to love Cynthia as much as he did. He was certain Kathryn could. She was halfway there already.

Then there was the matter of his career. Until Cynthia got pregnant, he hadn't considered cutting back, much less thought of doing something else. His work was the one thing that had never failed to give him that unqualified feeling of fulfillment.

But now it had.

He realized there were many things that were more important to him. He had begun to wonder if his own happiness didn't require him to make a change. The need to succeed, to be accepted, to be recognized by others, had driven him so relentlessly there hadn't been a question of doing anything else. Until a few weeks ago the need had been to find more ways to achieve even more spectacular successes.

While he was learning other things were more important to him, he also learned he didn't need the recognition of other people to know he was a success, to *feel* successful. And once he felt successful, the need to *be* successful began to ease. So many things had changed in these last few weeks, he hardly knew where to begin sorting out his feelings.

But he knew Kathryn was central to the changes. He also knew he couldn't imagine never seeing her again. He hadn't expected what he felt for her, but now he couldn't imagine going back to his life the way it used to be. In retrospect it seemed empty. He couldn't imagine how he could have felt it was full and satisfying. Maybe one of the reasons he'd worked so hard was to keep from facing the truth, from admitting he wasn't happy.

But he was happy now. He wanted to figure out how the courses of their far separated lives might be brought closer together. He still wanted to find out why Kathryn was unhappy, what she was hiding from, refusing to face. He was certain that would be important to his future happiness.

For the first time she could remember, Kathryn was reluctant to go home. She didn't want the plane to land, to have to walk out of the airport and back into her life in Charlotte. She was afraid that once she did that, the magic of the time she'd shared with Ron would slip away.

It wasn't that she had lost her interest in the girls. She was as determined as ever to help them. It wasn't that she'd lost her interest in the shelter. She couldn't imagine not being there when the next young girl found herself pregnant with nowhere to go. But it was no longer enough. She'd been telling herself for the last few years it didn't matter all that much that she couldn't seem to find a man she could love. She didn't need a husband to feel complete and happy. She had her work which was very important, and she had her girls. That was enough.

And it had been until Ron Egan came barging into her life. Nothing had been the same since. In the beginning she'd felt safe because she couldn't compromise with his interest in his career. But now that he was starting to consider change, she kept telling herself there had to be a way to compromise, that she could find it if she looked hard enough.

Now she was too impatient to wait. She knew what she wanted, and she wanted it now. She didn't, however, know if she could live with the price she would have to pay.

Ron had always looked forward to seeing Cynthia, but this time was special. For the first time in years, he felt he was really coming home. They had made a lot of progress that weekend in the mountains. Whatever they needed to figure out, they would be able to do it now.

"I bet you're anxious to get back," Ron said to Kathryn

as the limousine pulled into the driveway. "Have you ever been away from your girls this long?"

"Only once."

She had been so quiet ever since the plane landed he was worried she was upset. She had assured him she wasn't, but something was wrong. He didn't need to be halfway in love with her to figure that out.

"I'm sure they're fine," she said. "Ruby can take just as good care of them as I can."

"It's not the same. I'm sure they're all anxious for you to come back."

The car came to a stop. He opened the door and got out. He'd half expected the girls to come rushing out the door to meet her, but it was late and the house seemed unnaturally quiet. In fact, the entire neighborhood was quiet. The chauffeur got the luggage while Ron walked with Kathryn up to the house.

"It feels hot and muggy," she said.

The smell of wet, moist earth invaded his nostrils. "It must have rained," he said, opening the door and they stepped inside.

A young man across the room sprang to his feet. It was a boy Ron had never seen before, a tall, well-built kid, probably handsome if he hadn't looked so startled. Ron didn't understand why the boy should look practically frightened. He was here after hours, but he was in the living room keeping a reasonable distance from the girl sitting across from him. Ron was surprised when the girl turned and he recognized his daughter.

"I thought you were supposed to be in bed," he said.

"I am," she said, "but I had to talk to Arthur."

"I don't think I've met you before," Kathryn said. She moved toward the boy whose gaze didn't leave Ron. "I'm Kathryn Roper. I run this shelter."

Arthur took Kathryn's outstretched hand. His handshake was perfunctory. He didn't take his gaze off Ron. "I'm Arthur Peabody."

"What brings you here, Arthur?" she asked.

"I wanted to see Cynthia."

"I'm always pleased to have her friends visit, but I don't allow it after hours. And I don't allow them to sit alone with the girls."

"Mrs. Collias is chaperoning Kerry and Lisette," Cynthia said. "She said I could see Arthur as long as we stayed in this room."

"What's Kerry doing here? He knows it's too late for visiting."

"He says he's talked his father into letting him get married and go into the business with him after his graduates this summer. He and Lisette are trying to come up with wedding plans."

"I'd think her mother would want to do that."

"Lisette says it's her wedding, and she wants everything to be the way she wants it. She figures she'll have a better chance if she has everything worked out before she tells her mother."

"Leave home for just one day, and the whole place goes to pot," Ron said, teasing.

"It's not that bad, but I don't like rules being broken without a good reason. Maybe Lisette has a reason—I'll talk with her in a few minutes—but you have no business being here," Kathryn said turning to Arthur. "You'll have to leave."

"I can't," he said, apparently more calm than moments ago.

"Of course you can," Ron said. He wasn't going to allow this kid to defy Kathryn.

"No, he can't, Daddy," Cynthia said.

"Why not?" Ron asked.

"Because he's the father of my baby."

Ron didn't know what came over him. Thirty years of rigid self-control went out the window. The most uncontrollable anger he'd experienced in his whole life grabbed hold of him. And every bit of it was directed at the boy across from his daughter.

"I'm going to kill you for what you did to my daughter," he bellowed.

"Ron Egan," Kathryn said, stepping between the two men, "get a grip on yourself. Have you gone crazy?"

"No. I just want to get my hands on the—"

"Well you won't do it in my house."

"I don't care where I do it," Ron said, picking her up and setting her aside as though she didn't weigh anything.

Cynthia tried to get between the two men.

Ron grabbed hold of Arthur. The boy didn't try to get away. He just stood there, waiting for whatever was going to happen. "I know things have changed," Ron said to the boy, menace in his voice, "but you still don't get a girl pregnant then disappear, especially when she's only sixteen."

"I didn't mean to get her pregnant, sir."

"Haven't you ever heard of condoms?"

"Daddy—"

"You stay out of this, Cynthia. This is between me and Arthur."

"No, it's not. In case you've forgotten, I'm the one who's pregnant. It's between me and Arthur."

Ron had to give the boy credit. He didn't look scared, but he did look upset.

"What's going on in here?" Lisette asked. "It sounded like a fight."

Lisette and Kerry had entered the parlor, followed by Mrs. Collias.

"If he's a friend of yours, tell him goodbye," Ron said.

Lisette giggled. Kerry smiled like it was a joke, and Ron felt some of the rage flow out of him. He didn't feel any less angry that this boy had taken advantage of his daughter, but he realized he couldn't beat him to a pulp. He didn't know what he could do, but he had to do something. The kid couldn't do something like this and get away scot-free.

"That's enough, "Kathryn said. "I won't have my living room be turned into a brawling ring."

"There's no such thing as a brawling ring," Kerry said.

"Daddy's not going to brawl or anything else," Cynthia said. "He's going to take his hands off Arthur. Miss Roper is going to take Lisette and Kerry somewhere else, and the three of us are going to sit down and talk like sensible human beings."

Ron didn't see anything sensible about the situation, but he was proud of Cynthia for standing up to him.

"Come on," Kathryn said to Kerry, Lisette and Mrs. Collias. "Let's leave them alone."

Ron didn't like being left alone with his daughter and this *boy*.

"Before you start yelling at Arthur," Cynthia said, "I have something to say."

"It won't do you any good to defend him."

"I'm not because *I* seduced *him*, not the other way around."

"I don't know why you would say something like that," Ron said, "but it's not going to protect him."

"I'm not saying it to protect him. I'm saying it because it's true."

Ron couldn't believe her. She'd hardly dated. She wouldn't know how. Ron told himself to take it easy. He'd get to the bottom of this shortly. *Then* he'd see what he could do to make this kid wish he'd never been born.

"Maybe we'd better sit down," Ron said. "I don't think the blood is reaching your head."

"I wish you'd stop acting like I'm helpless and innocent," Cynthia said.

Ron wanted better communication with his daughter, but he hadn't bargained on this. "You're telling me you dragged this boy into the bushes against his will and had your way with him?"

Cynthia smiled suddenly, and he felt better. If she could smile, there had to be some other explanation.

Ron turned abruptly to Arthur who flinched visibly. "My daughter says she seduced you. Is that true?"

The boy's tongue seemed to stick to the roof of his mouth. Of course it wasn't true. Not even a feckless teenage mass of rampant hormones could tell a lie like that.

"It wasn't that I didn't want to," Arthur said, "but I didn't have any protection."

"But you had sex anyway?"

"It's easy to get a boy to have sex, even if he's trying to hold back," Cynthia said. "All you have to do is—"

"I can guess," Ron said before Cynthia could shatter what was left of his image of his innocent daughter.

"It wasn't all her fault," Arthur said. "I was willing enough when she said it wasn't her time, that she wouldn't get pregnant."

"You told him you wouldn't get pregnant?" Ron said, stupefied, to his daughter.

"He wouldn't have had sex with me if I hadn't."

Ron decided it would be easier to go back to Geneva and pull off the impossible negotiations than to deal with this daughter. "Did you do this more than once?" he asked Cynthia.

Arthur answered. "No, sir. I wasn't stupid enough to do it twice."

Ron's heart sank. He turned to his daughter. "You knew it was your time, didn't you? You were hoping to get pregnant."

The color drained from Cynthia's face, but she didn't turn away. "I didn't plan it. I'd been really depressed all week, and Arthur was so sweet I just wanted to stay with him forever. I didn't think I would get pregnant, but I knew I wouldn't be upset if I did." Her body seemed to slump, to sink within itself. "There, you know all my horrible, dirty, nasty little secrets. I'm not sorry for myself, but I am sorry for Arthur. I shouldn't have done this to him."

Ron wanted to ask if she felt sorry for him, but he realized she hadn't even considered his feelings. "Why wouldn't getting pregnant upset you?"

"I wanted something of my own to love, something that would love me back. A baby has to love its mother, doesn't it?"

Ron felt as if someone had just kicked him in the gut, knocked him down and stomped on him. It was worse than that morning so long ago when he realized he wasn't as good as other people. Almost as bad as learning of Erin's cancer. Now his daughter, the only person he had left in the world, had said she was so desperately lonely she'd gotten pregnant so she could have a baby that would love her.

How could he ever have thought he was a success when he'd been such a monumental failure as a father?

Never in his life had he felt as miserable as he felt now. He had to do something to make Cynthia realize he loved her, that he always would love her.

He walked around the coffee table, held out his arms and drew the stiff, resisting body of his daughter into his embrace. "Baby, I love you just as much as I loved your mother. I would have given up every meeting, every trip, if it could have kept her alive. I feel the same way about you."

She pushed against him, but he wouldn't release her. "Then why didn't you do it?"

"Because I thought you understood I was doing it for you, that you wanted it as much as I did."

"I never wanted it," she cried. "Even when Mama was alive, I begged her to make you stay home."

He remembered that, but he and Erin had thought it was just a child's desire to keep both parents close.

"Mrs. Norwood was always the one who went to my school programs, met with my teachers, took me to the doctor, read to me and sat up with me when I was sick or too frightened to sleep. It was never you. I wanted it to be you. Just once I wanted to be more important than your work.''

He hugged her again. ''You are more important. You always have been. I didn't know what I was doing to you, but I do now and I'll never do it again.''

''You'll go back to Geneva tomorrow. You'll—''

''I broke off negotiations this morning. I'm not going back.''

''You didn't do it because of me.''

''I realized the negotiations were not the most important thing in my life, and I didn't have the desire to stay there and pull them back together. I wanted to be back here with you.''

''Did you really walk out of that meeting?'' Cynthia obviously found it hard to believe.

''You can ask Kathryn.'' She had just returned to the room. ''She saw me do it.''

''Do you really mean to stay home?''

''I've decided to let Ben and Ted handle all trips abroad from now on. I don't know what I'll do, but I won't go far from home.''

''Promise?'' Cynthia looked like she didn't dare believe him.

''Promise. You'll never know what agony it has been to learn you wanted a baby to love you because you didn't feel your father loved you. If it takes the rest of my life, I promise to make you believe that was never true.''

Cynthia's resistance collapsed. She put both her arms around him and started crying, deep, hiccupping sobs that shook her body. Ron's arms tightened around her as he fought the unfamiliar feeling that he was about to cry himself.

Kathryn tugged at Arthur's sleeve. ''I think we should leave them alone for a few minutes,'' she whispered. She tiptoed out of the parlor, Arthur following.

''I need to talk to Cynthia,'' Arthur said as soon as they

were outside. "We didn't get a chance to say much before you two turned up."

"Tomorrow might be a better time."

"She won't see me. I had to threaten to climb in through the window tonight." He looked back at the door into the parlor. "I have to talk to her father, too."

"I think that ought to wait."

"No. I know what I did was terrible, but I've got to do what I can to make it right. I've got to talk to him. I'm going to wait."

"Do your parents know where you are?"

"They think I'm with a friend."

"Don't you think you ought to give them a call?"

"I guess so."

"There's a phone in my office." She pointed to a door down the hall then watched as Arthur moved as if he had the weight of the world on his shoulders. His shattered world, she thought to herself. Just like her sister so many years ago. Why did it have to happen over and over again? Was it impossible to make young people understand what they were doing before it was too late?

Probably. With Mother Nature doing all she could to propagate the species, man's efforts at restraint were puny by comparison.

Kathryn didn't think Arthur should talk to Ron tonight, but she admired the boy for having the courage to accept his responsibilities. But as hard as it would be to face Cynthia's father, she imagined it would be still harder to face his own parents. She remembered what happened when her sister tried.

"Did you get your parents?" Kathryn asked when Arthur came back into the hall.

"Yeah. It's okay for me to be late."

"Why don't you wait in the TV room?" Kathryn said.

"Will you wait with me?"

"Sure. Don't worry about Cynthia's father. His bark is worse than his bite."

Arthur attempted a weak smile. "Glad to hear that. His bark nearly killed me."

They talked about unrelated things until Ron found them twenty minutes later. He looked unhappy to see Arthur was still there.

"I thought you'd be gone," he said.

"I wanted to talk to you."

Ron couldn't revive his anger. Cynthia's admission that a lot was her fault made it Ron's fault. If he'd been the kind of father he should have been, the boy wouldn't be in this position now.

"Do your parents know?" Ron asked.

"I didn't know myself until today. I've been wondering what happened to her. If I hadn't overheard Leigh and Kerry talking at school I still wouldn't know. I knew it was my fault. Cynthia isn't the kind of girl to mess around with a lot of guys. Why didn't she tell me?"

"She didn't want it to ruin your life," Kathryn told him.

"That's what she said about me, too," Ron said, "but she has to realize this is your child, my grandchild. We've got to think about the baby as well as ourselves."

Arthur dropped his head into his hands. "I'm not ready to be a father. I haven't even finished high school."

"Biology doesn't know anything about high school," Ron said.

"My parents are going to kill me. They'll completely flip out."

"I'll leave you two to talk," Kathryn said. "I need to check on the girls."

"Don't go to bed before I get a chance to talk to you," Ron said.

"Okay."

She closed the door, wondering what Ron would say to the boy. Taking everything into consideration, from Geneva to walking out on the negotiations to meeting the father of his future grandchild, this had to be one of the most momentous days in Ron Egan's life. She was glad she'd been able to share it.

"Can I fix you a drink?" Kathryn asked when Ron found her in the kitchen more than an hour later. "Sorry, I forgot you don't drink."

"I'll take a glass of wine if you've got any."

"How about some brandy?"

"Okay. How is Cynthia?"

"She's upset about Arthur. I tried to tell her the baby is Arthur's as much as it's hers, but she won't listen. What did the boy have to say?"

"Poor kid, he reminds me so much of me. His family has too many children, not enough money. He's attending Country Day on a football scholarship and was hoping to win a scholarship to an Ivy League college. Now he says he wants to go to college here in town so he can work part-time and help support the baby."

"What did you tell him?" she asked as she handed him the brandy.

"I told him not to worry about Cynthia or the baby, that I would take care of them. He could go on to college, get his degree and start his life as if he didn't have anybody to worry about but himself."

"That was very forgiving of you."

"He said it was his baby, he wanted to help support it and he wanted to try to be its father."

"I think that's very admirable of him."

"So do I, but it won't work. If his parents don't convince him to turn his back on Cynthia and the baby, just trying to establish himself in life will." Ron took a sip of brandy and made a face. "This is awful! Why did you buy it?"

Kathryn laughed. "It was a gift."

"The person must have wanted to make you sick. I'll settle for coffee. Tell me where I can find everything."

"It'll be easier if I do it myself."

While she fixed his coffee and he drank it, he told her

most of what had passed between him and Arthur and between him and Cynthia.

"When this started, you were between me and Cynthia," Ron said to Kathryn. "Now it looks like I'm between Cynthia and Arthur."

"What are you going to do about him?"

"Help him, of course. I'm partially responsible for this mess. I can't leave him to sink or swim by himself."

"I didn't think you would."

"What did you think I'd do?"

"I don't know. Once you decided not to kill him, I knew you'd help him."

They were sitting side by side at the table in the breakfast room. Ron reached out and took her hand. "And what made you think that?"

"You're the kind of man who tries to take care of everything. That's probably why you went into merger negotiations, trying to convince people to do what's best for them."

"Not everybody thinks my motives are quite so pure."

"I didn't used to, either, but I know you better now."

Ron leaned over and kissed her on the lips. She kissed him back.

"If you know me all that well, then you know I'm in desperate need of some tender loving care. Why don't we sit in the TV room and cuddle for an hour or so?"

"What would the girls think if they knew?"

"That I'm lucky enough to be cuddling with the prettiest, smartest and nicest woman in Charlotte."

"I think they'd be more interested in you."

He stood and pulled her to her feet. "We can imagine we're in a plane by ourselves winging our way to some exotic spot."

"I don't dare," Kathryn said with a chuckle, "for fear I'll disgrace myself with you on the fireplace rug."

Ron couldn't wait to talk to Kathryn. For one thing, it had been more than thirty-six hours since he'd seen her.

For another, he had several pieces of very interesting news to share with her.

He had spent the better part of last evening with Arthur's family. He'd ended up being impressed that such an intelligent, responsible and honorable boy had come out of that household. Apparently they had been furious until they realized the father of the girl he got pregnant was very rich. After that they started putting pressure on him to get married. Arthur had made it clear neither he nor Cynthia loved each other, that they had no intention of complicating their lives any more than they already had. It hadn't taken Ron long to convince them he had no intention of giving any future son-in-law free access to his money, or a substantial bank account of his own. He expected Cynthia's husband to support her.

But maybe of more interest to Kathryn was that the largest bank in North Carolina had decided to embark on a series of mergers over the next several years, and they wanted Ron's firm to handle all of them. That meant he would be able to work in Charlotte and any trips out of town could be short.

He also had a new project he wanted to discuss with her, one he'd only thought of yesterday.

There was a van he didn't recognize in the driveway when he reached the house. He hardly paid any attention to that until Mrs. Collias answered the door instead of Kathryn.

"Her sister's here," Mrs. Collias said. Ron couldn't tell if she was angry or disapproving, but something had the woman's nose out of joint.

"Will she be here long?" Ron asked.

"However long, it'll be too long," Mrs. Collias said. "Do you want me to call your daughter? She's finished her studies for today."

"Sure."

Ron was unhappy when Cynthia entered the parlor looking just as upset as Mrs. Collias.

"What's wrong?" he asked.

"That woman is here again."

"What woman?"

"Miss Roper's sister."

"The one who had the baby?" He realized too late he might have divulged privileged information.

"She's got three horrible kids, and she comes here begging for money."

"How do you know?"

"Julia told me. She's been here the longest and was here when that woman came the last time. She's been putting the squeeze on Miss Roper ever since she opened this place."

"Kathryn doesn't strike me as the kind of person you can successfully put the squeeze on."

"That's just it. Her sister makes her feel guilty."

"How can she do that?"

"Julia listened at the door the last time. She says that Elizabeth—that's her sister's name—makes her feel guilty because Elizabeth always had to stand alone."

"That's nonsense. Kathryn's relationship with her parents was ruined because of what happened to Elizabeth."

"Then she brings in the fact that their aunt left this house and all her money to Kathryn."

"So?"

"So Elizabeth makes Kathryn feel guilty and she gives her money."

"Why does she need money?"

"She says her husband doesn't earn enough money to give the kids all the things they need. What they *need* is a year's tuition to obedience school."

"How do you know so much about her kids?"

"Her sister came one day when you were in Geneva. She talked Miss Roper out of some tickets to some really important reception downtown. Elizabeth said her husband needed to make the contacts for his business. She went through Miss Roper's closets and took her best gown, the one Miss Roper had bought especially for the reception and hadn't even worn yet. She said since Miss Roper wasn't going to the party, she wouldn't need it."

Ron wanted to go straight to where Elizabeth had Kathryn cornered and throw her out of the house. But he knew the relationship between Kathryn and her sister was none of his business. He was certain Kathryn would be angry if he interfered. If she felt guilty about what had happened, she probably didn't want him to know what was going on. He told himself to focus on Cynthia.

"I've been talking to Arthur and his family," he said, firmly pushing Kathryn's sister out of his mind. "He wants to help with the baby."

"He doesn't have any money."

"We can work around that."

Cynthia turned her face away from him. "I can take care of my baby by myself."

"Not without my help. You've got to realize that when you and Arthur decided to have unprotected sex, you started something that will have consequences far beyond the two or you. We're talking about another human being here, not you, not Arthur, not me. A baby that deserves everything in life every other kid wants. And one of the things it needs most is a father. Isn't that what you've been telling me you needed?"

"Yes, but—"

"No buts. Arthur's parents want him to marry you, but Arthur refused."

"Good."

"But you're both going to have to make compromises for the good of the baby. You understand that, don't you?"

She nodded, but he knew she didn't. She was so young, so naive, she had no idea what it meant to bring a child into the world, but she would learn. And Arthur. It didn't

look like the boy would get much guidance or support
from home.

"We've got a lot to talk about," Ron said. "I want you
to move back home. Would you consider it?"

She seemed fearful, uneasy. "I don't know."

"I know you like having Kathryn and the house between
you and me, but we have to learn to live together again.
The sooner we start, the better it'll be for you and the
baby."

"I'll think about it, but don't start putting pressure on
me."

"How can I help it? You're *my* baby. I feel about you
the same way you're going to feel about your baby. Would
you like having it living in somebody else's house where
you couldn't watch over it and make sure it was safe?"

"No."

"That's how I feel. If you—"

The door opened and Julia came into the room. She ignored Ron's presence.

"Do you know what *that woman* wants now? A new
car," Julia said without waiting for a response. "When
Miss Roper said she didn't have enough money to buy her
a BMW, that witch said she'd take Miss Roper's Jaguar
instead. She said her husband needs it to make the right
kind of impression on his clients."

Cynthia turned her to father. "Daddy, can you—"

"I'm on my way."

Chapter Thirteen

"Bill doesn't need a Jaguar," Kathryn told her sister. "Construction workers need a good truck."

"It's for his image," Elizabeth said.

"I wouldn't hire a builder who rode around in a Jaguar. I'd figure he was so afraid to get dirty he wouldn't know what was going on with my house."

"Not everybody is as persnickety as you."

"Besides, you'll use it as much as he does, and a Jaguar is not a family car."

"No, but a Lincoln Navigator would be," her sister snapped back, "but we can't afford that, either."

"Pardon me for overhearing," Ron said, entering the room, "but if you want your conversations to be confidential, you ought to keep the doors closed."

"Who are you?" Elizabeth asked. "Don't tell me. I'll bet you're the father of one of Kathryn's girls."

Her tone so condescending Kathryn felt mortified.

"Is that your van in the driveway?" Ron said, ignoring her comment.

"What concern is that of yours?"

"Seems like the perfect family car to me."

"When did you start letting men have the run of your house?" Elizabeth asked her sister.

"I haven't, but you never know when I might consider it," Kathryn snapped.

"Are you still grilling them with your list of questions before you'll date them?"

Kathryn knew her sister had never been any good at holding her tongue within the family, but she'd never had occasion to see that she didn't bother in front of strangers, either.

"Those questions were a breeze." Ron winked at Kathryn. "I passed them just like that," he said, snapping his fingers.

Elizabeth looked from her sister to Ron then back to her sister, her expression incredulous. "You're dating the father of one of your girls?"

Kathryn had always made allowances for her sister. Elizabeth had been hyperactive from birth, she had an attention deficit disorder, and she was saddled with a husband whose ambitions and income were far less than what Elizabeth thought she deserved, but she didn't have to insult people she didn't even know.

"I know I'm only a professional negotiator, not a family counselor," Ron said, "but it would seem to me that if you're asking your sister to give you something, you would probably have a better chance if you adopted a more conciliatory attitude."

"Butt out, mister. This is between Kitty and me."

Elizabeth knew Kathryn *hated* being called Kitty. She did it to make her feel guilty because that's what Aunt Mary had called her.

"I've heard about you," Ron said to Elizabeth, "but your press doesn't do you justice."

"What have you been saying about me?" Elizabeth demanded of her sister.

"She didn't say anything," Ron said. "My daughter was telling me about you."

"I'm not interested in what one of these brats has to say."

"I guess that's why your parents didn't pay much attention to what you said when you did the same thing," Ron replied.

"You have been talking!" Elizabeth yelled at her sister.

"You really need to learn to be more discreet," Ron said. "It's not advisable to yell when you are putting the squeeze on Kathryn for money, at least not when there are young girls around who look upon her as their guardian angel. They tend to resent it."

"I don't care what they think."

"And talk about it."

"I don't care—"

"It's never wise to ignore people you don't know. You never know when one of them might have the power to help you. Or hurt you."

"Who the hell are you?"

"He's Ron Egan," Kathryn said. "Maybe you remember the article in *The Charlotte Observer* a few months ago about a Charlotte man who was making a name for himself in managing international mergers and takeovers. Ron, let me introduce you to my sister, Elizabeth Rush."

Elizabeth directed a sharp, calculating gaze at him. "I take it you're rich."

"Elizabeth!" Kathryn exclaimed.

"Yes, I guess you could say that."

"Then you can afford to give me a car, "she said, turning back to Kathryn. "He can buy you anything you want."

"Mr. Egan is the father of one of my girls," Kathryn said, so angry she could hardly control her voice. "I'm not his mistress nor anything else that would make it acceptable for him to buy me a car."

"Don't be so stuffy."

"You'd better go. I'll think about the car."

"I need to know now."

"If you'd take the advice of a disinterested stranger, let me suggest that you've made your case. Now leave before you blow it."

Elizabeth looked as though she was going to ignore Ron's advice, but she looked at her sister then changed her mind. "Bill likes white, but I want something red. I'm tired of looking like the typical suburban housewife with the typical two point five kids."

She picked up her purse and left without saying a word to Ron.

"So that's your sister, the one you feel guilty about."

"Today wasn't a good day for Elizabeth. One of the boys is sick enough to be at home but not sick enough to stay in bed. Then her nine-year-old got into trouble in school."

"If he takes after his mother, I'm surprised he isn't in jail."

Kathryn knew her sister didn't make a good impression, but she never allowed anyone to criticize her.

"You have no right to make a remark like that. You don't know Elizabeth or what she's had to go through."

"You're right, and I don't want to get to know her, not when she treats people she thinks beneath her like trash. Nor do I see any excuse for her to treat you like you were her own personal lackey."

"She doesn't. She—"

"I heard the woman order you to buy her a car. No, two cars."

"She knows I don't have that kind of money."

"No, she thinks I do."

"She didn't mean that."

"I'm certain she did, as well as think the money you spend on this shelter would be better spent on her."

"You can't know that. You've only seen her for five minutes when she wasn't her best."

"Kathryn, it's my business to sum up people in five minutes. I can do it with men from Scandinavia to the Orient. Your sister wears her colors like a red flag. It's obvious she's made a habit of bullying people into doing what she wants them to do. Unfortunately it seems you've knuckled under. You bought her that van outside, didn't you?"

"My aunt left all her money to me, but Elizabeth is the one with three kids."

"And she reminds you of it all the time."

"They're my nephews and niece."

"Did your nephews and niece thank you for the nice van?"

"I gave it to their mother, not them."

"Did your sister thank you for it? Did her husband?"

"This is none of your business, Ron. You don't know anything about my family. You don't understand the pressures my sister lives under."

"And I bet she reminds you of them, too, every time she comes to ask for money."

"All three kids have A.D.D."

"They probably just need discipline."

"They're hyperactive."

"Too much sugar and junk food."

"Her husband has a difficult time making enough money for them to live on."

"Probably just doesn't make as much money as your sister *wants* to live on."

"Why are you so down on her?"

"Because she was so nasty to you. I won't allow anybody to treat you like that."

Kathryn didn't know quite why she was so angry at Ron. Maybe it was because he'd broken in on them. It was rude and he knew it. She suspected he'd done it intentionally. Maybe because she was angry at Elizabeth and was projecting that anger on Ron. Maybe she was feeling guilty— and stupid—because she suspected Ron was right, that Elizabeth was trying to make her feel guilty so she could get what she wanted.

But Kathryn didn't need Elizabeth to make her feel guilty. That was part of the reason she'd decided to open the shelter. Pressure from Elizabeth was also part of the reason her relationship with her parents was so strained. Elizabeth had forced her to make clear to her parents where her loyalties lay.

She truly did feel Elizabeth had been treated unfairly, but she resented the pressure Elizabeth kept applying every time she came to visit. And Kathryn had finally begun to accept the fact that Elizabeth only came to see her when she wanted something. That hurt, and made her want to strike out. But Ron was here, where he wasn't supposed to be, the perfect target.

"I won't allow you to talk about my sister like that," Kathryn said. "You don't know anything about her."

"I don't need a detailed life history to recognize a selfish, tyrannical woman when I see one. By giving her money, you're enabling her dysfunctional lifestyle. Let her stand on her own two feet."

"Stop it! I forbid you to talk about Elizabeth like that."

"Forbid me!" Ron looked amazed. "What makes you think you can stop me from speaking my mind?"

"You have no business giving advice. You've failed just as badly with your own daughter."

"That's beside the point."

"That *is* the point. You have no right to criticize her. If you can't stop, you can leave."

"This isn't like you. You're not one to deny an obvious truth. You didn't hesitate to pin my ears back when you thought I was wrong."

"This has nothing to do with being right or wrong. It has to do with the fact I have the greater resources and she has the greater needs."

"Her *greater needs* have nothing to do with money. If she were half the woman you are, she wouldn't dream of doing what she just did. And unless I'm badly mistaken, she keeps poisoning your mind about your parents, keeps reminding you that you owe her because they liked you better—or treated you better—than they did her.''

Kathryn couldn't take any more. She marched over to the door. ''You were right. I should never leave a door open when I don't want someone to come in. I'm going to close my door. I want you on the other side of it.''

''Are you throwing me out?''

''I think it's rather a case of me putting you back where you belong. You had no right to listen to my conversation with my sister, and you had no right to interrupt it.''

''When did a man cease to have the right to protect the woman he loves?''

His words nearly knocked Kathryn off her feet, but she managed to hold on. Men didn't mean the same thing as women when they spoke of being in love. Most of the time they meant they were in lust. That might even mean they were in temporary love—the length of time corresponding roughly to the length of time it was convenient—but they didn't mean the long-term commitment every woman meant when she said she was in love.

Kathryn knew she had been falling in love with Ron, but even she wasn't ready to use the commitment word. There were so many things they hadn't talked about, Elizabeth for one. If he loved her, he would have to accept her sister.

''You never said anything about love,'' she said.

''I didn't know until I heard your sister berating you. My immediate reaction was to protect you. I figure that's a really good sign I'm in love.''

''More likely the universal male drive to protect. But I don't need protecting, so you don't have to feel like you're in love.''

''Do you always talk like this after your sister visits you?''

''Like what?''

''Like you've suddenly lost your ability to think. That

woman has got you so screwed up you can't think straight.''

"That's enough," Kathryn said, pointing to the door. "Say good-night to your daughter. She needs to be in bed.''

"You don't believe I love you, do you?''

"I haven't had time to think about it.''

"It's not something you think about. Either you believe me or you don't.''

"I admit the attraction between us is very strong, but we haven't known each other very long. You've been under a lot of stress, both here and in Geneva. You probably see me as a relief from Geneva and as way to help you solve your problems with Cynthia.''

"I'm glad you hire professional psychologists," Ron said. "That's some of the worst nonsense I've ever heard come out of an intelligent woman's mouth.''

"Then I'm surprised you think I'm so intelligent.''

"I've attacked the one thing in your world you can't deal with rationally, your sister. And because you can't deal with it, you strike out at anyone who threatens this unbalanced, symbiotic relationship.''

"Why do you say unbalanced?" She was so coldly furious with him she didn't know why she asked.

"You do all the giving, she does all the taking.''

"I've told you—''

"You don't realize it, but your sister has ruined more than your relationship with your parents. She's made it impossible for you to deal with any man on a normal basis. If it's a male, he's either inadequate like her husband, wild like her kids, or a villain like your father. You can't look at any of us without filtering what you see through the mirror of your sister's narcissism.''

"I'm apparently not the only armchair psychologist.''

"I'm trained to study people. To do my job well, I have to be objective. I need to know what they think and why they think it, not what I *want* them to think. You've painted us all black and challenged us to prove otherwise.''

"So far no man has managed to meet the challenge."

She didn't mean that, but he'd made her so angry she couldn't control her tongue. He couldn't expect her to calmly accept his calling her a mindless sycophant—well, not that exactly, but he certainly thought she wasn't capable of making up her mind without Elizabeth's help—yet accept his word on people he knew nothing about.

"Would you admit it if he did?" Ron asked.

"Why wouldn't I?"

"Because it would challenge too many of your fears. As long are men as unreliable, you don't have to trust one of us."

"Why wouldn't I trust the right man if he came along?"

"Maybe because you think your mother got a raw deal. I know you think your sister did. Maybe you're attracted to the very kind of man you fear. I don't know. I thought I knew you until I saw you with your sister."

"And I thought I knew you. It looks like the physical attraction made us think we had more in common than we do. My father always said a woman should never let the chemistry between herself and a man blind her to reality."

"That's the first time I've ever heard you quote your father."

"You probably both think the same way." Suddenly she felt as though her body weighed an extra hundred pounds. She had to sit down, she had to rest, she had to be alone. "Now you'd better go."

"I came to tell you about a plan I thought of this afternoon."

"It's probably not a good idea. I would have to consult my sister before I could tell you what I thought. And you know you don't like my sister."

"If you were my wife, I'd ban her from the house until she learned to behave toward you with respect and courtesy."

"Then I guess it's a good thing I'll never be your wife." She hadn't meant to say that, either. But it was true. Even if he really did love her and want to marry her, she could never be his wife. She had refused to let her parents come between her and her sister. She couldn't let Ron do it. "Now please go. I'm really very tired."

"When can I see you tomorrow?"

"I don't know. Maybe you shouldn't—"

"I'll call."

"I have got a lot to do tomorrow."

"I'll call."

She wasn't prepared for him to take her in his arms and kiss her ruthlessly. She tried to resist, but it was impossible. She melted into his arms and returned his kiss.

"I'll call," he said when he broke the kiss. Then he was gone.

Kathryn closed the door and leaned against it before the sobs that had been building up erupted. She should have known not to let herself get involved with Ron. She also knew the old saying that a tiger can't change his strips. If ever a man was a tiger, Ron Egan was it. He went after life, got it in a throat latch, and shook it hard.

It was time she realized she'd allowed herself to get caught up in a dream that was impossible. It had been stupid, she knew it, but she'd done it anyway. Maybe this would help her remember next time.

She wasn't sure there would ever be a next time. You can't break a heart that's already broken.

"Are you sure you want to go home?" Kathryn asked Cynthia. "I'm not trying to keep you here, understand, but I know your father can be very persuasive."

It was three days later, and Kathryn had come upstairs to Cynthia's bedroom when Julia informed her Cynthia was packing to go home. In the short time she'd been there, Cynthia's room had become where the girls gathered when they wanted to talk.

"Daddy didn't talk me into it. I want to go home. I made a lot of mistakes, one of which was running away from everybody—Daddy, Arthur, Leigh and all my friends. I thought people only liked me because Daddy was famous.''

"I told you from the beginning you were a very likable girl. Everybody here liked you immediately.''

Cynthia hung her head. "I was acting like a baby. I wanted something I didn't get so I threw a tantrum. Only I threw the kind of tantrum you can't fix.''

"You'll fix it. It'll just be hard. Who's going to help you move?''

"Daddy and Arthur.''

"They're coming at the same time?''

"Daddy said they're going to see a lot of each other in the future, so they might as well start now. I think they actually like each other.''

"How do you feel about that?''

Cynthia wrinkled her nose. "I don't know. Arthur's a nice guy, but I don't love him. Besides, even if I did, I don't want to get married now. I don't know what I want to do, but I'll have my hands full with a baby and school. I don't need a husband even if I did love him so desperately I couldn't live without him.''

Kathryn didn't want to hear words like that. They made her think of Ron and the realization she loved him so desperately she didn't know how she was going to live without him. She hadn't thought of anything else for the last three days. She dreaded going out of the house for fear she might run into him. She checked the driveway before she went out. She listened for any car pulling up while she was with the girls. She couldn't decide whether she was more afraid he would find her or that he wouldn't want to.

"Then I think you're wise not to consider marriage at this point. Lots of women are single mothers.''

"It might be good for the mother, but it can't be good for the baby. I guess I'm glad Arthur wants to take an active part in the baby's life.''

Kathryn thought she heard a car pulling into the driveway, but when she looked out the window, it was pulling in across the street. "I'd better go."

"You don't have to run away."

The words stung. "I'm not running away."

"Daddy says you've been running away from him ever since the night your sister came here. He said you were furious at him for saying your sister was a mooch, that she tried to get money out of you by making you feel sorry for her."

"Your father shouldn't have said that."

"Why not? All the girls know it. We think she's hateful. It was Julia who sent Daddy in there to keep her from making you buy her that car." Cynthia made a rude noise. "I can just see what those heathens of hers would have done to a Jaguar."

"Cynthia! I'm surprised at you."

"You ought to hear Julia. She spent half the night trying to figure a way to get the police to arrest her."

"Elizabeth has had a difficult life. You don't understand—"

"What don't I understand? Having a father who doesn't understand me, didn't even know I was alive half the time, having my mother die when I was seven? Your sister is completely selfish. She isn't trying to make her life better. She's doing what I wanted to do in the beginning. I wanted to hurt everybody around me, my friends for not liking me enough, my father for not giving me more time and attention, Arthur for being so driven by his hormones he was stupid enough to have unprotected sex."

"It's not that bad."

"I even considered suicide—I wrote a note—because I thought it would hurt everybody. But I finally realized I would be hurting the baby most. If I really wanted to make things better, I had to start with myself. And I had to believe in other people. And the only way I could do that was by starting to believe in myself because if I can't believe I'm worth saving, how can I believe in anybody else?''

"That's some mighty deep thinking."

"I know. A sixteen-year-old kid isn't supposed to be able to think, but it's not hard really. It's just common sense. Anyway, I'm going home. Now that you won't see him, Daddy needs me. He's terribly lonely."

"It isn't that I *won't* see him," Kathryn said. "It's just that—"

"You know he's in love with you, don't you?"

"He told me."

"But you don't believe him?"

"I do, but..."

"But what?"

How had she ended up in this discussion? She didn't have to explain herself to anyone, least of all Ron's daughter. But if she couldn't explain to Cynthia, how could she explain to herself?

"I don't think we have enough in common for a meaningful relationship."

"Do you love him?"

"That's not a proper question to ask me."

"This is my Daddy we're talking about. Do you love him? If you don't, you've got to let him go. He's miserable thinking about you all the time."

"I'm not holding him."

"He says you love him, but you're afraid to let go for fear everything won't be perfect. Nothing is ever perfect. Even I know that."

"You don't understand."

"I understand a lot more than you think. All the girls think you're making a mistake. Even Mrs. Collias. And if *she* thinks Daddy is too good to throw away, then he's got to be something special. If you'd just talk to him..."

"We disagree on so many things."

"That's how I felt when I came here, but I was wrong. Maybe you'll find you've been wrong, too."

"Cynthia, do you realize you're talking about your father marrying again, about my being your stepmother?"

"I'm too old to feel like anybody's daughter. You'd just be Daddy's wife. Besides, I think you'd be a great wife. You're smart and beautiful, and you both love each other. What better start could you have?"

"You all packed?"

Kathryn nearly jumped out of her skin. She'd been so intent on her conversation with Cynthia she hadn't heard anyone come up the stairs. She turned to find herself facing Ron Egan.

Kathryn had to stop herself from backing into the corner. "I was helping Cynthia finish her packing." Three suitcases sat neatly on the floor, a carryall beside them.

"Is this everything?" Arthur asked.

"Yes."

"I'll take two suitcases."

"I'm glad you and Arthur are getting along," Kathryn said to Ron as Arthur worked his way out of the room with the two large suitcases.

"It appears I haven't lost all my skills. I can still reach some people."

"I'll meet you downstairs," Cynthia said. She grabbed the carryall and bolted through the doorway before Kathryn could stop her.

"Why won't you talk to me?" Ron asked.

"I have nothing to say."

"Then you could listen. I can talk enough for both of us."

"Why bother? We're too different."

"You're still sore about your sister, aren't you?"

Kathryn started to deny it. "I didn't like what you said."

"Would it make any difference if I took it back?"

"You wouldn't mean it."

Ron sighed. "You know me better than I thought." He reached inside his coat and drew out an envelope. "If you're mad now, this is going to make you furious."

"What is it?"

"It's a report." He held it out of her. "I think you'll find some of it very interesting."

"Where did you get it?"

"I have researchers on my staff. I had one of them look into your sister's background."

"You spied on my sister?"

"Most of the things are a matter of public record. When they aren't, that's noted."

"I can't believe you would investigate my sister."

"Consider it a preventive measure. I always like to know what I'm getting into."

"We're not getting into anything together."

"Cynthia tells me I shouldn't give up. I agree with her, so I won't."

He wrapped his arms around her and kissed her. Her resistance was weak and momentary. She would never kiss him again. She'd probably never see him again. Besides, she couldn't resist him. She never had been able to, not even in the beginning when she thought he was the personification of everything wrong with modern men.

Besides, she loved him. He didn't have to know. She had fallen in love with him weeks ago, probably the day he took her to the trailer park and she got a glimpse of the little boy who had decided right then to become a man. There was so much about him to admire, but every admirable trait was mirrored by something she couldn't accept. She knew it would never work. Why didn't he?

So she kissed him to make up for the days she hadn't seen him but thought of him constantly, for the evenings she wouldn't take his calls but lay awake thinking about him, for the nights she tossed in her bed dreaming of him. She kissed for all the years of happiness they would never have, for all the dreams that would never come true.

And she kissed him for himself, just in case he really did love her as much as he said.

* * *

"Why don't you call her again?" Cynthia asked her father as they sat eating dinner.

"She still won't talk to me."

Cynthia had been home for a week. With Ron not traveling to Geneva, they'd quickly developed a routine. He worked when she was at school. When she came home, they spent time together until after dinner when she had to do her homework. Afterward, they watched TV or talked until time to go to bed. They talked about Cynthia's future, Arthur and the baby. They talked about Kathryn, too.

Ron hadn't expected her to be pleased with the information he gathered on her sister. He'd known when he did it he was taking a chance. Pretty much everything Kathryn had done in the last ten years was predicated on her belief her sister had been cruelly treated by their parents.

To believe what he'd discovered about Elizabeth would mean she'd misjudged her parents, that her behavior and attitude for the last ten years was unfounded. That would throw her into even deeper guilt. Ron loved Kathryn enough to try to set her free from the misconceptions and guilt that had kept her prisoner for so long, but he also knew he risked losing her. Not every prisoner loved the person who set them free.

"Then go over to the shelter," Cynthia suggested. "She can't avoid you then."

"It wouldn't change the way she feels about me."

They were seated at the breakfast table which looked out onto a patio and the back lawn. They'd decided the dining room was too big and formal.

"I don't see why she can't see her sister is mean."

"For the same reason you feel free to criticize me but get angry when anybody else does. She loves her sister. She might admit she isn't perfect—"

"She's a witch!"

"—but she doesn't want anybody criticizing her."

"But you want to marry her."

"All the more reason she has to *want* to see me before

I go back. She's got to want me for myself, not because she feels motivated by guilt. She's lived with that too long."

"Are grown-ups always this stupid?"

Considering the mess they'd both gotten themselves into, he had to laugh. "A lot of the time. We're so sure we have the answers we don't listen. Speaking of having answers, those idiots in Geneva have decided maybe I do know what I'm talking about. Don't look like that. I won't go back unless you come with me."

"Me? What would I do in Geneva?"

"Enjoy being spoiled in a fancy hotel. Go shopping. Maybe even go to a meeting so you can see what your old man does for a living."

Cynthia looked confused. He didn't know if she was happy he had invited her or whether she was reluctant to leave school now that she'd settled back into classes.

"Won't they object to a kid being in the room?"

"They won't have any choice. If they want me, they get you, too."

"You'd do that for me?"

"I already gave up on this deal because of you. Either you go with me or I won't go. The bank wants me to start working with them right away. And I've got that new program I want to set up. I've got more than enough work to do right here. I don't need Geneva. They can make do with Ben and Ted. They'll have to from now on. I'm giving up international negotiations."

"But you like doing that."

"I like being here with you even more. And when the baby comes, I'll be too busy being a grandfather to worry about other people's problems. I'll have plenty of my own, like getting ready for the time *he's* a teenager."

"It could be a girl."

"Then I'll have to prepare doubly hard."

They laughed then fell silent.

"You really want me to go with you?" Cynthia asked.

"I won't go without you."

"What about Kathryn?"

"I'd like to keep this trip just for us."

"Okay. If you're sure."

"I'm sure."

Kathryn was in a vile mood, but she'd been in a vile mood ever since she read the report Ron handed her. That stuff couldn't be true. Elizabeth wasn't perfect, but Kathryn couldn't believe that of her sister. Yet she knew it had to be true. Ron's career depended on accurate and detailed information. His people weren't in the habit of getting things wrong. They wouldn't have gotten things wrong about Elizabeth.

She was furious at him for forcing her to learn she'd spent the last ten years making decisions based on lies and misrepresentations. Even worse, they were lies and misrepresentations she could have avoided if she'd been willing to listen to her father instead of assuming everything he said was wrong just because she was angry his work seemed more important to him than his family.

She didn't want to see Elizabeth today, but when Kathryn refused to buy her the car, Elizabeth insisted she had to talk with her. Elizabeth always did that when Kathryn was reluctant to give her what she wanted. And she'd always managed to make Kathryn feel so guilty she'd give in. She hadn't believed Kathryn when she said things had changed. She was coming up the walk now, dragging little Billy behind her.

When Elizabeth entered the TV room, it was obvious she was sailing with a full head of steam. "It was really rotten of you to make me come over here today," she said. "I've had to spend the morning with the school principal. Sit down, Billy. Don't move or I'll jerk a knot in you."

Billy ignored his mother.

"I didn't ask you to come over," Kathryn said. "I told you there was no point in it."

"You said you weren't going to buy me that car. What did you expect me to do?"

"Exactly what you have done. But before you start on your usual arguments, I think you ought to look at this."

"What's that?" Elizabeth asked when Kathryn held the papers out to her.

"I doubt you'll be surprised at their contents, but I was."

Elizabeth took the papers with ill grace. She glanced up, a perplexed expression on her face after an initial glance. "What is this?"

"Read it."

"How much longer are we going to be here?" Billy asked. "You said you'd buy me some new Nikes if I'd stay out of trouble for a week."

"Shut up. I can't read with you yammering at me."

Billy stuck out his tongue at his mother and went back to rifling through the videos. A moment later Elizabeth lifted her gaze to her sister.

"Where did you get this?"

"The company logo is on the letter."

"You had me investigated?"

"Someone else did."

"It's not true."

"There's more."

Twice in the next minute Elizabeth uttered a profanity before glancing up at her sister. "You don't believe any of this, do you?"

"Read the rest of it."

"It's all a bunch of lies." Elizabeth tossed the papers aside. "I don't know who's out to get me, but—"

"Nobody's out to get you."

"They have to be to make up this stuff."

"It's not all made up," Kathryn said. "I checked out some of it myself."

"What did you check out?"

For the first time she could remember, Elizabeth's confidence slipped. She didn't show the brazen front Kathryn was so used to. It wasn't fear. No, Elizabeth had never been afraid of anybody or anything. It was anger.

"I asked the lawyer about Aunt Mary's bequest to you. You said you didn't get anything."

"It was practically nothing," Elizabeth said. "It only lasted a few years."

"I think Aunt Mary expected a half millions dollars to last longer than that. I guess that's why she gave everything else to me."

"I should have gotten more than you instead of less."

"It was her money to leave any way she wanted."

"You were always her favorite."

"No, you were, but you were never even nice to her. You didn't even bother to visit."

"Billy, turn down that TV. I can't hear over the noise."

Billy ignored his mother. Kathryn walked over to the TV, turned it off, and ejected the video. "It's about time you learned to do what you're told. If you treat your teachers like you do your mother, I'm surprised they haven't expelled you from school. Now either sit quietly until your mother and I finish or go outside."

Billy took the opportunity to escape.

"You ought to discipline that child," Kathryn said.

"You don't know what it's like to have three children."

"If I had twice that many, I wouldn't let them grow up like hooligans."

"What's gotten into you? You've never acted like this."

"That report is what's gotten into me. You've been lying to me, not just about Aunt Mary's money. About Bill's construction company, about Daddy, about anybody who crossed you in the last ten years. And what makes me angriest of all is I was stupid enough to believe you."

"Most of this is lies," Elizabeth said. "They can't prove it."

"If *any* of it's the truth, you've been lying to me. You've manipulated me to get me to believe what you wanted, to do what you wanted. I can't believe I was so stupid I let you ruin my life.''

"Me ruin *your* life!" Elizabeth exclaimed. "You don't have a life. You've been Miss Goody Two-shoes your whole life, doing what Dad wanted, keeping your nose out of trouble, pretending butter wouldn't melt in your mouth so I would look even worse.''

"I defended you. I got in a huge fight with Dad and Mom over you.''

"Big deal. So now you only go over for Sunday lunch. They threw me out of the house.''

"Because you stole a set of Dad's company plans and gave it to the competition.''

Kathryn shrugged. "It was a dare. I couldn't refuse. Besides, after what he said about Bill, I didn't want to.''

"It cost Dad his job.''

"He got another that paid even more. Why should he care?''

Kathryn realized she and her sister had an entirely different ethical basis for making decisions. There was no way she could convince Elizabeth she'd done anything wrong.

"I've learned a man's career is important to him in a way it probably never could be for a woman. That's the way our society defines him, the way society values him. When you injure that, you're striking at the heart of who he is.''

"I don't know where you learned all this psychological bull, but don't try it on me. Dad is a selfish old man, and he's never going to change.''

"Are you going to change?''

"Why should I?''

"There are hundreds of reasons, but I won't bore you with them. But since you're here, let's set a few things straight. I'm not going to buy you or Bill a car. I'll send money to the kids for their birthdays and gifts for everyone at Christmas, but that's all.''

"You can't do that. I—''

"I can. According to that report, Bill makes more than two hundred thousand dollars a year. You can afford to buy anything you need."

"That's not true. You don't know how many places it has to go."

"Then get rid of some of those places. My money will go to the shelter."

"You'd give your money to those silly teenagers instead of your nephews and niece?"

"Yes. Now you'd better go collect your son. I don't trust him to stay out of serious trouble much longer."

"You haven't heard the last of this," Elizabeth said. "I'm going to—"

"I hope you're going to apologize to Dad. After ten years, it's about time."

Elizabeth threw her a furious look and stalked from the room.

"They've been talking about him on the news all week," Mrs. Collias said to Kathryn. "He's a real celebrity."

Kathryn hadn't been able to put Ron out of her mind, but having him appear on the news and in the newspaper practically every day was almost more that she could stand. After everyone had abandoned hope, he'd managed to bring off the biggest merger in European history. The financial commentators were calling him a genius.

They also made a point of showing him with his daughter, saying that even though he was an internationally important businessman, he still found time to be with his only child.

"He said he wanted to stay in Charlotte," Mrs. Collias was saying. "He's taken a new job."

Kathryn was drinking her coffee in the kitchen while Mrs. Collias cleaned up after dinner. They were watching a small TV on the counter. The girls were watching a movie on the big one in the TV room.

The bank had announced its expansion plans at the same

time they announced they had retained Ron's company to handle the negotiations. One vice president even went so far as to say the bank couldn't have undertaken such an aggressive program without Ron. Her father had called to see if she still had any connection with Ron. She had told him she didn't.

But the announcement that affected Kathryn the most had come just a few minutes earlier. Ron had appeared on TV, Cynthia at his side, to announce he was beginning a program for unwed fathers. "All the attention is focused on the mother and the child," he had said, "but the father is just as important. We've virtually ignored him except to take him to court to get child support. No one helps with their education, their getting a job and building a career. This kind of help could make all the difference in the boy becoming a productive member of society or a dropout." When the commentator asked who he planned to get to run the program for him, Ron said he intended to be personally involved at every level. He'd then cited Kathryn's shelter as an example of the kind of program he hoped to build.

"We'll have reporters on the phone within ten minutes," Kathryn said.

Mrs. Collias laughed. "Looks like you turned him around really good."

"I can't take credit for it."

"I didn't see anybody else sitting with him, talking to him, making sure he and his daughter started talking to each other again."

"Anybody else would have done the same thing if they'd had the opportunity."

"Would he have fallen in love with anybody else?"

Startled, Kathryn looked up.

"You don't think you could live in a house with five other women and not have every one of us know the minute it happened. Or that you're in love with him."

Kathryn felt the bottom drop out of her stomach. "I don't

think we're exactly in love. Besides, we have nothing in common.''

''You have Cynthia in common. From the first you liked her more than the others.''

''I try not to have favorites,'' Kathryn said, appalled.

''You didn't treat her different, but the girls could tell you two got along better.''

''That's not enough to build a life on.''

''Don't let your sister ruin the rest of your life. Don't look so surprised. I told you nothing goes on in this house we all don't know. We know she's been using you for years. I'm just glad Mr. Egan had the guts to show her up.''

''Why didn't somebody tell me before now?''

''People tried, but you wouldn't believe anybody else.''

Kathryn didn't remember anybody trying, but she'd always been so sensitive on that subject she wouldn't let anyone talk about it.

What was hard for her to understand, and even harder to accept, was how someone as smart, aware and perceptive about other people as she thought herself to be had failed to see through her sister's narcissism. She guessed not being narcissistic herself, she had no frame of reference. Elizabeth knew this and played on it. An even harder truth was that she had been playing rescuer-martyr, using the role to boost her own self-esteem and ego. It had taken confronting her own misperceptions, seeing her own contribution to the dysfunctional relationship, for her to be able to kick away the prop she'd been using.

Ron had taught her that everybody needs a bit of the narcissist to be able to cope with life. Her own lack of it was part of reason she had opened the shelter, had developed her questions so as not to allow a real man into her life. When Ron barged in and broke the barriers, she had started to see herself through his eyes, had started to see her whole life differently.

"I think you ought to take a piece of your own advice," Mrs. Collias said.

"What advice?"

"Don't let one mistake ruin the rest of your life. If these girls can straighten things out, you can, too."

Kathryn felt like a coward. She'd been doing exactly what she told her girls not to do, feeling sorry for herself.

"You're right. I'll begin by apologizing to my parents for being so blind."

"Then will you talk to Mr. Egan?"

"He may not call again."

Kathryn knew she probably should have waited for Ron to call her, but she was the one who was in the wrong. It was up to her to make the first move, but she wasn't sure going to his house was the right first move. But she couldn't shake the fear that after what she'd said and done he might never call again. She had to see him, no matter what the outcome.

She had driven by his house many times. It was the most impressive house on the street. She knew that's why he bought it. Everything about it was so perfect it almost intimidated her. She parked her car in the brick driveway and walked up to the front door. His doorbell sounded like cathedral chimes. A very pleasant-looking woman opened the door.

"My name is Kathryn Roper," Kathryn said. "I'd like to speak to Mr. Egan. Is he in?"

Much to her surprise, the housekeeper broke into a big smile and threw the huge, carved door all the way open. "Come in. He's in the pool. Cynthia's with him."

"I don't want to disturb him."

"You won't. I've seen him hold a staff meeting in that pool."

Feeling very uncomfortable, Kathryn followed the housekeeper through the entrance hall, across a huge living room, and through the French doors that opened onto a courtyard surrounded on three sides by the house. An enormous pool filled most of the space.

"You've got a visitor," the housekeeper announced. "A young woman, so make yourself decent."

There wasn't anything indecent about Ron unless you considered him indecently handsome. She felt her stomach lurch when Ron looked surprised to see her. She shouldn't have come. This wasn't a good time.

A slow smile spread over his face. "Come join us. Margaret can find you a bathing suit."

"I'll go look," Cynthia said.

"I can't stay," Kathryn said, but Cynthia climbed out of the pool and disappeared.

"I think she wanted to leave us alone," Ron said.

"Why?"

"She hopes I'll ask you to marry me and you'll agree."

"After all the things I've said, why should you marry me? Don't answer that," she said before he could speak. "That's not why I came."

Ron climbed out of the pool and reached for a robe. His expression sobered.

"Why did you come?"

"To apologize for the way I've acted. You were right about my sister. *Everybody* was right about her. I was the only one who couldn't see her for what she was, but I can't blame everything on Elizabeth. I made up my mind about some things because they fitted into my prejudices. My father left a lot to be desired as a father, but I didn't give him credit for what he did. I'm ashamed I didn't believe him when he told me Elizabeth had cost him his job. I figured it was another man refusing to admit he bore any responsibility for an unmarried girl getting pregnant."

"Feeling that way, I'm surprised you had anything to do with the fathers or the boys."

"I never did until you came along." She laughed self-consciously. "I told myself it was because Cynthia was so sweet and you were such a hopeless case."

He offered her a glass of lemonade. She accepted it and let him guide her to a lounge. "I was a hopeless case. I would never have come to see what I had become if it hadn't been for you. I didn't like anybody else enough to care what they said."

"That's something else I have to talk about."

"Are you going to tell me you never loved me, that you don't want to see me again?"

She felt a surge of hope. He didn't sound as if he wanted to get rid of her. She couldn't expect him to be happy about the way she'd treated him.

"You know I liked you. I would never have gone to Geneva or…"

"Made love to me?"

"Or made love to you," she said in a faint voice. "I don't know what you thought of me, but—"

"I thought you were wonderful. I never enjoyed myself as much as I did that trip. I've been dreaming about doing it over and over again."

So he didn't want marriage. He wanted someone who could go places with him, enjoy the same things, have a good time, but someone he could put aside when she got in the way.

"I can't do that."

"Why not?"

"I know I'm supposed to be a rich, sophisticated society woman, but I'm not. I want a husband who comes home to dinner, a house I can call my own, and some children to keep it messed up. I don't want to be a mistress or a party girl."

"Who said anything about that? I discovered that all the money and prestige didn't obliterate the lonely trailer park kid hiding inside. It took a while to figure out, but a house full of kids is exactly what I want. And I want it with you."

"You still love me after all this?"

"This was a minor misunderstanding. I expect we'll have some *real* fights down the road, but that won't change the way I feel about you.'' He got up and sat down on her lounge chair. She made room for him. ''I don't want you ever to feel you can't tell me when you think I've taken a wrong turn. I've found out I don't know very much about building a family. I want you to help me.''

''It'll be the blind leading the blind,'' Kathryn said, so happy she felt tears coming to her eyes. ''I made an even bigger mess out of mine.''

Ron took her lemonade out of her hands and set it on the table. He drew her hands to his lips and kissed them. ''We can learn together. Deal?''

''Are you sure you want to have more children?''

''I hated being an only child. I want Cynthia to have a couple of brothers and at least one sister.''

''I'm too old to be chasing after three kids.''

''I'll help you. I missed too much of Cynthia's growing up. I don't want to do it again.''

''I heard about your establishing a program to help un-wed fathers. I think that was a wonderful idea.''

''I got it from you, so you can compliment yourself.''

''If I do, I'll compliment myself on being lucky enough to have you fall in love with me. Why on earth did you do it?''

''I was bored and looking for something to do.''

She punched him and he pulled her into an embrace. ''Can you move in right now?'' he asked when he broke the kiss. Kathryn laughed at the foolishness of such a question.

''You're making the fatal mistake of marrying into high society. We have to have a formal engagement, hundreds of showers and a huge wedding with a reception at the country club. I figure it'll take at least a year to plan.''

Ron looked horror stricken. ''Let's elope.''

''Okay.'' She couldn't believe she'd just said that. ''When?''

''How about tonight?''

''Give me time to pack a suitcase.''

"You can get married just as you are. After that you won't need clothes for at least a week."

Cynthia came out of the house carrying a bathing suit.

"You won't need that," Ron said. "You have to help with an elopement."

"Lisette and Kerry?" she asked.

"No, us," her father said.

Cynthia grinned broadly. "Can I give the groom away?"

Epilogue

"Are you sure you want all of us to be in your wedding?" Julia asked Kathryn.

"Of course she does," Lisette said. "We're her friends. I want *all* of my friends to be in my wedding."

"I couldn't wish for three prettier bridesmaids," Kathryn said.

"Yeah, right, with all of us so pregnant we're showing."

Kathryn couldn't believe she was getting married to Ron with only three hours notice, the length of time it took them to get a license and blood tests. Her living room was crowded with the families of her sister and her older brother, Alan.

"I had to come," Elizabeth said when Kathryn expressed surprise at her arrival. "I had to see if the man you bagged was worth waiting so long."

Elizabeth's husband, Bill, had already congratulated Kathryn three times, so Kathryn figured Ron probably met her sister's approval, too. A bustling at the front door heralded another arrival. Kathryn's younger brother, Bruce, his wife and three children were making a noisy entrance, all wearing shorts, T-shirts and tennis shoes.

"Are you married yet?" Bruce called over the hubbub.

"No," Kathryn replied. "The preacher hasn't arrived. I thought you were camping in the mountains."

"We were," her brother said, working his way through relatives to reach her, "but when Alan called and said if I wanted to see my little sister get married *at last* I had a little over two and a half hours to get my butt back to Charlotte, I packed up the kids and broke every speed limit between here and the mountains." He gave Kathryn a bear hug. "Where is the poor guy?" he whispered in her ear.

Kathryn laughed happily. "He's standing right next to me." She turned to Ron. "This is my disreputable younger brother, Bruce," she said. "And this is—"

"I know who he is," Alan said, interrupting. "His picture has been in the paper half a dozen times this last week. How did you manage to catch such a big fish?"

"Now you know why I say he's disreputable," Kathryn said to Ron. "He'll say anything to embarrass me."

"Actually it was the other way around," Ron said, shaking hands with Bruce. "She tried to get away, but I whisked her off to Switzerland. I wouldn't let the plane land until she agreed to marry me."

"Not true. I caught him skinny-dipping in his swimming pool and threatened not to give him his bathing suit back unless he agreed to marry me before the sun went down."

"Is either of you telling the truth?" Bruce asked.

"No," Kathryn and Ron said in chorus.

Bruce beamed. "My kind of people. Never let the truth stand in the way of a good story."

Kathryn had barely finished introducing Ron to Bruce's wife and children when the door opened and her parents entered. Suddenly her throat was tight and she had trouble swallowing.

"Is that your father?" Ron asked.

"Yes," Kathryn said as she watched her father work his way toward them through a room full of family excited to see him.

"I thought you said he couldn't come, that he was in Pinehurst at a company golf tournament," Ron said.

"He was." Kathryn's reconciliation with her father had been difficult for both of them, difficult for her to admit she'd been wrong, difficult for him to forget the things she'd said. She hoped for a much better relationship in the future but expected it would take a while to recover from the scars of the past twelve years. She found herself almost holding her breath until he reached her.

"I wasn't sure you could make it," she said, not giving voice to her real fear, that he wouldn't want to come. "I didn't give you much time."

"I had to be here to give the bride away," her father said, smiling. "And to make sure the groom was good enough for you."

"I'm not," Ron said, "but my daughter's promised to help me work on it."

"Dad!" Cynthia said with a typical teenage mixture of exasperation and embarrassment.

"I'm glad you could be here." Kathryn gave her father a kiss, hoped he didn't notice the tears in her eyes. "You, too," she said as she gave her mother a hug.

"It was a close call," her mother said, "but he was able to get a ride with the mayor."

"He doesn't usually do that," her father said, "but I told him I had an engagement I couldn't miss."

Kathryn was so sure she was going to cry she was relieved when the preacher came bustling in.

"I'm told there's going to be a wedding here. Who's the lucky bride?"

Nearly every person in the room turned and pointed to Kathryn. "She is," they chorused in unison.

The preacher looked at his watch. "Time to begin. Are you ready?"

"Yes," Kathryn said turning to Ron and looking into his eyes. "I'm very ready."

Four months later

"He's such a big boy," Lisette said. "I can't believe you didn't demand a C-section."

"I didn't have any trouble at all," Cynthia said, looking down at the sleeping baby in her arms. "The doctor said I was made to have babies."

Lisette, Julia and Betsy had all had their babies, two girls and a boy. Kathryn had five new girls at the shelter, and Cynthia's father's pilot program had recently gotten underway with the first four unwed fathers enrolled. Arthur had been the first to sign up.

"I've got to run," Lisette said. "I was suppose to meet Kerry downstairs fifteen minutes ago."

"Will she ever change?" Ron asked Kathryn as Lisette disappeared through the doorway.

"Yes, but not right away," Kathryn said. "Now I want to hold my grandson. Are you ready to give him up yet?"

"I get him first," Ron said. "Us boys have got to bond."

"You've been reading too many books," Kathryn said.

"I had to get prepared," Ron said reaching out for his grandson. "Being a grandfather is serious business. I don't know why everybody thinks he's so big," he said, carefully settling the baby in the crook of one arm. "I can practically hold him in one hand."

"Don't try it," Kathryn said, laughing.

"He's nearly twenty-three inches long and weighs over eight pounds," Cynthia said, indignantly defending her baby. "He's huge. If you're going to find fault with him you can give him back."

"He's so proud of you and the baby he doesn't know what to do with himself," Kathryn said. "He'll probably give him a football and a set of pads for his first birthday."

"I'm not going to let you and Arthur push him into sports if he doesn't want to," Cynthia said.

"He's going to be a quarterback," her father said. "See his long arms?"

"I thought you said he was small," Cynthia said, grinning.

"Don't pay attention to anything he says," Kathryn said. "He's already planning his schedule around the baby's naps and feeding times."

"Are you sure you don't have some companies that need merging," Cynthia asked, "maybe somewhere like Timbuktu?"

"Don't worry," Kathryn said. "He'll soon have a lot more to worry about."

"Is the unwed father program expanding?"

"No. I am."

"You mean you're—"

"Pregnant. Your father is going to be a father again in six months. Ron, don't you dare drop that baby!"

* * * * *

Don't miss the latest miniseries from award-winning author Marie Ferrarella:

Meet...

Sherry Campbell—ambitious newswoman who makes headlines when a handsome billionaire arrives to sweep her off her feet...and shepherd her new son into the world!

A BILLIONAIRE AND A BABY, SE#1528,
available March 2003

Joanna Prescott—Nine months after her visit to the sperm bank, her old love rescues her from a burning house—then delivers her baby....

A BACHELOR AND A BABY, SD#1503,
available April 2003

Chris "C.J." Jones—FBI agent, expectant mother and always on the case. When the baby comes, will her irresistible partner be by her side?

THE BABY MISSION, IM#1220, available May 2003

Lori O'Neill—A forbidden attraction blows down this pregnant Lamaze teacher's tough-woman facade and makes her consider the love of a lifetime!

BEAUTY AND THE BABY, SR#1668,
available June 2003

The Mom Squad—these single mothers-to-be are ready for labor...and true love!

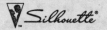

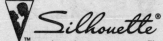

USA TODAY bestselling author

LINDSAY McKENNA

**brings you a brand-new series
featuring Morgan Trayhern and his team!**

WOMAN OF INNOCENCE
(Silhouette Special Edition #1442)

An innocent beauty longing for adventure. A rugged mercenary
sworn to protect her. A romantic adventure like no other!

DESTINY'S WOMAN
(Silhouette Books)

A Native American woman with a wounded heart. A strong, loving
soldier with a sheltering embrace. A love powerful enough to heal…

Available in Feburary!

HER HEALING TOUCH
(Silhouette Special Edition #1519)

A legendary healer. A Special Forces paramedic in need of faith
in love. A passion so strong it could not be denied…

Available in March!

AN HONORABLE WOMAN
(Silhouette Books)

A beautiful pilot with a plan to win back her honor. The man who
stands by her side through and through. The mission that would
take them places no heart should dare go alone…

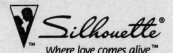

Where love comes alive™

If you enjoyed what you just read,
then we've got an offer you can't resist!

Take 2 bestselling love stories FREE!

Plus get a FREE surprise gift!